F. S. McDonald

Fogazzaro

SHORT STORY CLASSICS

(FOREIGN)

VOLUME TWO
ITALIAN AND
SCANDINAVIAN

EDITED BY

William Patten

WITH
AN INTRODUCTION
AND NOTES

P. F. COLLIER & SON
NEW YORK

CONTENTS—VOLUME II

ITALIAN

SCANDINAVIAN

CONTENTS

ii

THE LOST LETTER

BY ENRICO CASTELNUOVO

Enrico Castelnuovo, who was born at Florence in 1839, is one of the earliest of Italian writers of the modern short story, and a link between the group of poets, dramatists, and novelists, beginning with Manzoni (1785-1873), and the group of his own immediate contemporaries, including Carducci, Fogazzaro, Barrili, Farina, Verga, D'Annunzio, De Amicis, Serao, and other disciples of Carducci.

His literary career began with a little romance called "Il quaderno della zia"; it struck not only his first note of popularity, but the rich vein of h's talent, which consists in minute observation and keen dramatic insight, softened by a sympathetic, almost sentimental, style—a rare combination traced from his first little romance to his later volumes of short stories, and especially marked in the story given here, "The Lost Letter."

THE LOST LETTER

A STORY OF WHAT MIGHT HAVE BEEN

BY ENRICO CASTELNUOVO

PROFESSOR RANIERO CERVIALE, then an old Extraordinary Member of the Lincei, the complement of numerous other academies, of the Lincei, Corresponding Fellow of an infinite number of Italian and foreign societies and academies, was having his servant Pierapondo open two cases of books, arrived the evening before from Padua.

The books were the residue of a library that he had gathered at Padua when twenty years before, he had filled the chair of neo-Latin in that university. Afterward he had devoted much for scientific purposes, had been called successively to the chairs at higher learning in Florence to the University of Naples, and finally the Ministry had solicited his presence in Rome at the Suprema, creating a chair especially for him, and offering him high emoluments.

For some time, during the Professor's peregrinations, the library, packed up and left with a colleague, had remained undisturbed at Padua. Then Cerviale had sent for a part of it when he was in Florence, another part later on when in Naples. Now having to come to Rome, with the intention of fixing there his

Translated by Florence McIntyre Tyson. Copyright, 1901, by The Current Literature Publishing Company

THE LOST LETTER

A STORY OF WHAT MIGHT HAVE BEEN

BY ENRICO CASTELNUOVO

PROFESSOR ATTILIO CERNIERI, distinguished Egyptologist, Senator of the Kingdom, commander of numerous orders, active member of the Lincei, Corresponding Fellow of an infinite number of Italian and foreign societies and academies, was having his servant, Pomponio, open two cases of books arrived the evening before from Padua.

The books were the residue of a library that he had gathered at Padua when, twenty years before, he had filled the chair of neo-Latin in that university. Afterward he had traveled much for scientific purposes, had been called successively to the institute of higher learning in Florence to the University of Naples, and finally the Ministry had solicited his presence in Rome, at the Sapienza, creating a chair especially for him, and offering him high emoluments.

For some time, during the Professor's peregrinations, the library, packed up and left with a colleague, had remained undisturbed at Padua. Then Cernieri had sent for a part of it when he was in Florence; another part later on when in Naples. Now having to come to Rome, with the intention of fixing there his

Translated by Florence McIntyre Tyson. Copyright, 1903, by The Current Literature Publishing Company.

permanent residence, he had determined to send for the two last cases.

To be sure, these books were not absolutely necessary to a man who, besides having recently refurnished his own library, had at his disposition the public and private libraries of the capital.

We live in a century in which everything proceeds by steam, even science. What is true to-day can readily be false to-morrow; and a volume runs the risk of being useless over night.

But in spite of its ten years of life, the monograph in which our hero had demonstrated, with ponderous arguments, relegated to the Finnish Family a group of roots hitherto believed to be of Celtic origin, had not grown old. The book, small in weight, but heavy in thought, had been translated into all the languages of Europe, and the genial information had placed our professor "at the top of the scientific pyramid," to quote the words of an enthusiastic disciple, by the side of the principal living philologist, the famous Lowenstein of the University of Upsala. But whether because the top of a pyramid is an uncomfortable place for two or not, Cernieri and Lowenstein had at first offered the interesting spectacle of two contestants who are vigorously striving to throw one another off, until, finally convinced of the uselessness of their struggles, they had changed rivalry into friendship.

The two learned men were, of course, two strugglers in the scientific arena, but instead of struggling with each other, they struggled with the world at large. If by chance any mortal could be found rash enough to raise his crest and dare to endeavor to seat himself, too, on the top of the famous pyramid; had it been possible to penetrate the depths of the minds of the two "chers confrères," as they styled themselves in correspondence, it would probably have been discovered that each placed a very moderate estimate upon the virtues of the other. Lowenstein had very little faith in the Finnish roots; and Cernieri believed still less in the revolution brought about by Lowenstein in the study of the Hindu-Persian.

But let us leave Lowenstein in peace in distant Norway and turn our attention entirely to our illustrious compatriot. And, to begin with, upon the afternoon in which Pomponio is opening the case of books, the Professor was but forty, though looking much older.

He was slightly stoop-shouldered and his ample forehead was seamed with premature wrinkles; his near-sighted eyes were hidden behind glasses, and were generally half-closed, like those of a sleepy pussy-cat. His hair was thin and gray, his beard straggling, ill-cared for, and nearly white. When he was young, Cernieri used to shave; but after it had happened several times that he in his absent-mindedness had shaved but half his face, and in that unusual condition had entered his classes, he had thought best to leave well enough alone. For the rest, the abstraction of professors is proverbial, and need not be dwelt on here, though upon one occasion he had lost his train by persisting in looking through the whole station at Bologna for a package he had in his hand.

Absent-minded people are generally very good-

natured, but our professor was an exception to the
rule. Ordinarily his lips were visited but by the
scientific smile, made up of the superiority and com-
miseration with which a learned man hears of the
absurdities committed by a brother colleague or the
world at large. In society, upon the rare occasions he
forced himself to enter it, he preferred standing aside,
avoiding women with horror, for he had not the faint-
est idea what to say to them, and the dear creatures
themselves were equally at a loss what to say to him,
though five or six years ago, owing to the scarcity of
husbands in this vale of tears, more than one mother
had cast her eyes over him as a convenient parti for
one of her daughters.

So at one time the Countess Pastori had been brave
enough to invite him to dinner, hoping to make him
marry her second daughter, who had bad teeth and
weak eyes, and had not found any one who would have
her. The young girl, properly coached, had received
the professor with marked deference, had prepared
with her own hand an exquisite peach marmalade, and
had even gone to the length of evincing interest in
Finnish roots. Cernieri, however, did not take the
bait; but, at once on guard, shortened his visit and was
careful never to set foot inside the doors of the Pastori
mansion until the little Countess was betrothed to an
importer of salt fish, who joined the cultivation of
salmon with veneration for the titled nobility.

So warned by experience, he became gruffer than
before, and more than ever inaccessible to any ideas
of gallantry.

Every man has in the book of his life a secret page that a woman has made joyous or gloomy; as far as Professor Cernieri was concerned, this page had remained a blank. At least so his friends said; so would he have answered himself had he been asked, and he would have spoken in good faith. Absorbed as he was in research, he forgot things near at hand. Oh, why must he be made to remember the distant past?

. . . .

"Mercy on us!" exclaimed Pomponio, who had begun to take the books out of the box. "Mercy on us, what a dust!" Then added: "Really, it would be much better if you would let me take them all downstairs, and dust them there."

But the Professor vigorously opposed the proposition. He wished it all to take place in his study, under his own eyes. He wanted, after they were dusted, himself to put the books in a case ready for their reception. And Pomponio, resigned to the inevitable, continued taking them out, dusting them as best he could, and handing them to his master, who, having glanced at the title, put them in place.

The air was surcharged with dust, which covered the furniture, penetrated the pores, making both master and servant cough and sneeze constantly. "There is a spider's web on this," said Pomponio as he lifted a large folio. It proved to be an antique atlas of the world, printed at Gotha by Justus Perthès; and it so happened that while the man was dusting it a little square envelope, yellowed with age, dropped from its leaves and fell upon the floor.

"Gracious, what is that?" said Pomponio. "It looks like a letter." And putting down the atlas, he stooped to pick it up.

But the Professor had anticipated him, and, half-dazed, was turning the letter round and round. Without doubt it *was* a letter, and one of his own at that, still sealed, the stamp uncanceled, addressed in his own writing; the heavy, weighty writing of a man born to be a cavaliere of many orders; a fellow of many societies. It was a too distinct hand, giving assurance that the letter should reach its destination if it had been mailed!

"Alla gentile Signorina Maria Lisa Altavilla, Firenze, Via dei Servi, No. 25—1 Floor."

That name appearing so unexpectedly under his eyes carried Professor Cernieri back twenty years, forcing from the mists of oblivion a slender, graceful girl, whose lovely countenance was crowned with an expression of rare sweetness. For her alone had his heart ever quickened. For her sake alone had he once for one day, for an hour, thought seriously of taking a wife. And then?—

Pomponio, who was consumed with curiosity, had noiselessly approached the professor and murmured: "But how in the world did it get hidden in that book?"

Cernieri turned bruskly—"What business have you here? Leave the room."

"Shall I not go on?"

"No, not now. Go away."

"Has anything happened?"

"Nothing. If I need you, I will ring."

Pomponio reluctantly retired. He would have given anything to know what sort of a letter that was which had so disturbed his employer.

When he was gone, the Professor sat down in his great armchair, and, with trembling fingers, broke the seal that Maria Lisa Altavilla had never been allowed to do. And this was what he had written in Padua, October 15, 1875:

"Cara Signorina—I have just received the sad announcement, and hasten to assure you of my sincere sympathy in your great grief. Last July, when I had the honor in Venice of being often with your father and yourself, I was a witness of your solicitude for that precious, highly esteemed soul.

"Do you remember (I can never forget it) that morning's trip to the sea? We had first visited San Lazzaro, where he had been good enough to listen with interest to my explanation in regard to the mummy preserved in the Museum of the Mechitaristi Fathers; then having crossed to Sant' Elizabeth on the Lido, we repaired to the baths lately established there. Your father, feeling rather tired, remained in the hotel with a friend while we went to walk on the beach.

"The day was deliciously balmy, the sun's rays tempered behind little clouds, so that you closed your red silk umbrella. The wavelets lapped the shore softly at our feet where our footprints marked the sand. You confided to me that for several years your father's health seemed to grow worse; how the various doctors, who had been called in, had suggested this rem-

edy and that without being at all able to arrest the
course of the disease, which was overwhelming you
with terror. You told me of the tender affection that
led him to hide his suffering from you; he who had
never before concealed anything. Growing more con-
fidential, you told me of your happy home life, of the
full accord of your mutual thoughts and feelings, of
your deep love each for the other, cemented by sorrow;
for, from a large family, there now remained but you
two in the world. Then, overcome by emotion, you
ceased speaking, your eyes full of tears.

"What words struggled for utterance on my part!
I can not express all that was in my heart. I am naturally timid, and I will acknowledge a great horror of
anything that will distract me from my studies or interfere with my habits; but I feel sure I made you
understand, Signorina, how deeply I sympathized with
you. I know I told you I was at your service whenever you might choose to call upon me. 'Thanks,'
you murmured gently while your hand trembled in
mine. Then you insisted upon going back to your
father.

"We spoke no word as we went, but it seemed to
me that our souls understood one another. In a day
or two you had quitted Venice without my having the
opportunity of seeing you again alone.

"Now, Signorina, the greatest of sorrows has come
to you. Now is the time for you to test the true value
of your friends.

"I would wish to come myself to Florence, but I am
forced to leave in a few hours for London, in order to

be present at the Congress of Orientalists, which opens
there on the 19th inst.

"From England I may possibly start on a long journey out of Europe. My movements will depend upon
you; one word from you will take me back to Italy.
In any event, I shall be in London all October, and I
beg you will let me have a line from you, Poste Re-
stante. Think that I, too, and for a much longer
period than you, have been alone in the world. Believe
me always,   Yours sincerely,

"ATTILIO CERNIERI."

Twice the Professor read the four pages through,
forcing himself to recall the day, the hour, the place in
which he had written it; seeking to explain to himself how he could have forgotten to post it, as well as
that the absolute silence of Maria Lisa Altavilla had
not aroused some suspicion in his mind; why he had
never written again to make sure. And this is what
he remembered.

The mortuary notice had arrived one morning as he
was in the midst of packing, and his thoughts had
turned persistently to the young girl he had known
three months before in Venice, and who had shown
such perfect confidence in him. All day he had de-
bated within himself whether he should merely send
her his condolences or if he ought to say something
more in regard to the sentiments with which she had
inspired him, in which perhaps she shared. She was
not an ordinary girl, this Maria Lisa. She seemed
created to be the companion of a scholar.

Had she not been her father's secretary and could she not be his? To learn two or three languages so that she might help him; to take notes for him; to keep his work in order; to correct printer's proofs, and when he was leaving for a congress or scientific mission, to pack his trunks and accompany him to the station; perhaps sometimes go along to look after the nuisance of tickets, to treat with hotel proprietors, cabmen, et cetera. Viewed in this light, matrimony did not seem such a terrible abyss; but a tranquil port, in which to take shelter from storms. And that evening, at the same time with other letters, he had written that one to Maria Lisa; had written with an expansion and an abandon that had filled him with wonder; even now he was amazed, as he felt once again the unaccustomed sweetness of the thing.

Once again he was in his little room in his apartment at Padua; on the table an oil lamp was burning; spread out before him lay the atlas of Menke at the page that told of "Egyptus ante Cambysii tempus." He had been consulting it before answering his friend Morrison of the University of Edinburgh, who was insisting that they should together visit the ruins of Thebes in Upper Egypt, and he leaving his decision until after the Congress had, on the chance of the journey, corrected and amplified the itinerary to take in Ithaca, Apollonapolis, Syene, and then Cernieri remembered his landlady had knocked at his door to tell him the carriage was there and that she had already put his luggage, his plaid, and his umbrella in. He had shut the atlas and put it back upon the shelf hur-

riedly, hurriedly he had pushed the letters already
stamped into his pocket; hurriedly had rushed down
and thrown himself into the cab.

By what strange fate had one of the letters been
shut in the atlas? By what carelessness, in putting
the rest in the mail-box, had he not noticed that one
was missing, the most important of all, was an enigma
the learned professor was unable to solve? He was
ready to swear that never for an instant had the
thought occurred to him that he had not posted the
letter; indeed, he remembered, how for a number of
days he was dumfounded at his own rashness.

Why had he not considered the matter more fully?
Why, with one of those words which can not be taken
back, had he run the risk of sacrificing that greatest
of blessings—independence? Why had he played all
his future on one card? He was a man of honor; had
he received a favorable reply from Maria Lisa, nothing would have induced him to draw back. If she
said no, then he had invited a needless repulse.

Dio buono, what madness had taken possession of
him? It was more than likely that a girl, who was
not beautiful and hadn't a penny of dot, would remain
single for two or three years at least and then he
could have sought opportunities of seeing her and
knowing her better, and of weighing the pros and
cons.

So during the first week in London, while the temptation was increasing for the journey to the Orient
with Morrison and a young "docente" from Heidel-
berg, who had offered himself as a companion, he was

upset and nervous, and trembled at every distribution
of letters, not knowing what he wished or feared.
Then as time passed and he read his two theses, and
became absorbed in the work of the Congress and
drawn within the circle of illustrious scholars, who
were greeting him as a new luminary in the world of
science, the image of the poor absent orphan faded
gradually away and a secret hope sprang up in his
heart that he had regained his liberty through the continued silence of Maria Lisa without the humiliation
of a refusal.

He could always remember he had done his
duty; it was not his fault if his offer had not been
accepted.

So one day, early in November, he could exclaim
with Julius Cæsar:

"Alea jacta est."

A rapid flight through Europe brought him with his
companions to Brindisi, whence they embarked for
Alexandria. Two years were passed in Upper Egypt
and Abyssinia in the study of hieroglyphics and ruins,
and in sending learned treatises to the principal Euro-
pean Reviews. Magazines, journals, letters from men
of science, elections to academies poured in from Italy,
from France, from Germany; some silly letters even
came from his landlady in Padua. From Florence,
from Maria Lisa Altavilla not a word. Then when
he got home, he almost forgot all about her. Only
two years had passed, but they were worth a century
to him, and preceding events assumed to his eyes a
vague, nebulous distance. So when he had heard that

three months before Maria Lisa had married a "Pretore residente" in an out-of-the-way corner of Sicily, he had not troubled himself more than he could help about it. He had to choose from the various offers of the Ministry, he had to write an article for the "Edinburgh Review" on Assyrian Antiquities; finally, he had to finish a weighty thesis on those Finnish and Celtic roots, for whose sake he had resolved to devote himself entirely to philology at the expense of everything else.

Maria Lisa was so small in comparison and matrimony might have been such a nuisance. Only some time afterward, as he was on the point of accepting a Chair in Florence, he was assailed with scruples. Suppose through the changing of her husband's jurisdiction the lady were now in Tuscany? How ought he to act? To seem indifferent and pretend not to recognize her, or to reproach her with the rudeness with which she had treated him?

Alas! the professor was soon relieved of all doubts. La Maria Lisa Altavilla? the daughter of the Chevalier Altavilla? Who had married the pretore Carlucci? Poor thing! she had died in Sicily of malarial fever before she had been married more than ten months.

Dead! Attilio Cernieri felt penetrated through with pity and regret. Dead, so young; she, who might have been his wife! Then he would now be alone with his life all wrecked about him! Ah! it was indeed a thousand times better that Maria Lisa had not answered him! Better not to have gotten into habits that would

now have to be broken! Better not to have grown
accustomed to having a woman by his side. Those
who know declare it is difficult to do without them
then.

In a word, Cernieri had not been slow to comfort
himself. And then, too, Time had fulfilled her part,
spreading a thick veil over the fleeting episode; covering even the name of Maria Lisa with oblivion.

Now the old letter found within the pages of the
ancient atlas had brought it all back. Before the
middle-aged man, grown old in study, hardened with
egotism, rose an enchanting picture of youth, clothed
in shining colors, full of intangible sweetness. Pressing the poor, little yellow sheet between his hands, he
beheld once more Maria Lisa's sweet face. As she
sadly gazed at him she seemed to say: "Why in my
hour of need did you not send me a word of sympathy? Chance acquaintances pitied my grief; thou,
who hadst let me believe didst love me, alone remained
mute and insensible. I called upon thee too. Ah!
wretched indeed is she who trusts in a man!"

Cernieri seemed to hear Maria Lisa's voice pro-
nounce the words.

And she had died without hearing his vindication,
without knowing the truth. It is indeed, "Sorrow's
crown of sorrow," to be faded with the irrevocable,
to be tormented with wrongs that can not be repaired,
with misunderstandings that can not be removed.

But the letter, which the grave professor continued
to hold unfolded before him, told, not only that Maria
Lisa was dead, believing him worse than he deserved,

but also that in his life there had been a moment of
poetry, of abandon, and of love, and that that moment
had remained barren. Never again could life bring
him such another. Never again would his heart
quicken for a woman's sake. Never again could flow
from his pen words which might seem to us cold and
conventional, but to him seemed burning with ardor
and love. And he asked himself: "Suppose the letter
had gone, had arrived at its destination and Maria
Lisa had answered: 'I understand what thou wishest;
I consent. I love thee and am willing to be thine.
Come.'" Then certainly, he should not have undertaken his great journey to Egypt and Assyria. Would
not have deciphered hieroglyphics or interpreted the
language of the ruins. Perhaps, though, he would
have had sons of his own. Perhaps domestic cares
might have retarded his fame, his activity might have
been clogged and honors and decorations might not
have fallen so abundantly upon his head. He might
not even have made his luminous discovery about the
Finnish roots. Perchance another would now occupy
his enviable position on the very top of the scientific
pyramid by the side of Lowenstein of the University
of Upsala. If all that might have happened, a man
like Professor Attilio Cernieri ought to rejoice that it
had not. And still—and still!—A persistent, hungry
doubt would not allow him to quiet his soul with this
philosophic consolation. Would it not have been better to have sacrificed a little glory to have had a little
love?

The Professor Attilio Cernieri lacked courage to

tear or destroy the letter. He placed it in his desk, recalled Pomponio, and desired him to resume his interrupted labor.

But that evening in his study, the temptation to again behold those words of twenty years ago overcame him anew. And afterward there did not pass a day in which he did not take the poor little worn sheet from its envelope and read it over and over.

Then he would look at the envelope, at the stamp, upon which the Post had impressed no mark and murmur once more:

"If the letter had only gone!"

CAVALLERIA RUSTICANA

BY GIOVANNI VERGA

Giovanni Verga was born at Catania, Sicily, in 1840. He was at first a romanticist, carrying on the traditions of Manzoni. Between 1874 and 1880, he produced two masterpieces, dealing with the life of the Sicilian peasant, in which he found his true bent, abandoning his earlier romanticism. With his fellow townsman, Capuana, he now stands at the head of the Italian "veristi," or naturalists, often compared with Zola. His style is singularly vigorous and sincere, especially in describing the customs and analyzing the souls of the Sicilian peasants. But his plots are often confusing and long drawn out; he has attempted drama, but with little success. Yet, strangely enough, his short story, "Cavalleria Rusticana," which he afterward developed into a novel, has been made into one of the most popular, dramatic, concentrated one-act operas of the world— the "Cavalleria Rusticana" of the composer Mascagni.

CAVALLERIA RUSTICANA

BY GIOVANNI VERGA

AFTER Turridu Macca, Mistress Nunzia's son, came home from soldiering, he used to strut every Sunday, peacock-like, in the public square, wearing his rifleman's uniform, and his red cap that looked just like that of the fortune-teller waiting for custom behind the stand with the cage of canaries. The girls all rivaled each other in making eyes at him as they went their way to mass, with their noses down in the folds of their shawls; and the young lads buzzed about him like so many flies. Besides, he had brought back a pipe, with the king on horseback on the bowl, as natural as life; and he struck his matches on the back of his trousers, raising up one leg as if he were going to give a kick. But for all that, Master Angelo's daughter Lola had not once shown herself, either at mass or on her balcony, since her betrothal to a man from Licodia, who was a carter by trade, and had four Sortino mules in his stable. No sooner had Turridu heard the news than, holy great devil! but he wanted to rip him inside out, that was what he wanted to do to him, that fellow from Licodia. However, he did nothing to him at all, but contented himself with going and singing every scornful song he knew beneath the fair one's window.

Translated by Frederic Taber Cooper. Copyright, 1907, by P. F. Collier & Son.

"Has Mistress Nunzio's Turridu nothing at all to do," the neighbors asked, "but pass his nights in singing, like a lonely sparrow?"

At last he came face to face with Lola, on her way back from praying to Our Lady of Peril; and at sight of him she turned neither white nor red, as though he were no concern of hers.

"It is a blessing to have sight of you!" said he.

"Oh, friend Turridu, I was told that you came back around the first of the month."

"And I too was told many other things besides!" he answered. "So it is true that you are going to marry Alfio the carter?"

"If such is the will of God!" answered Lola, drawing together beneath her chin the two corners of her kerchief.

"You do the will of God by taking or leaving as it pays you best! And it was the will of God that I should come home from so far away to hear such fine news, Mistress Lola!"

The poor fellow still tried to make a show of indifference, but his voice had grown husky; and he walked on ahead of the girl with a swagger that kept the tassel of his cap dancing back and forth upon his shoulders. It really hurt the girl to see him with such a long face, but she had not the heart to deceive him with fair words.

"Listen, friend Turridu," she said at length, "you must let me go on to join the other girls. What would folks be saying if we were seen together?"

"That is true," replied Turridu; "now that you are

to marry Alfio, who has four mules in his stable, it won't do to set people talking. My mother, on the other hand, poor woman, had to sell our one bay mule, and that little bit of vineyard down yonder on the high-road, during the time that I was soldiering. The time is gone when the Lady Bertha span; and you no longer give a thought to the time when we used to talk together from window to courtyard, and when you gave me this handkerchief just before I went away, into which God knows how many tears I wept at going so far that the very name of our land seemed forgotten. But now good-by, Mistress Lola, let us square accounts and put an end to our friendship."

Mistress Lola and the carter were married; and on the following Sunday she showed herself on her balcony, with her hands spread out upon her waist, to show off the big rings of gold that her husband had given her.

Turridu kept passing and repassing through the narrow little street, with his pipe in his mouth and his hands in his pockets, pretending indifference and ogling the girls; but inwardly he was eating his heart out to think that Lola's husband had all that gold, and that she pretended not even to notice him as he passed by.

"I'd like to take her from under his very eyes, the dirty dog!" he muttered.

Across from Alfio's house lived Master Cola, the vine-grower, who was rich as a porker, so they said, and had an unmarried daughter. Turridu said so much, and did so much, that Master Cola took him into his employ; then he began to haunt the house and make pretty speeches to the girl.

"Why don't you go and say all these fine things to Mistress Lola?" Santa answered him.

"Mistress Lola is a big lady! Mistress Lola is wife of one of the crowned heads now!"

"I suppose I am not good enough for the crowned heads."

"You are worth a hundred such as Lola; and I know one fellow who would never so much as look at Mistress Lola or her patron saint when you are around. For she isn't fit even to carry your shoes for you, indeed she isn't!"

"When the fox found that he couldn't reach the grapes—"

"He said, 'how lovely you are, you sweet little grape!'"

"Oh! come, hands off, friend Turridu."

"Are you afraid I am going to eat you?"

"No, I am not afraid of you nor of him you serve."

"Ah! your mother was from Licodia, we all know that. Your blood boils quickly! Oh! I could eat you up with my eyes!"

"Then eat me up with your eyes, and leave no crumbs; but meanwhile pick up that bundle of twigs for me."

"For your sake I would pick up the whole house, that I would!"

To hide her blushes, she threw at him the fagot she happened to have in her hands, but for a wonder missed him.

"Cut it short! Talking doesn't bind fagots."

"If I was rich, I should be looking for a wife just like you, Santa!"

"I shall not marry a crowned head, as Mistress Lola did; but I shall have my dower, as well as she, when the Lord sends me the right man."

"We know that you are rich, yes, we know that!"

"If you know so much, then stop talking, for my father will soon be here, and I don't care to have him catch me in the courtyard."

The father began to make a wry face, but the girl pretended not to notice, for the tassel of the rifleman's hat had set her heart-strings quivering and was forever dancing before her eyes. After the father had put Turridu out of the door, the daughter opened her window to him, and would stand chatting with him all the evening, until the whole neighborhood could talk of nothing else.

"I am crazy about you," Turridu would say; "I am losing my sleep and my appetite."

"I don't believe it!"

"I wish I was the son of Victor Emanuel, so that I could marry you!"

"I don't believe it!"

"By our Lady, I could eat you up, like a piece of cake!"

"I don't believe it!"

"On my honor!"

"Oh, mother mine!"

Lola, listening night after night, hidden behind a pot of sweet basil, turning first pale and then red, one day called down to Turridu: "How is it, friend Turridu, that old friends no longer greet each other?"

"Alas!" sighed Turridu, "blessed is he who may greet you!"

"If you care to give me greeting, you know where my home is," answered Lola.

Turridu came back to greet her so often that Santa took notice of it, and closed her window in his face. The neighbors pointed him out with a smile or a nod of the head when he passed by in his rifleman's uniform. Lola's husband was away, making a circuit of the village fairs with his mules.

"On Sunday I mean to go to confession, for last night I dreamt of black grapes," said Lola.

"Wait a while! wait a while!" begged Turridu.

"No, now that Easter is so near, my husband would want to know why I have not been to confession."

"Ahah!" murmured Master Cola's Santa, waiting for her turn on her knees before the confessional where Lola was washing herself clean of her sins. "On my soul, it is not to Rome I would send you to do penance!"

Friend Alfio came home with his mules and a pretty penny of profit, and brought his wife a present of a fine new dress for the holidays.

"You do well to bring her presents," his neighbor Santa said to him, "for while you are away your wife has been trimming up the honor of your house!"

Master Alfio was one of those carters who wear the cap well down over one ear, and to hear his wife talked

of in this fashion made him change color as though
he had been stabbed. "Holy big devil!" he exclaimed,
"if you have not seen aright, I won't leave you eyes
to weep with, you and your whole family!"

"I have forgotten how to weep!" answered Santa;
"I did not weep even when I saw with these very eyes
Mistress Nunzia's son, Turridu, go in at night to your
wife's house."

"Then it is well," replied Alfio; "many thanks to
you."

Now that the husband was home again, Turridu no
longer wasted his days in the little street, but drowned
his sorrow at the tavern with his friends; and on
Easter eve they had on the table a big dish of sausage.
When Master Alfio came in, just from the way he
fastened his eyes upon him, Turridu understood what
business he had come on, and laid his fork down upon
his plate.

"How can I serve you, friend Alfio?" he asked.

"Nothing important; friend Turridu, it is some time
since I have seen you, and I wanted to talk with you
of the matter that you know about."

Turridu had at once offered him a glass, but Alfio
put it aside with his hand. Then Turridu arose and
said to him: "Here I am, friend Alfio."

The carter threw an arm around his neck.

"If you will come to-morrow morning down among
the prickly pears of Canziria, we can talk of this affair,
friend Turridu."

"Wait for me on the highroad at sunrise, and we
will go together."

With these words they exchanged the kiss of challenge. Turridu seized the carter's ear between his teeth, and thus solemnly bound himself not to fail him.

The friends had all silently withdrawn from the dish of sausage, and accompanied Turridu all the way to his home. Mistress Nunzia, poor woman, was accustomed to wait for him late every night.

"Mother," said Turridu, "do you remember when I went away to be a soldier, and you thought that I was never coming back! Give me a kiss, such as you gave me then, for to-morrow I am going on a long journey!"

Before daybreak he took his clasp-knife, which he had hidden under the straw at the time he went away as a conscript, and started with it for the prickly pears of Canziria.

"Holy Mother, where are you going in such a rage?" sobbed Lola in terror as her husband started to leave the house.

"I am not going far," answered Alfio, "but it will be far better for you if I never come back."

Lola, in her night-gown, prayed at the foot of her bed, and pressed to her lips the rosary which Fra Bernadino had brought her from the Holy Land, and recited all the Ave Marias that there were beads for.

"Friend Alfio," began Turridu after he had walked quite a bit of the way beside his companion, who remained silent, with his cap drawn over his eyes, "as true as God himself, I know that I am in the wrong, and I ought to let you kill me. But before I came here, I saw my old mother, who rose early to see me start, on the pretext that she had to tend the chickens; but her heart must have told her the truth. And as true as God himself, I am going to kill you like a dog, sooner than have the poor old woman weeping for me."

"So much the better," replied Master Alfio, stripping off his jacket, "strike your hardest, and so will I."

They were both worthy foes. Turridu received the first thrust, and was quick enough to catch it on his arm. When he paid it back, he gave good measure, and aimed for the groin.

"Ah, friend Turridu, you have really made up your mind to kill me?"

"Yes, I told you so; ever since I saw my old mother going out to feed the chickens, her face floats all the time before my eyes."

"Then open your eyes wide," Alfio called to him, "for I am going to square accounts with you."

And as he stood on guard, crouching ever, so as to hold his left hand upon his wound which was aching, and with his elbow almost touching the ground, he suddenly caught up a handful of dust and threw it into his opponent's eyes.

"Oh!" howled Turridu, "I am done for!"

He sought to save himself by making desperate leaps backward; but Alfio overtook him with another blow in the stomach and a third in the throat.

"And the third is for the honor of my house, that

you made free with. Now, perhaps, your mother will
forget to feed her chickens."

Turridu stumbled about for a moment, here and
there among the prickly pears, and then fell like a log.
The blood gurgled in a crimson foam out of his throat,
and he had no chance even to gasp out, "Oh, mother
mine!"

THE SILVER CRUCIFIX

BY ANTONIO FOGAZZARO

*Fogazzaro is the author of the most dis-
cussed of modern Italian novels, "The Saint."
This poet, novelist, orator, and senator was
born at Vicenza in 1842. He studied law at
Turin, and by a collection of lyrics in 1876
established his reputation as a poet, drawing
from the spirit of the past, as opposed to
D'Annunzio, who draws from the future.*

*Though thoroughly modern in his prose, in
his novel, "Piccolo Mondo Antico," he makes
a link with the romantic school of Manzoni,
many considering this story a companion
piece to the latter's "I Promessi Sposi."*

*Though frank in tone and tendency, Fogaz-
zaro's writings always aim at the highest
morality. His most striking quality, perhaps,
is love of the beautiful in nature.*

*Between 1887 and 1894 he published two
volumes of short stories, from which "The
Silver Crucifix" has been selected as, on the
whole, the best representative.*

THE SILVER CRUCIFIX

BY ANTONIO FOGAZZARO

"YOUR coffee, milady," said the maid.

The Countess did not reply. But although the curtains were closed, her thin, sere young face could be dimly discerned on the white pillow. The maid standing tray in hand at the foot of the bed, repeated more loudly:

"Your coffee, milady."

The Countess sat up, while she yawned, with eyes still unopened, "Yet in some light."

Her maid went to the window without putting down the tray, and, in turning the handle of the shutters, managed to knock over the empty cup on its saucer.

"Keep quiet," whispered the mistress in a tone of irritation. "What is the matter with you this morning? Don't you see you are waking the baby?"

And as a matter of fact the infant was now awake and crying in its crib. The lady turned toward the child's bed, and peremptorily called out "Hush!"

This silenced her offspring at once, excepting for a few faint moans.

"Now, then, I will have my coffee," commanded the Countess. "Have you seen your master yet? Why, you are trembling all over! What is the matter with you?"

Translated by Lionel Strachey. Copyright, 1901, by P. F. Collier & Son.

THE SILVER CRUCIFIX

BY ANTONIO FOGAZZARO

"YOUR coffee, milady," said the maid.

The Countess did not reply. But although the curtains were closed, her handsome young face could be dimly discerned on the white pillow. The maid, standing tray in hand at the foot of the bed, repeated more loudly:

"Your coffee, milady."

The Countess sat up, while she yawned, with eyes still unopened, "Let in some light."

Her maid went to the window without putting down the tray, and, in turning the handle of the shutters, managed to knock over the empty cup on its saucer.

"Keep quiet!" whispered the mistress in a tone of irritation. "What is the matter with you this morning? Don't you see you are waking the baby?"

And as a matter of fact the infant was now awake and crying in its crib. The lady turned toward the child's bed, and peremptorily called out "Hush!"

This silenced her offspring at once, excepting for a few faint moans.

"Now, then, I will have my coffee," commanded the Countess. "Have you seen your master yet? Why, you are trembling all over! What is the matter with you?"

Translated by Lionel Strachey. Copyright, 1907, by P. F. Collier & Son.

What, indeed, ailed the girl? Cup, saucer, sugar-bowl, and coffee-pot were rattling on the tray. "What is it?" repeated the Countess.

If the maid's face showed signs of alarm, no less was the mistress disturbed by doubts and fears.

"Nothing," replied the servant, still trembling.

The Countess hereupon seized her by the arm, shook it roughly, and exclaimed:

"Tell me!"

Meanwhile the pretty little head of a child of four was peering over the edge of the crib.

"It's a case," said the maid, half in tears, "it's a case of cholera."

Pale as death, the lady started up, and instinctively looked at her listening son. She jumped out of bed; by a single gesture she imposed silence on the girl, while motioning her to go into the next room. Then she darted to her child's crib.

The little fellow had begun to cry again, but his mother kissed and petted him, played and laughed with him until he forgot his woes, and stopped weeping. She pulled on her dressing-gown in great haste, and joined the servant, shutting the door behind her.

"Oh, my God, my God!" lamented the girl between her sobs, while the other woman too began to shed tears.

"Hush, for Heaven's sake! On no account must baby be frightened! What about this case—where is it?"

"Here, milady! Rosa, the steward's wife. She was taken ill at midnight."

"Heavens! And now—?"

"She is dead. She died half an hour ago."

The baby was shrilly clamoring for his mother.

"Go," said the Countess; "go in and play with him. Keep him happy; do anything you like. Be quiet, darling!" she exclaimed. "I shall be back in a moment." Upon which she rushed to the Count's room.

The lady was blindly, insanely afraid of the cholera; nothing but her passion for her child could have been more intense than this feeling. At the first rumors of the epidemic she and her husband had fled the city, escaping to their splendid country seat—her marriage portion—in the hope that the disease would not spread thither. The place had been spared in 1836, and had even remained untouched in 1886. And now there it was, in the farmyard attached to the villa.

Disheveled and untidy, she flew into her husband's room. Before speaking she gave two violent tugs at the bellrope.

"Have you heard?" she said, with flaming eyes.

The Count, who was phlegmatically shaving his beard, turned round, inquiring, with the soapy brush in his hand: "What?"

"Don't you know about Rosa?"

"Oh, yes, I know," was his calm response.

If, in the first place, the Count had cherished some vague illusion that his wife was ignorant of Rosa's death, it now also seemed proper to reassure her by his cool demeanor. Instead, however, her ladyship's eyes shot fire, and her features were savage with anger.

"What!" she shouted, "you know, and you can

think of nothing better to do than shave? What sort
of man are you—what sort of father—what sort of
husband?"

"Good Lord!" cried the Count, throwing up his
arms.

But before the poor man, soaped up to the eyes, and
wrapped round with a towel, could add another word,
in came the valet. Her ladyship commanded that not
a peasant from the farmyard should be admitted to
the house, and that no one should go thence to the
farmyard. After this she gave orders for the coachman to be ready within an hour; he must harness to
the landau the horses which his lordship would select.

"What are you going to do?" asked the latter, who
had recovered himself meanwhile. "Nothing rash, I
must insist."

"Rash—how dare you say that? I am willing to
be obedient to you in everything, but when it comes
to a question of life and death—my son's life, you
understand—then I will listen to no parley from any
one. I wish to leave here at once. Order the horses,
please."

The Count grew annoyed. How could matters have
come to such a pass as this? Was there any propriety
in running away after such a fashion? And then, what
about business affairs? In two days, or one day, or
maybe in twelve hours, he would be ready to start.
But not before—no. His wife, however, interrupted
him violently: "Propriety, indeed, and business! For
shame!"

"And clothes?" objected the husband. "We must

certainly take some with us. You see, we shall really need more time."

The Countess made some contemptuous answer. She would see to it, she assured him, that the trunks were packed in an hour.

"But where do you expect to go?" persisted the Count.

"To the railway station, first of all, and then wherever you like. Now order the horses."

"I have had enough of this!" cried the other. "I'll give such orders as I choose! I'll let the business affairs go, and everything else! Your clothes, too! The sorrels," he added, enraged, to the domestic who was standing by impassively.

The Countess dressed and did her hair with the utmost speed, at moments clasping her hands in silent prayer, distributing commands, summoning servants from various parts of the house by frantic pulls at the bell. There was running up and down stairs, banging of doors, shouting, laughing, calling out of names, suppressed swearing. All the windows facing the fatal farmyard were immediately closed. Thus the cries of the unfortunate children who had lost their mother were shut out; besides a disagreeable odor of chlorin had penetrated into the villa, and even into the Countess's room, smothering the delicate Viennese perfume she habitually used.

"Heavens!" she exclaimed angrily, "now they are doing their best to ruin everything! Pack up quickly, and get those trunks locked! This frightful smell is enough to kill one! Don't they know that chlorin has no effect? They ought to burn the things. The steward will be dismissed if any thieving goes on."

"Some things are being burnt already, milady," observed one of the maids. "The doctor is having sheets, coverlid, and mattress burnt."

"That's not enough!" snapped the Countess.

Here the Count, shaved and dressed, entered his wife's apartment. He began talking to her aside.

"What shall we do with these servants? We can't take all of them with us."

"Anything you please. Send them away. Nothing will be safe in the house if they remain. I don't want them to get the cholera, and then fumigate the rooms with that vile chlorin, and perhaps burn up some of my best gowns. They have no respect whatever for their masters' property, and——"

Furious at having yielded, the Count now broke in with:

"A pretty state of things! A shame, I tell you, a scandal, to sneak off like this!"

"That's it!" retorted the woman. "That's just how you men always are! To appear strong and courageous is more important to you than the life and safety of your family. You are afraid of becoming unpopular. Well, if you want to keep up your reputation, why don't you send for the mayor, and present him with a hundred lire for the cholera patients of the place?"

He thereupon suggested that he would stay at the villa alone, and that she should go with the child. Only he had not enough stability to carry out his own idea.

During this conversation the trunks were being filled. The little boy's playthings, his most expensive apparel, prayer-books, bathing-suits, jewelry, crested note-paper, furs, underlinen, many superfluous and few necessary articles were thrown in helter-skelter, and the lids closed down by sheer force. Then the Countess, followed by her spouse—who made a great show of activity, but really accomplished nothing—hurried through the whole house, opening drawers and cupboards, taking a last look into them, and locking them up with their own hands. The Count stated his opinion that it might be advisable to partake of some refreshment before commencing the journey.

"Yes, yes!" ironically said his consort, "we'll take some refreshment! I'll show you what to take!"

And she drew up her husband and all the servants, including those who were going home for a holiday, and dosed each one with ten drops of laudanum. Her son she regaled with some chocolates.

At last the landau stood before the door. Prior to actually departing, her ladyship, who was extremely pious, withdrew to the seclusion of her bedchamber for a final prayer. Kneeling at a chair, in her tight-fitting costume of white flannel, her black, eight-button gloves reaching to the elbows, and her gold and platinum bracelets, she raised her eyes devoutly to heaven —under the overshadowing plume of her black velvet hat—and murmured a feverish supplication. Not a word did she say to God about the poor wretches who had lost their mother; nor did she ask that the cholera might spare the humble workers chained to the rich soil which had given her this house, her jewels, clothes, Viennese perfume, her education, her dignity, her husband and child, her accommodating God. Neither did she ask anything for her own person. She, who already saw herself and her family smitten down with the dread disease on the journey, offered up no prayers excepting for her son. In fact, her lips simply muttered Paters and Aves and Glorias, while her mind was altogether with the child, thinking of the fearful fate which might befall him, of the danger to his health in this precipitate journey, of his possible loss of appetite, sleep, spirits, or color. Oh, if he could but be kept unconscious of any peril or pain assailing others!

Rapidly she crossed herself, donned a long, gray cloak, and shut a window that had remained open. Before the strong morning breeze clouds were chasing across the sky, the grass was bending on the lawn, and the tall poplars were swaying in the avenue leading to the villa. But the Countess, though brought up on family traditions, had no thought for reminiscences of her youth belonging to this country estate. She merely closed the window and went downstairs.

The mayor was conversing with his lordship by the carriage door.

"Have you just come from there?" she asked the official, and, being informed that he had come from his home, she upbraided him for not having kept off the epidemic. He excused himself with polite smiles, to which the lady confusedly replied: "Never mind, then; never mind," as she hastened her child into the vehicle.

"Did you give him the money?" she whispered to her husband as soon as she was seated beside him. He made a sign in the affirmative.

"I should like to thank her ladyship, too," began the obsequious mayor, "for the generosity with which—"

"Oh, it was nothing—nothing!" interrupted the Count, scarcely knowing what he said.

Established in the carriage, the Countess made a rapid survey of bags and boxes, coats and shawls, umbrellas and parasols. Her husband in the mean time turned round to see if all the luggage was in its place in the barouche, which had been fastened on behind to the landau. "But," he suddenly remarked, "what is the matter with that little boy?"

"Yes, who is that crying?" excitedly called out the Countess, leaning far out of the carriage.

"All ready!" exclaimed the peasant who had been assisting the servants with the luggage, and to whose side clung a small, ragged urchin. "Stop, can't you?" his father bade him, sharply, then repeating the words, "All ready!"

The Count, with his eye on the boy, plunged into one of his pockets. "Don't give way, my boy; you shall have a soldo all to yourself."

"Mother is ill," whined the lad sorrowfully; "mother has the cholera."

Up jumped the Countess. Her face livid and contorted, she brought down her folded sunshade across the coachman's back:

"Drive on!" she shrieked; "drive on—quick!"

The menial whipped up the horses. They began to prance, and then went off at a gallop. The mayor barely had time to leap out of the way, and his lordship to fling out a handful of coppers, which scattered on the ground at the peasant's feet. He stood motionless—while the boy continued weeping—and stared after the flashing wheels of the carriage that rolled swiftly away, whirling up the dust.

"Damn those rich pigs!" he said.

Pretending not to hear, the mayor discreetly departed.

The peasant, a man of middle age and stature, pale, meagre, evil-looking, and as rugged as his offspring, made the youngster pick up the coins. Then they went home together.

They inhabited, in the yard belonging to one of the Countess's farmhouses, a tumble-down, unplastered brick hovel, situated between a dunghill and a pigsty. Before the door gaped a dark ditch, from which issued an indescribable stench, and which was bridged by a single rough plank. Upon entering, one found one's self in a dingy, unpaved sort of cavern. There was no flooring, either wood or stone, but there was an irregular brick fireplace, and in front of it the ground had been depressed by poor wretches kneeling to cook their mess of cornmeal. A wooden stair—three steps missing—conducted to the room, foul with dirt and rubbish, where father, mother, and son were wont to pass the night in a single bed. Standing by this article of furniture, one might look down into the kitchen below through the broken boards. The bed occupied the only spot not soaked by the rain that dripped from the roof.

Crouching on the floor, her head leaning against the edge of the bed, sat the peasant's cholera-stricken wife. Although but thirty, she looked old; at twenty she had been a blooming girl, and even now preserved remnants of mild beauty. At the first glance her husband understood; he swallowed an imprecation. The child, frightened by his mother's discolored face, kept in the doorway.

"For Christ's sake, send him away," she moaned feebly. "I have the cholera; send him away. Go to your aunt's, dear. Take him away, and send me the priest."

"I'll go," said the man to her; and to the boy, motioning toward the farmyard gate, "You go to your aunt's."

From the porch of the yard he fetched an armful of straw, carried it into the kitchen, and went upstairs to his wife, who by exerting all her strength had contrived to get on the bed.

"Listen," said the man, in accents of unusual tenderness; "I am sorry, but if you die in the bed it will have to be burnt. You understand, don't you? I have brought some straw into the kitchen—a nice lot."

Too weak to answer, she made a mute signal of assent, and then a faint effort to rise from her couch. But the man took her up in his arms. By a gesture she begged him to reach first for a small silver crucifix hanging on the wall; she pressed it fervidly to her lips while her husband carried her down to the kitchen. Here he made her as comfortable as he could on the straw, before going for the priest.

And now she, too, this poor creature lying alone like a beast in a cage on the already infected straw—she, too, before departing to an unknown world, began to pray. She prayed for the salvation of her soul, convinced that she was guilty of many sins, and tormented by her inability to remember them.

When the timid doctor, sent by the mayor, arrived, he asked in great fright whether there was any rum or marsala in the house. There was neither; so he recommended hot bricks for her stomach, put up a notice of quarantine, and left her. The priest, who knew no fear, carelessly reeled off what he termed "the usual things," obscuring the divine message with words of his own. Nevertheless, though benighted and ignorant, the dying woman derived comfort and serenity therefrom.

His task done, the priest went. Meanwhile the husband had put a few more handfuls of straw under her back, and lit the fire to heat the bricks. His wife went on praying—less for her child than for the man whom she had pardoned so often, and who was embarked on the road to perdition. Finally, kissing the cross, her mind turned to its giver. She had received it sixteen years back, at her confirmation, from the Countess, the mistress of the splendid manor where it was a joy to live and of the wretched hovel where it was a joy to die. At that time the Countess was a young girl, and had presented the silver crucifix to the laborer's daughter at the suggestion of her mother, then mistress of the estate, a kind, gentle lady, long dead, but unforgotten by her humble tenants.

The dying woman acknowledged having thought ill of the new mistress, of having complained sometimes, so that *her* husband had cursed because, despite repeated petition, neither roof, nor flooring, nor staircase had ever been repaired, and because the window frames had not been filled with linen panes. Feeling truly penitent, in her heart she implored forgiveness of his lordship and her ladyship; and she besought the Holy Virgin to bless them both.

At the moment when her husband placed the scorching bricks on her stomach, a spasm ran through her body, and she gave up the ghost. The man flung some straw over her blackening face, wrenched the little cross out of her hand, stuffed it into his pocket with a scowl at its small value, mumbling some customary pious sentiment the while.

But he did not say, for he did not know, and we do not know, how much good this poor woman's crucifix had done, invoked and kissed by her on so many occasions. Still less can we tell how much benefit may yet spring from that charitable thought of an old lady, descending to an innocent child, and afterward reascending as a prayer from a pure heart to the Throne of Infinite Mercy.

The same evening the servants at the villa, who had been given leave of absence during the journey of the Count and Countess, got drunk in the drawing-room on rum and marsala.

THE LITTLE SARDINIAN DRUMMER

BY EDMONDO DE AMICIS

*Edmondo de Amicis, Italian publicist with a
military training, born in 1846, is principally
known as the author of "Il Cuore" ("The
Heart of a Boy"), a simple classic intended
for children, and which has had an incredible
influence on school life in Italy. It pretends
to be a child's own day to day record of his
school year.*

*His style has not crystallized into originality
—it suggests on one page Washington Irving,
with gentle, smooth, playful humor, broad tol-
erance, and on the next it suggests the word-
painters like Théophile Gautier, with their
keen observation and warm, rich coloring.*

THE LITTLE SARDINIAN DRUMMER

BY EDMONDO DE AMICIS

ON the 24th of July, 1848, the first day of the battle of Custoza, sixty soldiers belonging to one of our regiments of infantry, ordered to garrison a lonely house on a height near by, were suddenly attacked by two companies of Austrians, who, assaulting them on several sides, scarcely gave them time to take refuge within the house, and hastily barricade the door, leaving their dead and wounded on the field.

The door being well secured, our soldiers hastened to the windows on the ground floor, as well as to those on the upper floor, and opened a deadly fire on the besiegers, who replied vigorously as they slowly approached in the form of a semicircle.

The sixty Italian soldiers were commanded by two subaltern officers, and by a tall, silent, grim old captain, with white hair and whiskers.

With them was a little Sardinian drummer, a boy scarcely more than fourteen years old, but who did not look even twelve, with his dark, olive skin, and black, deep-set eyes that flashed fire.

From a room on the upper story the captain directed

Translated by Clou. E. Hard. Copyright, 1898, by The Current Literature Publishing Company.

the defense, every order sounding like a pistol shot, his iron countenance showing not the slightest emotion.

The little drummer, pale, but with his feet firmly planted on the table, and holding fast to the walls, stretched out his head and neck to look from the window, and saw through the smoke the Austrians steadily advancing over the fields.

The house was near the top of a very steep hillside, so that but one small high window in the upper story looked out over the crest. The Austrians did not threaten that side, nor was there anybody on the hilltop. The fire was directed against the front and the two sides.

The firing was infernal—a close, heavy hailstorm of balls rained upon the walls and through the broken roof, tearing out the ceiling, shattering the beams, doors, furniture, filling the air with fragments, plastering, and clouds of lime and dust, utensils and broken glass whizzing, clattering over their heads, rebounding from the walls with a noise and clash that made the hair stand on end.

Now and then a soldier stationed at the windows fell inward, and was pushed one side; others staggered from room to room, stanching their wounds with their hands. In the kitchen lay one soldier, pierced through the forehead. The enemy was closing in. At last the captain, until then impassible, began to show signs of uneasiness, and hurriedly left the room, followed by a sergeant. In a few moments the sergeant came rushing back, called the drummer, telling him to follow.

The boy raced up the stairs after him, and entered a dilapidated garret, in which he saw the captain with pencil and paper in hand, leaning on the window sill, and lying on the ground at his feet was a rope belonging to the well.

The captain folded the paper, and, fixing on the boy those cold, gray eyes before which every soldier trembled, said abruptly:

"Drummer!"

The little drummer's hand went up to his cap.

The captain said:

"Thou art brave."

The boy's eyes flashed.

"Yes, captain," he answered.

"Look down yonder," said the captain, taking him to the window, "on the ground, near the house of Villafranca, where those bayonets glisten. There is our regiment, motionless. Take this paper, grasp this rope, let yourself down from the window, cross the hill like lightning, rush through the fields, reach our men, and give this paper to the first officer you see. Take off your belt and knapsack."

The drummer took off his belt and knapsack, and hid the paper in his breast pocket; the sergeant threw out the rope, holding fast one end; the captain helped the boy jump through the window, his back toward the fields.

"Be careful," said he, "the salvation of this detachment depends on thy valor and thy legs."

"Trust me, captain," said the drummer, sliding down.

"Crouch low when you drop," again said the captain, taking hold of the rope, too.

"Have no fear."

"God speed thee!"

In a few moments the boy was on the ground, the sergeant drew up the rope, and disappeared, while the captain hastened to the little window, and saw the drummer racing down the hill. He now hoped he would escape unseen, but five or six little clouds of dust rising from the ground warned him that the boy had been discovered by the Austrians, who were firing down from the top of the hill. Those little clouds were the earth torn up by the balls. But the drummer continued running at full speed. After a while the captain exclaimed in consternation: "Dead!" but scarcely was the word out of his mouth when he saw the little drummer rise.

"Ah, it was but a fall!" said he, and breathed again.

The drummer again ran on, but he limped.

"He has sprained his foot," said the captain.

A little cloud of dust rose here and there around the boy, but always farther from him.

He was beyond their reach. The captain uttered a cry of triumph; but his eyes followed him, tremblingly, for it was a question of minutes. If he did not soon reach the regiment with the note, asking for immediate succor, all his soldiers would be killed, or he would be obliged to surrender, and become a prisoner of war with them.

The boy ran for a while rapidly, then he stopped

to limp; again he ran on, but every few minutes he stopped to limp.

"Perhaps a ball has bruised his foot," thought the captain, and he tremblingly noted all his movements, and in his excitement he talked to the drummer as if he could hear him. Every moment his eyes measured the distance between the boy and the bayonets that glistened below on the plain, in the midst of the golden wheat fields.

Meantime he heard the whistling and the crash of the balls in the rooms below, the voice of command, the shouts of rage of the officers and sergeants; the sharp cries of the wounded, and the noise of broken furniture and crumbling plaster.

"Courage! Valor!" he cried, his eyes following the drummer in the distance. "Forward! Run! Malediction! He stops! Ah, he is up again, forward!"

An officer out of breath comes to tell him that the enemy, without ceasing the fire, wave a white handkerchief, demanding their surrender.

"Let no one answer!" shouts the captain, without taking his eyes from the boy, who was now in the valley, but who no longer ran, and who seemed hopeless of reaching the regiment.

"Forward! Run!" cried the captain with teeth and fists clenched. "Bleed to death, die, unfortunate boy, but reach your destination!" Then he uttered a horrible oath. "Ah, the infamous idler has sat down!"

In fact, up to that moment the boy's head, that could be seen above the wheat, now disappeared as if he had fallen. After a moment his head was again seen, then he was lost behind the wheat field, and the captain saw him no more.

Then he hastened down. The balls rained, the rooms were full of wounded, some of whom rolled over like drunken men, catching at the furniture; the walls and floors were covered with blood. Dead bodies lay across the threshold; the lieutenant's arm was broken by a ball. Smoke and powder filled the rooms.

"Courage!" shouted the captain. "Stand to your post! Succor is coming! Courage a little longer!"

The Austrians had approached closer. Their disfigured faces could be seen through the smoke. Through the crash of balls could be heard the savage cries insulting them, demanding their surrender, and threatening to cut their throats. A soldier, terrified, withdrew from the window, and the sergeants again pushed him forward.

The fire of the besieged slackened. Discouragement showed on every face; resistance was no longer possible. The moment came when the Austrians redoubled their efforts, and a voice thundered, at first in German, then in Italian:

"Surrender!"

"No!" shouted the captain from a window. The fire became more deadly, more furious on both sides. Other soldiers fell. There were more than one window without defenders. The fatal moment was imminent. The captain's voice died away in his throat as he exclaimed:

"They do not come! They do not come!"

And he ran furiously from side to side, brandishing his sabre convulsively, ready to die. Then a sergeant, rushing down from the garret, shouted with stentorian voice:

"They come!"

"Ah, they come!" joyfully shouted the captain.

On hearing that cry all—the well, the wounded, sergeants and officers—crowded to the windows and again the fierceness of the defense was redoubled. In a short while there was noticed among the enemy a species of vacillation and a beginning of disorder. Suddenly the captain gathered a few soldiers together on the lower floor to resist with fixed bayonets the impetuous attack on the outside. Then he went upstairs. Scarcely had he mounted when he heard the sound of hurried footsteps, accompanied by a formidable "Hurrah!" and the pointed hats of the Italian carbineers appeared through the smoke, a squadron at double-quick, a brilliant flash of swords whirled through the air above their heads, their shoulders, their backs; then out charged the little detachment, with fixed bayonets, led by the captain. The enemy wavered, rallied, and at last began to retreat. The field was evacuated, the house was saved, and shortly after two battalions of Italian infantry and two cannon occupied the height.

The captain and the surviving soldiers were incorporated with their regiment, fought again, and the captain was slightly wounded in the hand by a spent ball during the last bayonet charge. The victory on that day was won by the Italians.

But the following day the battle continued. The

Italians were conquered, in spite of their heroic resistance, by superior numbers, and on the morning of the 26th they were in full retreat toward the Mincio.

The captain, though wounded, marched at the head of his company, weary and silent, arriving at sunset at Goito on the Mincio. He immediately sought his lieutenant, who, with his arm broken, had been picked up by the ambulance, and who must have arrived before he did. They pointed out to him a church in which the field hospital had been installed. He went there, the church was filled with the wounded lying in two rows of cots, and mattresses laid on the floor. Two physicians and several practitioners were busily coming and going, and nothing was heard but groans and stifled cries.

Scarcely had the captain entered when he stopped and glanced around in search of his subordinate.

At that moment he heard, near by, his name called faintly:

"Captain!"

He turned. It was the little drummer. He was stretched upon a wooden cot, covered up to the neck with a coarse old red and white check window curtain, his arms lying outside, pale and thin, but with his eyes burning like two coals of fire.

"What! is it thou?" asked the captain in a surprised, abrupt manner. "Bravo! thou hast fulfilled thy duty."

"I did all that was possible," replied the drummer.

"Art thou wounded?" asked the captain, glancing around at the beds, in search of his lieutenant.

"What could you expect?" replied the boy, who was

eager to speak of the honor of being wounded for the first time, otherwise he would not have dared to open his lips before his captain.

"I ran as long as I could with my head down, but, though I crouched, the Austrians saw me immediately. I would have arrived twenty minutes earlier had they not wounded me. Fortunately I met a captain of the general's staff, to whom I gave the note. But it was with great effort I got along after that. I was dying with thirst. I was afraid I could not arrive in time. I cried with rage, thinking that every minute's delay sent one of ours to the other world. But at last I did all I could. I am content. But look, captain, and excuse me, you are bleeding!"

In fact, from the palm of the badly bandaged hand the blood was flowing.

"Do you wish me to tighten the bandage, captain? Let me have it for a moment."

The captain gave him his left hand, and stretched out his right hand to help tie the knot; but scarcely had the little fellow risen from the pillow when he turned pale, and had to lie back again.

"Enough! enough!" said the captain, looking at him, and withdrawing his bandaged hand, which the drummer wished to retain. "Take care of yourself instead of thinking of others, for slight wounds, if neglected, may have grave consequences."

The little drummer shook his head.

"But thou," said the captain, looking attentively at him, "thou must have lost much blood to be so weak."

"Lost much blood?" repeated the boy, smiling.

"Something more than blood. Look!" and he threw down the coverlet. The captain recoiled in horror.

The boy had but one leg; the left leg had been amputated above the knee. The stump was wrapped in bloody cloths.

Just then a small, fat army physician in shirt-sleeves passed.

"Ah, captain," said he rapidly, pointing out the little drummer; "there is an unfortunate case. That leg could have been easily saved had he not forced it so much, caused inflammation; it was necessary to amputate it. But he is brave, I assure you. He shed not a tear, nor uttered a plaint. I was proud, while operating, to think he was an Italian boy, my word of honor. Faith, he comes of good stock."

And he went on his way.

The captain wrinkled his bushy white eyebrows, and looked fixedly at the little drummer while covering him up with the coverlet. Then, slowly, almost unconsciously, yet still looking at him, his hand went to his képi, which he took off.

"Captain!" exclaimed the astonished boy. "What, captain, for me?"

Then that rough soldier, who had never spoken a gentle word to an inferior, replied in a soft and exceedingly affectionate voice:

"I am but a captain, thou art a hero."

Then he threw his arms about the little drummer and kissed him with all his heart.

LULU'S TRIUMPH

BY MATILDA SERAO

Matilda Serao was born in 1856 at Patras, Greece. She is Italy's foremost woman writer, adopting a career very unusual with her countrywomen. Up to her thirtieth year she contributed sketches to periodicals.

In her early work she distinctly shows the influence of French realists like Zola. Few writers know Balzac as she does. Later she developed a liking for the psychological problem novel, and later still, in "Christ's Country," she seems to have joined that neomystic school represented in Italy by Fogazzaro, especially in his "Saint." Her style is slovenly, and, though not strong-minded, more like that of a man. But her stories are told with great spirit. The heroine of one of her very latest stories is an American, but she does not at all sympathize with the American reader's "absurd wish for happy endings." "Lulu's Triumph" combines the singular merits of a "happy ending" according to the American idea, with a sad ending according to the author's.

LULU'S TRIUMPH

BY MATILDA SERAO

I

SUFIA did not raise her eyes from her work, and her chin drooped easily down over the delicate cambric. But Lulu wandered about the room, moving the ornaments on the shelves or peering eager to react nervously [the ?]. It was clear that she wished either to do or to say something, but checked by fear. First softly, then to another, hummed a few bars of a song, trilled a valse, even attacked air to beat... tune but also who was annoyed with her friend's reserve, decided to put the question boldly; and, planting herself in front of her sister, she asked:

"Lulu, do you know what Mademoiselle Jeannette told me?"

"Assuredly nothing very interesting."

"Now that is an answer dry and cold enough to give one a chill even in summer! Where do you get your ice, oh, my glacial sister?"

"Lulu, you are a veritable baby!"

"Now, that is just where you mistake, idol of my heart. I am not a baby, for I am going to be married."

LULU'S TRIUMPH

BY MATILDA SERAO

I

SOFIA did not raise her eyes from her work, and her slim fingers fairly flew over the delicate lace. But Lulu wandered about the room, moving the ornaments on the shelves or opening a drawer to gaze absently into it. It was clear that she wished either to do or to say something, but was abashed by her elder sister's grave manner. She hummed a few bars of a song, recited a verse, but Sofia appeared not to hear. Then Lulu, who was not blessed with too much patience, decided to put the question boldly, and, planting herself in front of her sister, she asked:

"Sofia, do you know what Mademoiselle Jeannette told me?"

"Assuredly nothing very interesting."

"Now that is an answer dry and cold enough to give one a chill even in summer! Where do you get your ice, oh, my glacial sister?"

"Lulu, you are a veritable baby!"

"Now, that is just where you mistake, idol of my heart. I am not a baby, for I am going to be married."

Translated by Elise Lathrop. Copyright, 1907, by P. F. Collier & Son.

"What?"

"And that is just what Jeannette told me."

"What nonsense! I do not understand a word of
what you are saying."

"Very good, I will now tell you all, as they say in
plays. It will be a narrative—but will Your Seriousness lend me your whole attention?"

"Yes, yes, but be quick."

"The day of the races at the Field of Mars is the
time and place. You were not there; you preferred
your everlasting books."

"If you wander so from the subject I will not listen
to you any longer."

"You must listen to me; this secret is suffocating
me, killing me."

"Are you beginning again?"

"I will stop, I will stop. Well, then, at the races we
sat in the front row on the grand stand. Paolo Lovato
came and presented a handsome young man to us,
Roberto Montefranco. After the usual greetings and
vague compliments, they found places directly behind
us; we exchanged a few words until the signal for the
start of the horses was heard. You remember that I
favored Gorgon, without foreseeing how ungrateful
she was to be to me—one must resign one's self to
ingratitude even with beasts. A cloud of dust quite
hid the horses. 'Gorgon wins!' I cried. 'No,' said
Montefranco, smilingly, 'Lord Lavello.' I was vexed
at his contradiction; but he continued smiling and con-
tradicting me; we ended by making a wager. Finally,
after half an hour of palpitation and anxiety, I learned

that Gorgon had played me false, that I had lost and
Montefranco had won; only fancy! I tell him that I
will pay at once; he bows and replies that there is
plenty of time. I meet him on the Chiaja, throw him
an interrogative glance, and he contents himself with
bowing and smiling in a mysterious manner. It is the
same at the theatre, everywhere. I live in the greatest
curiosity. Roberto is handsome, twenty-six years old,
and this morning Montefranco *père*, my future father-
in-law, had a two hours' conference with mama."

"Oh!"

"Signs of attention on the part of my audience?
Well, I knew about his visit from Jeannette. So the
marriage is arranged. One momentous detail remains
to be settled; when shall I go to the mayor's office, and
shall I wear a gray or a tan colored gown? Shall I
wear a hat with streamers or without?"

"How you run on!"

"Run? Why, of course; there are no obstacles.
Roberto and I will love each other madly, our parents
are content—"

"And you would marry a man that way?"

"What does 'that way' mean? It is such an elastic
word."

"Without knowing him, without loving him?"

"But I do know him, I have seen him at the races
and when out walking. I adore him! Day before
yesterday I refused to take luncheon because I had
not seen him, and instead drank three cups of coffee,
trying to commit suicide."

"And he?"

"He wishes to marry me, therefore he loves me!"
replied Lulu, triumphantly. But seeing Sofia's face
pale, she repented of this imprudent remark, and bending over her sister, asked affectionately:

"Have I said anything wrong?"

"No, dear, no; you are right. When one loves one
marries. It is difficult to awaken love," and she sighed
softly.

"Awaken love, awaken love!" repeated Lulu, in an
irritated manner. "It is very easy, Sofia; but when
one has a serious brow, like you, sad eyes, and unsmil-
ing lips; when one goes and sits in a corner thinking,
while every one else is dancing and jesting; when
one reads instead of laughing, and instead of living,
dreams; and when one cultivates an old and lacka-
daisical manner, though still young, then it is difficult
to be loved."

Sofia lowered her head and made no reply. Her
lips quivered slightly, as though she were suppressing
a sob.

"Have I hurt you again?" asked Lulu. "It is because I should like to see you beloved, surrounded with
affection, to see you a bride— How nice it would be
if we were to be married on the same day!"

"That is foolish; I shall be an old maid."

"No, miss, I forbid it, you wicked creature. If
Roberto is a nice fellow he absolutely must have a
bachelor brother; I wish it!"

At this moment their mother entered the room in
walking dress.

"Are you going out, mama?" asked Lulu.

"Yes, dear, I am going to the notary's."

"Oh! to the notary's. That is a serious business."

"You will soon learn, Miss Tease. Sofia, come with me for a moment."

"And has Sofia, too, some dark dealings with the notary?"

"Lulu, when will you learn to be serious?"

"Very soon, mama; you will see."

She opened the door for her mother and sister to pass out, made two low courtesies, murmuring: "Madame, Mademoiselle!" When they had left the room she called to them from the threshold, with a burst of laughter:

"Talk, talk away! I will pretend that I know nothing about it."

II

As a general thing Roberto Montefranco was not a great thinker; he had not time to be. What with luncheons, horseback rides, calls, and dinners, his days flew by, and his evenings he passed pleasantly with his fiancée, Lulu. Then there were tiresome matters to be attended to, some appointments with his lawyer, contracts to be signed, some old debts to be settled, to say nothing of preparations for his house and for the wedding trip. .He had barely time even for his half-hour's reading and fifteen minutes' loitering at the door of his café. So he was never seen absorbed in profound reflection, nor was he ever known to be engaged in solving some social problem, for Roberto had nothing of the tragic or heroic in his character.

Rather, he was of a serene temperament, and many
envied him for it.

But this afternoon he lay stretched out in an armchair, one leg crossed over the other, a book in his
hand, with the fixed determination of reading. The
book was interesting; yet, new and strange as it may
seem, the reader had become very absent-minded. In
fact, he was more than that; he was nervous and restless. He never turned a page, because after reading
a couple of lines the letters seemed to leave their
printed places, to dance about, become confused, disappear. Roberto had involuntarily taken a journey into
the unknown regions of thought.

"Papa is satisfied, my aunts all have sent me their
blessings, my girl cousins are angry, my friends at the
café congratulate me ironically, my true friends clasp
my hand; therefore I am doing well to marry. I can
not deny that Lulu is very pretty; when she fixes her
eyes so full of mischief upon me, when she laughs and
shows her little white teeth, I want to take her charming little head between my hands and kiss her over and
over again. And she has an excellent disposition, a
character of gold, always merry, good-natured, ready
for a jest, witty, full of pranks, never melancholy.
We shall agree excellently. I can not endure serious
looks, especially in people I love. It always seems to
me that such looks conceal a secret grief, a grief with
which I am unacquainted, and which I can not alle-
viate, or of which I am perhaps the involuntary cause.
Sofia, my future sister-in-law, has the faculty of irri-
tating me with her cold, impassive face. Whenever

she appears my intelligence seems to shrivel up, the smile leaves my lips; and even should the most beautiful spring sun be shining, for me it turns into a gray November day. I no longer have the courage to joke even with Lulu; that Sofia drives all joy away. She may have noticed the unpleasant impression she makes upon me, for she speaks to me without looking at me, does not shake hands, answers in the fewest possible words. She has noticed my dislike for her. Perhaps she is offended by it.

"Lulu always laughs. She is very young. She never says a serious word to me, and even if she wishes to it always seems as though she were ridiculing. She loves me, but not madly. To be frank, mine is not a mad passion either; better so. For my part, I have two theories firmly established in my mind: an engaged couple should be of like dispositions, and, secondly, they should never begin with a violent passion. This is our case, and Lulu and I will be very happy. We shall take a trip through Italy, but without haste, taking short journeys, enjoying every comfort, stopping where we please, seeing even the most insignificant things. We will thus occupy three months; no, that will not be enough, let us say four months; I shall be glad to get Lulu away for a certain time from the doleful society of Sofia. But, I ask, is it natural that that girl should be so serious at her age? She must be twenty-three. She is not plain. In fact, she has beautiful eyes, and the carriage of a queen. If she were not so severe she would please. I wager that she will be an old maid; perhaps

that is her secret torment, perhaps a love affair, some
unfortunate love affair—I am curious to know the
cause of her seriousness—I shall ask Lulu when we
are alone—

"Lulu is fond of bonbons, she told me so that second evening I went to her house. How she nibbles
them! How they disappear between her little red lips,
and after a moment what a false air of compunction
she assumes—because there are no more. She is
dear, dear, dear! She confided to me in a low tone
that when it thunders she is frightened, and goes and
hides her head among the pillows; that she has always
dreamed of having a gown of black velvet, with a very
long train, and with white lace at the neck and sleeves.
She assures me that she shall be jealous, jealous as a
Spaniard, and that she shall buy a little dagger with a
handle inlaid with gold, with which to take vengeance.
She is adorable when she repeats these absurdities to
me, with her childish air of conviction. Even Sofia
is forced to smile sometimes, and how it brightens her
face! That Sofia, that Sofia! who will ever learn to
know her!"

The book fell from his knees to the floor, the young
man started at the sound, looked about in surprise, as
though unable to recognize himself. It was actually
he, Roberto Montefranco, caught in *flagrante delicto*,
meditating.

III

Twilight was descending like a rain of gray ashes.
Sofia, standing at the window that opened out on to

the balcony, was gazing down into the crowded, noisy street. It was the hour in which the Via Toledo becomes dangerous because of the great number of large and small carriages that pass up and down in a continuous stream. Sofia seemed looking for some one; suddenly a vivid flush passed over her face, she bent her head slightly, then suddenly paled, and turned back into the room. A minute later Lulu entered like a whirlwind, slamming doors, overturning chairs that she might hurry the more.

"What are you doing here, Donna Sofia Santangelo? Are you reading?"

"Yes, I was reading."

"And you did not even care to stand on the balcony?"

"And if I had?"

"Pshaw! I had to stay upstairs, for Albina, the dressmaker, had brought my gown for this evening, and all the while I was trembling with impatience, for I wanted to be here. Yesterday evening I told Roberto to wear his gray overcoat, to have Selim harnessed to the cart, and to pass at half-past six. Who knows if he obeyed me!"

"Roberto passed here in the cart, and wearing his gray overcoat."

"Good gracious! How do you know all this? I thought you were reading?"

"I was in the window."

"And you recognized Roberto, although you never look at him? Wonderful! Did he bow to you?"

"Yes."

"How did he take off his hat?"

"Why—as he always does."

"And you bowed to him?"

"Do you think me lacking in manners?"

"At least you smiled at him?"

"No—that is, I do not know."

"You are not nice, Sofia. And yesterday evening Roberto spoke to me about you."

"Telling you that I was not nice?"

"No, but asking me the cause of your reserved character, so different from mine. Then I recited a fine panegyric to him; I told him that you were better, more amiable, more loving than I, that your only fault was in concealing all these good qualities. Only fancy, he listened to me with the greatest interest; finally, he asked me about your aversion to him—"

"Aversion!"

"That is what he said, and, do you know, he is not so entirely wrong; you treat him with so little cordiality. But even on this point I defended you; I told a fib, for I said that you liked him very much indeed, and that you esteemed him greatly—"

"Lulu!"

"I know that it is not true, but Roberto is so fond of you, is it not ungrateful of you to treat him like a stranger?"

Sofia threw her arms around her sister's neck and kissed her; Lulu held her for an instant, and murmured in a caressing voice:

"Why do you not love Roberto a little?"

The other made a sudden abrupt movement and drew away, without saying a word.

"Oh, well!" said Lulu, shrugging her shoulders and changing the subject. "Are you really not coming with us this evening?"

"No, I have a headache; you can go with mama."

"As usual. I shall go just the same, because I shall have a very good time."

"Is—Roberto going with you?"

"No; he is going to his club, where there is a directors' meeting. I am going to profit by it and go to the Dellinos' ball, and shall dance until to-morrow morning."

"And when he knows of it?"

"So much the better. He will learn from now on to leave me free; I do not wish him to acquire bad habits."

"You love him very little, it seems to me."

"Very much, in my own way. But I must hurry away to dress. It will take me at least two hours."

Sofia stood listening to the noise of the departing carriage which bore away her mother and sister. She was left alone, quite alone, as she had always wished to be left. As a child, when some wrong or injustice had been done her, she had cried all alone, when she was in bed, in the dark, and the habit had remained with her. Now, alone in the great drawing-room, beneath the brightly lighted chandelier, her hands inert, her head resting against the back of her chair, her face wore an expression of great sorrow, the vivid reflection of a serious inward conflict. Certainly in these moments of complete solitude the consciousness of a great grief came over her; the sentiment of the reality, long repulsed, became clear, distinct, cruel.

The sound of footsteps startled her. It was Roberto. Seeing her alone, he paused, hesitating; but supposing the rest of the family to be in another room, he advanced. Sofia had risen at once, agitated.

"Good evening, Sofia."

"Good evening—"

They were both embarrassed.

"Heavens, how unpleasant this Sofia is!" thought Roberto.

Meanwhile the girl recovered herself, composing her features, which once more took on a severe expression. They sat down at some distance from each other.

"Your mother is well?"

"Quite well, thank you."

"And—Lulu?"

"She, too, is very well."

There was silence. Roberto experienced a strange sensation as of joy filled with bitterness.

"Lulu is occupied?" he asked.

Sofia checked a slight movement of impatience.

"She is at the Dellinos' ball with mama," she continued rapidly, as if to anticipate other questions.

Since Sofia was alone, then, and if he did not wish to be the most discourteous of men, he ought to remain and chat with her. At this thought Roberto was seized with an almost irresistible desire to flee. Yet he did not move.

"I came here because there was not the required number of us at my club," he finally said, as if to excuse his presence.

"Lulu did not expect you—I am sorry—"

"Oh, it does not matter," interrupted Roberto.

The interruption was too quick, and hardly flattering to the absent one.

"And you did not go?" he resumed.

"No, you know I am not very fond of balls."

"Do you prefer reading?"

"Yes, very much."

"Are you not afraid of doing yourself harm?"

"I have good eyes," replied Sofia, raising them to the face of her questioner.

"And beautiful ones," thought Roberto, "but expressionless. I meant—"

"Moral injury, perhaps. I do not think so. From the books that I read I always derive great peace."

"Do you need peace?"

"We all need peace."

Sofia's voice was grave, resonant. Roberto took pleasure in it, as though he were hearing it for the first time. He seemed to find himself face to face with a woman hitherto unknown to him, and who was revealing herself to him in every word and gesture. Sofia had lost her coldness, she even looked at him, smiled at him, and spoke to him as to a friend. What had been between them before this? What was happening now?

"When I like a book," continued Roberto, "I always feel the greatest desire to know the author, to know if

he or she is good, if he has suffered, if he too has
loved—"

"Perhaps you would be disillusionized. Authors
always describe the love of others, never their own."

"Possibly out of respect?"

"From jealousy, I think. There are cases in which
love is the only treasure hidden in a soul."

But the voice of Sofia did not change as she said
these words. Her face wore such a frank expression,
her tone was so simple, so pure, so convinced, that
Roberto felt no surprise at hearing her discuss love
with such sureness. Nothing now surprised him;
everything seemed natural, to be expected. Even
this evening, passed alone with this strange girl,
seemed to him something predestined and long awaited.
When they separated they gazed directly into each
other's faces, as though they wished to be sure of
recognizing each other again. Sofia held out her
hand, Roberto took it and bowed over it; a portière
fell heavily behind him. They were parted.

When the charm of Sofia's presence and conversation had ceased, Roberto felt confused, his brain in a
turmoil. He was both gay and melancholy, would
have liked to die, and was yet full of life. He did
not know what to think of Lulu, of himself, or of his
future.

Sofia was very happy, very happy. For this reason
she wept, sobbing heartily, her head buried in her
pillow.

IV

Three months had passed, Lulu's marriage was still postponed. Every once in a while her mother, who did not understand this delay, would call her daughter aside and ask her the cause.

"I wish to wait," Lulu always replied; "I need to know Roberto better."

In fact, the girl had become observing. She went about as usual, sang as usual, laughed, joked, but often interrupted these pleasant occupations to study her sister, or to listen closely to Roberto's every word. The former was often seen with lips compressed, her eyebrows drawn together with an air of great attention.

Then Lulu looked about her. And about her strange things were happening. Roberto was no longer serene and hilarious as usual, but thoughtful, pale, and agitated. He spoke briefly and absently; to many things in which he had formerly been interested he now seemed quite indifferent; sometimes with a great effort he succeeded in controlling himself, and becoming once more what he had been before, but only for a short time. He had never been accustomed to dissimulation, and succeeded badly; his passion and inner torment were revealed in his eyes.

A different Sofia, too, made her appearance at this time; that is to say, a nervous, restless Sofia, who at times embraced her sister with effusion, sometimes remained for hours without seeing her, rather avoiding her. Fleeting blushes rose to her cheeks, feverish

flushes; a flame burned in her eyes; her voice was now
deep and full of emotion, now dry and strident; her
hands shook. At night she did not sleep. Lulu often
rose, and went with bare feet to listen at her door, and
heard Sofia toss about and weep. If questioned, Sofia
declared that there was nothing the matter; always
the same reply.

When Roberto and Sofia met—and this happened
every day—the change that had taken place in both
of them became evident. Remarks were rare, replies
were either too prompt or too vague, there were odd
glances; sometimes for whole evenings they did not
speak, but each studied the movements of the other.
They never sat beside each other; yet Roberto always
found an excuse for picking up the work or the book
that Sofia had touched. Sometimes when she did not
come into the room, Roberto, always more and more
uneasy, stared at the closed door, answering absently
to what was said. Sometimes only five minutes after
Sofia's appearance he would take his hat and leave.
The girl was growing pale, black circles appeared
under her eyes. Finally, she decided not to let herself
be seen. Every evening for a week she shut herself
in her room, trembling with impatience, trying to
smother her unhappiness.

One evening Lulu entered her room. "Will you do
me a favor?" she asked.

"What do you want?"

"I have a note to write," said Lulu. "Roberto is
alone, out on the terrace. Will you go and keep him
company?"

"But I—"

"Do you wish to stay shut up here? Does it cost you so much to please me?"

"Will you come back soon?"

"I only want time to write four lines."

Sofia turned toward the terrace, trying to summon courage for the ordeal. She paused on the threshold. Roberto was walking up and down; she went up to him.

"Lulu sends me," she said in a low voice.

"You forced yourself to come?"

"Forced—no."

She trembled throughout her whole frame; Roberto was near her, his face transfigured with passion.

"What have I done to you, Sofia?"

"Nothing, you have done nothing. Do not look at me like that," she implored, terrified.

"You know then, Sofia, that I love you very dearly?"

"Oh! hush, Roberto, for pity's sake hush! If Lulu were to hear us!"

"I do not love Lulu. I love you, Sofia."

"That is treachery."

"I know it, but I love you. I will go away—"

"Well?" cried Lulu in the distance, appearing from another door. "Well, have you two made peace?"

But there was no reply. Sofia fled, hiding her face in her hands; and Roberto remained motionless, silent, as though stunned.

"Roberto!" cried Lulu.

"Lulu."

"What has happened?"

"Nothing; I am going."

And without even taking leave of her, he too went away with a despairing gesture. Lulu followed him with her eyes, and stood there absorbed in thought.

"One here, the other there," she murmured; "and previous to that? Enough! I must take a hand in it."

V

"And so for all these excellent reasons I can not marry Roberto Montefranco," Lulu finally said to her mother.

"They are absurd reasons, my daughter," replied the mother, shaking her head.

"In short, must I tell you frankly and plainly that Roberto does not please me, and that I am not going to marry him?"

"It is at least frank; but it is no more than a whim. Roberto loves you."

"He will console himself."

"You have exchanged promises."

"We can retract them. We are no longer living in the days when people were married by force."

"What will the world say?"

"Mother, let us define the world."

"People."

"And who is Mr. People? I do not know him; I am not obliged to be unhappy for the sake of Mr. People."

"You are a terrible girl! But how am I to arrange it with Roberto? What am I to say to him?"

"What you wish. That is what you are my mother for."

"Oh, indeed! To remedy the wrongs you have done. There will be a scandal."

"I do not think so; you can say it politely, with pretty manners. Indeed, I think you might even speak badly of me—call me capricious, frivolous, childish; say that I would be a very bad wife, that I am not at all serious, that I am lacking in dignity, that my sister is—"

"Your sister? Are you losing your mind, Lulu?"

"Pshaw! you could easily say that. At present Roberto and Sofia are indifferent to each other, but if they come to know each other better they might appreciate each other, and then—who can say? You would be praised as a good mother for having married off the elder daughter first."

"In fact—"

"I shall not go husbandless; I am barely eighteen years old. And I wish to amuse myself; I wish to dance a great deal; I wish to enjoy my happy youth with my dear, kind little mother—"

"You are a little rogue," replied the mother, moved, and embracing her daughter.

"Then we understand each other? Announce the ugly news to Roberto politely, but add that we must always be friends, that we hope to see him often. If these two are to fall in love with each other they will do so; it is predestined."

"But do you believe, naughty Lulu, that matters will all come right? You know that I hate quarrels."

"Oh, unconvinced mother! Oh, mother, more unbelieving than Saint Thomas! Yes, yes, out of my wide experience I assure you that there will be no scandal. Roberto is a gentleman, and will not expect me to marry him without loving him."

"What seems to me impossible is the affair with Sofia—"

"Nothing is more possible than the impossible," gravely replied Lulu.

"My dear, so many axioms! Enough. Let us leave it all to time; perhaps time will regulate our affairs. All of which does not change the fact that you are a scatterbrain."

"And very capricious—"

"Lacking in judgment—"

"And a whimsical creature. I am everything you like; lecture me, I deserve it. Come; have you nothing to say? I am waiting."

"Give me a kiss, and go to bed. Good night, baby."

"Thank you, mama. Good night."

"It is better so," thought the good mother. "Lulu is too young yet. Every day one sees the sad consequences of these marriages of convenience. May Heaven free us from them! It is better so."

"Uff!" said Lulu, taking a deep breath. "What diplomacy I was forced to use, what art in order to convince mama! I would make a perfect ambassador. What a triumph! Not like a triumph of love, to be sure, but it is Lulu's triumph!"

She paused outside her sister's door and listened. She heard every now and then a repressed sigh. Poor Sofia had lost her peace of mind.

"Sleep, Sofia, sleep," Lulu murmured softly, kissing the lock of the door almost as though she were kissing her sister's brow; "calm yourself and rest. I have worked for you this evening."

And the generous girl fell asleep, happy and content in the thought of the happiness of the sister she loved.

Time, good old time, the eternal wise old gentleman, accomplished his task. Lulu asked herself whether this unmarried sister who acted as bridesmaid should wear a gown of blue silk or a simple one of straw-colored foulard with lace. She asked Roberto if there would be a great many bonbons for her, and Sofia if she would give her that pretty embroidered handkerchief that was like a zephyr, a cloud. Roberto and Sofia, knowing what the girl's heart was capable of, smiled at her gay thoughtlessness, and loved her, and looked upon her as their Providence.

"For I have always maintained," said Roberto Montefranco to a friend, speaking of his marriage, "that a couple should be of opposite tastes. Extremes touch. Thus they will understand each other, will mingle, will form a complete whole, while those of similar tastes are like two parallel lines; they walk on together, but never meet. And then when there is love—! I have always said so."

THE END OF CANDIA

BY GABRIELE D'ANNUNZIO

Gabriele d'Annunzio, Italian poet and novelist, whose real name is Rapagnetta, was born
on the Adriatic in 1864. In 1898 he was
chosen member of the Chamber of Deputies,
when he announced himself a social demo-
crat. His first poems, which appeared in
1879, showed great talent, but it is as a
writer of richly colored, vivid, voluptuous
prose, which is at the same time classic in
form and correct, almost finikin, in its perfect
style, that he ranks among the best of Italy's
authors. His later stories grow deeper, more
sombre, and unpleasant in theme, and are full
of gruesome realism, borrowed from the modern French and Russian. He is a symbolist
whose love of musical cadence sometimes
leaves little room for sound thinking. But he
is a master of style. His earlier stories, one of
which is given here, are not so unpleasant as
the later ones, and are frank imitations of De
Maupassant—in this case of "The String."

THE END OF CANDIA

BY GABRIELE D'ANNUNZIO

I

THREE days after the Easter banquet, which was traditionally a great occasion in the Lamonica household, both in its lavishness and in the number of its guests, Donna Cristina Lamonica was counting the table linen and silver service, and replacing them one by one, methodically, in drawer and cupboard, in readiness for future banquets.

As usual, she had with her, to help in the task, the chambermaid, Maria Bisaccia, and the laundress, Candida Marcanda, familiarly known as Candia. The huge hampers, filled with fine linen, stood in a row upon the floor. The silver platters and other table service gleamed brightly from the sideboard—massive vessels, somewhat crudely wrought by rustic silversmiths, and of more or less liturgical design, like all the plate which rich provincial families hand down from generation to generation. A fresh fragrance of soapy water pervaded the room.

From the hampers Candia took tablecloths, napkins, and towels; she made the mistress take note that each piece was intact, and then passed them over to Maria, who laid them away in the drawers, while the mistress sprinkled lavender between them and entered the num-

Translated by Frederic Taber Cooper. Copyright, 1907, by P. F. Collier & Son.

bers in a book. Candia was a tall, lean, angular woman
of fifty, with back somewhat bent from the habitual
attitude of her calling, with arms of unusual length,
and the head of a bird of prey mounted on a turtle's
neck. Maria Bisaccia was a native of Ortona, a trifle
stout, with a fresh complexion and the clearest of
eyes; she had a soft fashion of speech, and the light,
leisurely touch of one whose hands were almost always
busy over cakes and sirups, pastry and preserves.
Donna Cristina, also an Ortonese, and educated in a
Benedictine convent, was of small stature, with a somewhat too generous expanse of bosom, a face over-
strewn with freckles, a large, long nose, poor teeth,
and handsome eyes cast downward in a way that made
one think of a priest in woman's clothing.

The three women were performing their task with
the utmost care, giving up to it the greater part of the
afternoon. All at once, just as Candia was leaving
with the empty baskets, Donna Cristina, in the course
of counting the small silver, found that a spoon was
missing.

"Maria! Maria!" she cried, in utter dismay, "count
these! There's a spoon missing! Count them yourself!"

"But how could it? That's impossible, Signora!"
replied Maria, "let me have a look." And she in turn
began to count the small pieces, telling off the numbers
aloud, while Donna Cristina looked on, shaking her
head. The silver gave forth a clear, ringing sound.

"Well, it's a fact!" Maria exclaimed at last, with a
gesture of despair; "what's to be done about it!"

She herself was safe from all suspicion. For fifteen years she had given proofs of her fidelity and honesty in this very household. She had come from Ortona together with Donna Cristina at the time of the wedding, almost as though she were a part of the marriage settlement; and from the first she had acquired a certain authority in the house, through the indulgence of her mistress. She was full of religious superstitions, devoted to the saint and the belfry of her birthplace, and possessed of great shrewdness. She and her mistress had formed a sort of offensive alliance against Pescara and all pertaining to it, and more particularly against the saint of the Pescarese. She never missed a chance to talk of her native town, to vaunt its beauty and its riches, the splendor of its basilica, the treasures of San Tommaso, the magnificence of its religious ceremonies, as compared with the poverty of San Cetteo, that possessed only one single little silver cross.

Donna Cristina said:

"Take a good look in there."

Maria left the room to extend the search. She explored every nook and corner of the kitchen and the balcony, but in vain. She came back empty-handed.

"It isn't there! It isn't there!"

Then the two together tried to think, to make conjectures, to ransack their memories. They went out upon the balcony that communicated with the court, the balcony back of the laundry, to make one last research. As they talked together in loud tones, women's heads began to appear at the windows of the surrounding houses.

"What has happened, Donna Cristina? Tell us about it."

Donna Cristina and Maria related the occurrence with many words and many gestures.

"Lord, Lord! Then there have been thieves here?"

In a moment the report of the theft had spread through the neighborhood, through all Pescara. Men and women fell to discussing, to imagining who could have been the thief. By the time the news had reached the most distant houses of Sant' Agostino, it had gathered volume; it was no longer a question of a mere spoon, but of all the silver plate in the house of Lamonica.

Now, since the weather was fine and roses were beginning to bloom upon the balcony, and a pair of linnets were singing in their cage, the women lingered at their windows, for the pleasure of gossiping across the grateful warmth of the outdoor air. Female heads continued to appear from behind the pots of sweet basil, and a chatter arose that must have rejoiced the cats upon the housetops.

Clasping her hands, Donna Cristina asked: "Who could it have been?"

Donna Isabella Sertale, nicknamed the Pole-cat, who had the lithe and stealthy movements of a beast of prey, asked in a strident voice: "Who did you have with you, Donna Cristina? It seems to me that I saw Candia on her way—"

"Ahah!" exclaimed Donna Felicetta Margasanta, nicknamed the Magpie because of her continuous garrulity. "Ahah!" repeated the other gossips.—"And

you hadn't thought of it?"—"And you never noticed?"
—"And you don't know about Candia?"—"We can
tell you about Candia!"—"Indeed we can!"—"Oh, yes,
we can tell you about her!"

"She washes clothes well, there is no denying it.
She is the best laundress in Pescara, there's no question about it. But the trouble with her is that she is
too light-fingered—didn't you know that, my dear?"

"She got a couple of towels from me once."—"And
a napkin from me."—"And a night-gown from me."
—"And three pairs of stockings from me."—"And a
new petticoat from me."—"And I never got them back
again."—"Nor I."—"Nor I."

"But I didn't discharge her. Whom could I get?
Silvestra?"

"Oh! oh!"

"Angelantonia? The African?"

"Each one worse than the other!"

"We must put up with it."

"But it's a spoon this time!"

"That's a little too much!"

"Don't you let it pass, Donna Cristina, don't you
let it pass!"

"Let it pass, or not let it pass!" burst forth Maria
Bisaccia, who in spite of her placid and benign appearance, never let an opportunity pass for displaying her
superiority over her fellow servants. "That is for us
to decide, Donna Isabella, that is for us to decide!"

And the chatter continued to flow back and forth
from windows to balcony. And the accusation spread
from lip to lip throughout the whole countryside.

II

The following morning, Candia Marcanda already had her arms in a tubful of clothes, when the village constable, Biagio Pesce, nicknamed the Little Corporal, appeared at her door.

"His Honor, the mayor, wants you up at his office right away," he told the laundress.

"What's that?" demanded Candia, wrinkling her brows into a frown, yet without interrupting the task before her.

"His Honor, the mayor, wants you up at his office, right away."

"Wants me? What does he want me for?" Candia demanded rather sharply, for she was at a loss to understand this unexpected summons, and it turned her as stubborn as a horse balking at a shadow.

"I can't tell you what for," replied the Little Corporal, "those were my orders."

"What were your orders?" From an obstinacy that was natural to her, she would not cease from asking questions. She could not convince herself that it was a reality. "The mayor wants me? What for? What have I done, I should like to know? I'm not going. I haven't done anything."

The Little Corporal, losing his temper, answered: "Oh, you won't go, won't you? We'll see about that!" and he went off, muttering, with his hand upon the hilt of the ancient sword he wore.

Meanwhile there were others along the narrow street who had overheard the conversation and came

out upon their doorsteps, where they could watch
Candia vigorously working her arms up and down
in the tubful of clothes. And since they knew about
the silver spoon, they laughed meaningly and inter-
changed ambiguous phrases, which Candia could not
understand. But this laughter and these phrases
awoke a vague forboding in the woman's mind. And
this forboding gathered strength when the Little Corporal reappeared, accompanied by another officer.

"Step lively," said the Little Corporal preemptorily.

Candia wiped her arms, without replying, and went
with them. In the public square, people stopped to
look. One of her enemies, Rosa Panura, called out
from the door of her shop, with a hateful laugh:
"Drop your stolen bone!"

The laundress, dazed by this persecution for which
she could find no reason, was at a loss for a reply.

Before the mayor's office a group of curious idlers
had gathered to watch her as she went in. Candia, in
an access of anger, mounted the steps in a rush and
burst into the mayor's presence, breathlessly demanding: "Well, what is it you want of me?"

Don Silla, a man of peaceful proclivities, was for
the moment perturbed by the laundress's strident
tones, and cast a glance at the two faithful custodians
of his official dignity. Then, taking a pinch of
tobacco from his horn snuff-box, he said to her: "My
daughter, be seated."

But Candia remained standing. Her beak-like nose
was inflated with anger, and her wrinkled cheeks
quivered curiously. "Tell me, Don Silla."

GABRIELE D'ANNUNZIO

"You went yesterday to take back the wash to Donna Cristina Lamonica?"

"Well, and what of it? What of it? Was there anything missing? All of it counted, piece by piece —and not a thing missing. What's the matter with it now?"

"Wait a moment, my daughter! In the same room there was the table silver—"

Candia, comprehending, turned like an angry hawk, about to swoop upon its prey. Her thin lips twitched convulsively.

"The silver was in the room, and Donna Cristina found that a spoon was missing. Do you understand, my daughter? Could you have taken it—by mistake?"

Candia jumped like a grasshopper before the injustice of this accusation. As a matter of fact she had stolen nothing.

"Oh, it was I, was it? I? Who says so? Who saw me? I am astonished at you, Don Silla! I am astonished at you! I, a thief? I? I?"

And there was no end to her indignation. She was all the more keenly stung by the unjust charge, because she knew herself to be capable of the action they attributed to her.

"Then it was you who took it?" interrupted Don Silla, prudently sinking back into the depths of his spacious judicial chair.

"I am astonished at you!" snarled the woman once more, waving her long arms around as though they had been two sticks.

"Very well, you may go. We will see about it."

Candia went out without a salutation, blindly bump-
ing into the doorpost. She had turned fairly green;
she was beside herself. As she set foot in the street
and saw the crowd which had gathered, she realized
that already public opinion was against her; that no one
was going to believe in her innocence. Nevertheless,
she began to utter a vociferous denial. The crowd
continued to laugh as it dispersed. Full of fury, she
returned home, and hopelessly began to weep upon her
doorstep.

Don Donato Brandimarte, who lived next door, said
mockingly: "Cry louder, cry louder! There are people
passing by!"

Since there were heaps of clothing still waiting for
the suds, she finally calmed herself, bared her arms,
and resumed her task. As she worked, she thought
out her denials, elaborated a whole system of defense,
sought out in her shrewd woman's brain an ingeni-
ous method of establishing her innocence; racking her
brain for specious subtleties, she had recourse to every
trick of rustic dialectic to construct a line of reasoning
that would convince the most incredulous.

Then, when her day's work was ended, she went out,
deciding to go first to see Donna Cristina.

Donna Cristina was not to be seen. It was Maria
Bisaccia who listened to Candia's flood of words, shaking her head but answering nothing, and withdrawing
in dignified silence.

Next, Candia made the circuit of all her clients. To
each in turn she related the occurrence, to each she
unfolded her defense, continually adding some new

argument, amplifying her words, growing constantly more excited, more desperate, in the face of incredulity and distrust. And all in vain; she felt that from now on there was no further defense possible. A sort of blind hopelessness took possession of her—what more was there to do? What more was there to say?

III

Meanwhile Donna Cristina Lamonica gave orders to send for Cinigia, a woman of the people, who practised magic and empirical medicine with considerable success. Cinigia had several times before discovered stolen goods; and it was said that she was secretly in league with the thieves.

"Find that spoon for me," Donna Cristina told her, "and you shall have a big reward."

"Very well," Cinigia replied; "twenty-four hours are all I need."

And twenty-four hours later she brought back her answer; the spoon was to be found in a hole in the courtyard, near the well.

Donna Cristina and Maria descended to the courtyard, made search, and, to their great amazement, found the spoon.

Swiftly the news spread throughout Pescara.

Then triumphantly Candia Marcanda went the rounds of all the streets. She seemed to have grown taller; she held her head erect; she smiled, looking every one straight in the eye, as if to say, "I told you so! I told you so!"

Gabriele D'Annunzio

The people in the shops, seeing her pass by, would murmur something and then break forth into a significantly sneering laugh. Filippo La Selvi, who sat drinking a glass of liqueur brandy in the Café d'Ange, called Candia in.

"Another glass for Candia, the same as mine!"

The woman, who was fond of strong spirits, pursed up her lips covetously.

"You certainly deserve it, there's no denying that!" added Filippo La Selvi.

An idle crowd had gathered in front of the café. They all had the spirit of mischief in their faces. While the woman drank, Filippo La Selvi turned and addressed his audience:

"Say, she knew how to work it, didn't she? Isn't she the foxy one?" and he slapped the laundress familiarly upon her bony shoulder.

The crowd laughed. A little dwarf, called Magnafave, or "Big Beans," weak-minded and stuttering, joined the forefinger of his right hand to that of his left, and striking a grotesque attitude and dwelling upon each syllable, said:

"Ca—ca—ca—Candia—Ci—ci—Cinigia!" and he continued to make gestures and to stammer forth vulgar witticisms, all implying that Candia and Cinigia were in league together. His spectators indulged in contortions of merriment.

For a moment Candia sat there bewildered, with the glass still in her hand. Then in a flash she understood —they did not believe in her innocence. They accused her of having brought back the silver spoon secretly, by agreement with the sorceress, to save herself further trouble.

An access of blind anger came upon her. Speechless with passion, she flung herself upon the weakest of them, upon the little hunchback, in a hurricane of blows and scratches. And the crowd, at the sight of this struggle, formed a circle and jeered at them in cruel glee, as at a fight between two animals, and egged on the two combatants with voice and gesture.

Big Beans, badly scared by her unexpected violence, tried to escape, hopping about like a little ape; and held fast by the laundress's terrible arms, whirled round and round with increasing velocity, like a stone in a sling, until at last he fell violently upon his face.

Some of the men hastened to pick him up. Candia withdrew in the midst of hisses, shut herself within her house, and flung herself across her bed, sobbing and gnawing her fingers, in the keenness of her suffering. The new accusation cut her deeper than the first, and all the more that she knew herself capable of such a subterfuge. How was she to clear herself now? How was she to establish the truth? She grew hopeless as she realized that she could not allege in defense any material difficulties that might have interfered with carrying out the deception. Access to the courtyard was perfectly simple; a door, that was never fastened, opened from the ground floor of the main stairway; people came and went freely through that door, to remove the garbage, or for other causes. So it was impossible for her to close the lips of her accusers by saying, "How could I have got in?" The means of successfully carrying out such a plan were many and easy.

Candia proceeded to conjure up new arguments to convince them; she sharpened up her wits; she invented three, four, five different cases to prove that the spoon never could have been found in that hole in the courtyard; she spilt hairs with marvelous ingenuity. Next she took to making the rounds of the shops and the houses, seeking in every possible way to overcome the people's incredulity. They listened to her, greatly entertained by her captious reasoning; and they would end by saying, "Oh, it's all right!"

But there was a certain tone in their voice that left Candia annihilated. So, then, all her trouble was for nothing! No one would believe her! Yet with marvelous persistence she would return to the attack, spending whole nights in thinking out new arguments. And little by little, under this continued strain, her mind gave way; she could no longer follow any sustained thought but that of the silver spoon.

Neglecting her work, she had sunk to a state of actual want. When she went down to the river bank, under the iron bridge, where the other wash-women congregated, she would sometimes let slip from between her fingers the garments that the current swept away forever. And she would talk continually, unweariedly, of the one single subject. In order not to hear her, the young laundresses would begin to sing, and would mock her with the improvised rimes of their songs. And she meanwhile would shout and gesticulate like a crazy woman.

No one could give her work any longer. Out of pity, some of her former employers would send her food. Little by little she fell into the habit of begging, and wandered through the streets, bowed over, unkempt, and all in rags. The street urchins would tag behind her, shouting: "Tell us the story of the spoon, 'cause we never heard it, Auntie Candia!"

She would stop strangers sometimes as they passed by, to tell them the story and to argue out her defense. Young fellows would sometimes send for her, and pay her a copper to tell it all over, two, three, or four times; they would raise up difficulties against her arguments; they would hear her all the way through, and then at last stab her with a final word. She would shake her head, and go on her way; she found companionship among other beggars and would reason with them endlessly, indefatigably, invincibly. Her chosen friend was a deaf woman, whose skin was a mass of angry blotches, and who limped on one leg.

In the winter of 1874 she was at last stricken with serious illness. The woman with the blotches cared for her. Donna Cristina Lamonica sent her a cordial and a scuttle of coals.

The sick woman, lying on her pallet, still raved of the silver spoon. She would raise herself on her elbow and struggle to wave her arm, to give emphasis to her fevered arguments.

And at the last, when her staring eyes already seemed overspread with a veil of troubled waters that rose from within, Candia gasped forth:

"It wasn't I, madam—because you see—the spoon—"

SIGNORA SPERANZA

BY LUIGI PIRANDELLO

Luigi Pirandello, master of style, the humorist of a group of young Italian writers who are said to be inaugurating a renaissance in Italian literature, was born at Girgenti, Sicily, in 1867. He appeared first as a poet, pure in style, severe in inspiration, but later "found himself" in the writing of humorous tales. His humor, though at bottom sad and almost pessimistic, is not of the quiet sort. To him man appears as a creature more miserable than grotesque, eternally made sport of by the irony of fate. Such is the philosophy in his lugubriously fanciful "Mathias Pascal," skeptical in spirit, in "Il Turno," with its cruel pictures of Sicilian peasant life, and in "Signora Speranza," one of the latest and most characteristic of his novelettes. For the purpose of this work the discursive passages have been here and there condensed and made more direct.

SIGNORA SPERANZA

BY LUIGI PIRANDELLO

THE family boarding-house of Signora Carolina Pentoni (Big Carolini, or Carolinona,
as she was called, because of the excessive
flesh which distressed her) was patronized by certain
scatterbrains, droll fellows, who were the delight of
the well-behaved who frequented the table, not so
much because of the good cooking perhaps, but that
they might be present at the gratuitous gaiety offered
them during the meals.

One of these excellent, well-mannered people, without the least suspicion that he might be included
among the so-called amusing types of the pension, had
been for some time the butt of the scatterbrains, Biagio
Speranza and Dario Scossi, who played all sorts of
tricks on him; but he remained calm; so calm and
obstinate that they were finally forced to let him alone.
"Laughter is healthy. You gentlemen make me laugh,
so I shall remain."

And he did remain, cordially disliked by all. His
name was Cedebonis; he was a physician, professor of
philosophy in the *liceo*, and of pedagogy in a normal
school for girls; he was a Calabrian, short, thick-set,
dark, bald, with an oval-shaped head, with no neck
to speak of; mulish, with a leather-colored face,

Translated by Elise Lathrop. Copyright, 1907, by P. F. Collier & Son.

enormous bushy eyebrows, and mustache the color of ebony. As the resigned victim of his many scientific doctrines, both philosophical and pedagogical, he had come to live almost automatically, with a brain like a warehouse, in which his thoughts, precise, well-weighed, and classified, were arranged in perfect order according to their various categories. Possibly his robust and vigorous body would gladly have lent itself to violent exercises, but Cedebonis made himself a storehouse for archives, or so said Scossi, and did not permit himself any expansiveness that was not according to the dictates of science, philosophy, and pedagogy. "To live is not enough; live to do good," he used to say placidly, in his big, oily voice. And he would ask: "Reason, reason, gentlemen, for what was it given us?"

"That we might be worse than beasts," once replied scornfully the music teacher Trunfo, who could not endure him.

Separated with much scandal from his wife, always scowling, gloomy, grumbling, and at times explosive, Trunfo passed almost the whole day in the house of Carolinona, in the dining-room there, intent, like a dog who licks the bruises he has received, on correcting and rewriting the most hissed parts of his opera, for the production of which he had half beggared himself. He smoked continually. Biagio Speranza called him "Vesuvius."

Sometimes Cedebonis would go quietly up behind him, and sit beside him in order to inhale the odor of the tobacco, which he delighted in. Trunfo, grumbling, would squint at him a couple of times, then fuming, fidgeting with annoyance, would draw a cigar from his pocket, and offer it to him rudely: "Pray take it. Smoke, for Heaven's sake!"

"No, thank you," Cedebonis would reply, without the least discomfiture. "You must know that nicotine is very injurious. I only like to inhale the smoke, to smell its fragrance."

"At my expense," Trunfo would then burst out furiously. "How about the damage to *my* health? Get out of here, I say! Shame on you! If you want your pleasure you can pay for it!"

"Cedebonis," said Scossi—who every time he began to speak would shove out the tip of his terrible tongue like an arrow-head—"Cedebonis, with that face of his, like a happy monk, would be quite capable of presenting himself calmly in the house of our dear Martinelli, and, with the pretext that woman, like nicotine, is injurious, ask him to lend him, yes, I say, for a moment—"

"His wife?" asked Biagio Speranza.

"Oh, shocking! Her powder puff."

"But what has my wife to do with the matter?" exclaims harmless Martino Martinelli, hit when least expecting it, his eyelashes quivering rapidly over his round, owl-like eyes, very close together, separated by an extremely long, thin nose, and which seemed to draw up and leave his upper lip suspended in the air.

"Calm yourself," replied Scossi; "I merely mentioned her because I know that your excellent wife is in Sicily, Signor Martinelli." And good Martinelli

became calm, sighed, and shook his head bitterly.
Ah, he thought continually of his poor wife, banished
to a normal school in Sicily, and he spoke of her always in his own peculiar manner, groping along in his
discourse, half helping himself, half covering every
pause with a "Yes, I say," an interjection which they
all imitated, without his perceiving it. The poor fellow could not resign himself to the bureaucratic
cruelty which, at a blow and without cause, had separated him at sixty-four from his wife, thus destroy-
ing his home and family, forcing him to live alone,
in a furnished lodging, and to dine there at the
boarding-house of Carolinona, whom he alone called
Signora Carolina.

King of Romancers was Momo Cariolin, a little
dwarf, who seemed like a living joke. To look at
him, it seemed impossible that such a tiny frame could
conceive such enormous lies, uttered imperturbably,
with the air of a diplomat.

"But tell me," Biagio Speranza once asked him seriously, "have you ever looked in a mirror?" because
Momo Cariolin boasted with particular pride of the
favor which women showed him. They had been
women of his own rank at the very least, or ladies
of the nobility; or they were of royal blood or impe-
rial archduchesses (notably Austrian), these victims
of Cariolin. And such adventures had befallen him
during the various congresses of Orientalists in the
capitals of Europe! For Cariolin professed himself,
although a dilettante, a profound student of Oriental
languages.

"But for Heaven's sake, look at Martino's nose!" Biagio Speranza would suddenly cry out, interrupting the marvelous narrations of Cariolin. And good Martinelli, abruptly roused amid the laughter of the others, would begin to smile.

Biagio Speranza's jokes, Dario Scossi's sarcasms, Trunfo's outbursts and sneers did not disturb Martino Martinelli. But another of the boarders frightened him, and this was none other than the poet Giannantonio Cocco Bertolli, who undoubtedly was the most ridiculous type of the house. But the poet had been absent for nearly a month, owing to a serious misfortune which had befallen him. A single one? No. All the misfortunes in the world had befallen the poor poet Cocco Bertolli, who for this reason was given to railings against injustice, both human and divine. What worse misfortune could befall him than this? To defend himself from celestial and terrestrial perfidies he had had only his powerful voice, his tongue of fire, and now he could not even whisper. Everybody knew it; those who had declared they were his friends had even done it purposely; they had teased him, tormented him, that they might utterly ruin him, might actually kill him; he roared, roared, until it seemed as though his enormous bovine eyes would burst out of his congested face. His bile accumulated. "My muse is bile! It was with bile that Shakespeare created Othello, King Lear!"

And he prepared a poem, "Erostratus," a tremendous poem. Ah, the magnificent temple of Imposture, the temple of so-called Civilization, where infamous

Hypocrisy was enthroned and adored, he would kindle it with his verses. But as soon as people knew that he was at work on this poem he was attacked on all sides. Though deprived of his professorship at the *ginnasio* because of these tragic bestialities, thrown out on the streets, until a short time before, Giannantonio Cocco Bertolli had not been cast down. Sleep? Why, for two cents he could sleep at a resort of beggars and of sublime, ragged, louse-covered fellows. Eat? Good Carolinona had given him credit for more than a year already. "And I, Carolina, I will make you immortal," he would repeat to her. "You only love me, you who beneath a rough exterior conceal a heart of gold, a most noble soul, Carolina!"

"Yes, sir, do not worry," Carolina would hasten to reply, for she, like good Martinelli, was afraid of those great eyes which opened so widely whenever he began to speak, while his mouth wore so complacent a sneer that one never knew, even when he paid a compliment, but that he was satirizing in his own way.

Signora Pentoni also feared that her other patrons, those who paid, would stay away because of him, would be annoyed or disgusted by his presence at table; and although, whether from good-heartedness or from fear, she could not show him the door, she lovingly advised him to be calm, prudent, sought with all politeness to tame him, and also took care of him and the garments in which he draped himself, mended them, brushed them, and finally even made him cravats out of the ribbons from her discarded hats.

Not understanding why all this care was taken of him, Giannantonio Cocco Bertolli finally—and why not?—fell in love with Signora Pentoni. He took to composing odes, sonnets, anacreonic songs, and read them while she sewed buttons on his coat or vest, or brushed them. Carolinona did not comprehend that these verses were addressed to her, and why he read them; but since she thought him mad, she did not ask for a reason, and allowed him to read on.

Giannantonio Cocco Bertolli, violent and bestial in everything else, was most timid in love. Not knowing how to confess directly to Pentoni the passion she had inspired, he poured it out in poetry, hoping to arrive by means of the monstrous flowery paths of his limping metaphors. But seeing that Carolinona remained impassive, he became frenzied, violent.

"And what is the matter with you now?" the poor woman asked him in amazement.

"What?" cried Cocco Bertolli in a trembling voice, folding the paper on which he had scrawled the poetry, and opening his eyes very wide, as usual, and stamping his feet. "You ask me? Nothing! But I know! This is to be my lot! Thus my accursed fate has decreed! I am to be understood by no one! Not even by you!"

"I? Why?"

"She does not even say that she seems to understand!"

"Understand what? The poetry? But good gracious! I understand nothing. You know that. Be good, come now! Why do you act thus?"

"Because—because—" In vain! He could not pour out his heart in a declaration.

For this was needed the impelling force of an odious suspicion that came upon him suddenly, during one of these scenes, while poor Pentoni was urging him to be quiet, at least to speak softly, since nearby was the musician correcting his music.

"Ah, so it is for him?" Cocco Bertolli had thundered forth. "You love him? He is your lover? Confess! Viper, viper, viper—and why, then, have you flattered me until now?"

"I? Leave me!" Pentoni had cried, trembling with fear. "You are mad!"

"Cry; yes, cry out so that he will hear! I wish to see your knight; he too is a viper!"

"But be quiet, hush!" Carolinona had implored him. "Are you speaking seriously, Signor Bertolli? What do you want of me? Let me alone!"

"I can not! I love you. Do you love another? We shall see."

"But I love no one. Are you trying to make fun of me? At my age? This is the last straw! And pray who would fall in love with me, Signor Bertolli?"

"I! And I have told you so!"

"Pardon me, but this is madness. And not even laughable. Let me be—I am a poor woman."

The Pentoni knew very well the vile calumnies which had been circulated about her, but she had not even tried to contradict them. What did it matter to her? She was conscious of her virtue, long re-

signed to discretion because of her sad lot, and that
sufficed her. And how could calumnies harm her
now? She knew that she was ugly; she was already
thirty-five years old, and might have been fifty as far
as she was concerned; she had never flattered herself
that a man could fall in love with her; she had never
even had the time to think that fate might perhaps
concede her a different lot, the compensation of some
affection in the dark poverty which had always oppressed her, weighed upon her, and against which she
had sought courageously to defend herself with every
means in her power. Did people believe that in her life
there had been some slip from the path of virtue, or
even more than one? Very well, let them believe it!
At heart this not only no longer offended her, but
almost flattered her self-love, her deep-rooted femi-
nine instinct. She closed her eyes. But it was not
true. No one had ever cared for her, save this insane
Cocco Bertolli. It would have been laughable had the
poor fellow not worn such a tragic expression.

"Must I go away then?" he asked.

"Why, no; stay!" she hastened to reply. "But you
must think no more of such madness."

"I can not help it! When an idea has taken root
here, it will not leave me, even if my head were to
be broken open with Vulcan's hammer. You know
that. And know that my proposals were honest, and
always will be. Carolina, will you be my wife?"

She had begun to laugh at such a precipitate proposal, but Cocco Bertolli, furious, checked the laugh
on her very lips.

"Do not laugh, do not laugh, by Heaven! At least believe me, you who are a woman of heart. Save me! I have need of some one who loves me and calms me. I will resume my position as professor; you shall be the wife of a great poet, who is now miserably wasting his talent. And if you do not understand the poet, no matter; you shall be the wife of a professor; does that content you? and I will liberate you from all these good-for-nothings who came to play the buffoon at your table. Listen; I will give you the greatest proof of my love, of the seriousness of my proposal. When I leave here I must go to the hospital and submit myself to a terrible operation. The doctors have told me that it may kill me. So be it! But if I recover, I will be yours, Carolina. Leave me this hope. Farewell!" And he rushed away without giving the poor woman time even to try to dissuade him.

At the hospital he had compelled the physicians to risk the terrible operation, declaring: "I neither can nor will go on living thus. It would kill me! Therefore operate on me without fear, without remorse. At the worst I am but anticipating my death by a few days."

Two days after the operation good Martinelli, to whom Pentoni had weepingly confided this fresh outburst of madness on the part of Bertolli, was despatched to the hospital for news. Poor Signor Martinelli returned with his great nose pale with terror, his eyes round and glassy.

Cocco Bertolli was dying, and had asked him as a favor to persuade "his" Carolina to see him for the last time. The physician had assured Martinelli that the dying man would not outlive the night. Signora Pentoni, overcome with pity, had gone to the hospital, and there had been obliged to promise, solemnly to swear to the dying man, that if he should escape death she would be his wife.

"But there will be no danger, you will see, there will be no danger!" good Martinelli had said to her, reassuringly, as they were returning from this visit. "Because—yes, I say—"

And he had raised one hand as though to bless the dying man.

II

All the boarders were at table when Biagio Speranza entered the dining-room, announcing gaily:

"Safe! Sound! I come from the hospital. In about three weeks we shall once more have at our table the magnificent poet. Gentlemen, I invite you to cry: Long live Giannantonio Cocco Bertolli!"

No one echoed this cry. Signor Martinelli bent his long nose over his plate. Trunfo cast a side glance, and went on eating. Signora Pentoni wept.

Cedebonis was the only one who rejoiced at sight of Biagio Speranza, who made him laugh quite as much as hygiene required, and exclaimed: "Oh, bravo! Now you must tell us all about it."

But Biagio Speranza did not assent. He looked at the mistress of the house.

"In Heaven's name!" implored Signora Pentoni, "leave me in peace this evening!"

Biagio Speranza glanced round at his friends, and with a gesture asked what had happened.

"Martinelli," explained Cariolin, "has been to the hospital before you to get news, and Carolinona has learned—"

"And regrets it?" cried Biagio Speranza, feigning surprise. "Ah, excuse me, Carolinona; what ingratitude! I have seen your poet, and by a miracle restrained myself from kissing his brow. What a hero of love! He spoke to me only of you. He asked me—"

Signora Pentoni rose to her feet, convulsed; she pressed her handkerchief to her eyes, tried to say "Excuse me," but a burst of sobs smothered the words in her throat, and she rushed toward the door of her room.

Cariolin, Scossi, ran forward and stopped her; all except Cedebonis and Trunfo rose to their feet and surrounded the weeping woman.

"Rubbish! Absurd!" sneered Trunfo from the table.

But the others, all in chorus, exhorted Carolinona to be of good courage. Was she really afraid that Cocco Bertolli would compel her to marry him? Preposterous, if she did not wish to! Disturbances? But were there not the police to keep him in order? Her promise as he lay at the point of death? What promise? Oh, nonsense! He should be made to understand, willy-nilly, that she had but uttered a pious lie. No? How was that?"

"See here!" Biagio Speranza cut short the discussion, becoming fervent. "Be quiet, Carolinona, I will marry you myself." All burst out laughing.

"What is there to laugh at?" cried Speranza, in earnest. "I am speaking seriously. Are we, or are we not, gentlemen? A hawk, gentlemen, threatens this dove; I will defend her. I shall marry her, I tell you. Who wishes to wager on it?"

"I do; a thousand francs!" suddenly proposed Cariolin. And Biagio Speranza cried as promptly: "Out with your thousand francs!" Then Cedebonis too rose from the table, rubbing his hands with delight: "Excellent! Excellent! Do you wish me to hold the stakes, gentlemen?"

"Out with the thousand francs!" repeated Biagio Speranza more emphatically.

"I have not got them with me," said Cariolin, feeling in his pockets. "But I give my word. Here is my hand on it. A thousand francs and the wedding breakfast."

"You will lose!" affirmed Speranza, clasping Cariolin's hand. "All of you gentlemen are witnesses of the wager: I shall marry Carolinona. Come, come, hush, my betrothed. Dry your tears, smile, look at me! Do you not like me?"

With affectionate violence he drew her fat, puffy hands from her face. Pentoni smiled amid her tears. Applause and cries of "Bravo!" broke forth. Biagio Speranza, growing more and more ardent, embraced his betrothed, who struggled: "In Heaven's name, let me go! let me go!"

"Let the engaged couple sit side by side!" some

of them proposed. "Here, here! at the head of the table!" And Biagio Speranza and Carolinona were escorted in triumph, and made to sit side by side.

Good Martinelli was confounded. His nose seemed to grow visibly. Trunfo continued to sneer. "Rubbish! Rubbish!"

"Are you jealous perhaps?" Biagio cried to him, rising to his feet, and striking his fist on the table. "Will you do me the great favor of stopping that? If you gentlemen believe that at this moment I am jesting, you are mistaken. If you think that I am committing a mad act in marrying Carolinona, I have the honor of telling you that you are crazy yourselves. I, who know my poor clay, am aware that at this moment I am wiser than I have ever been before in my life. I am a poor man, gentlemen, who, as a punishment from God, must fall in love with every beautiful woman I see. In love I at once become capable of the greatest follies. Quite different from Cariolin's lies. Twice, gentlemen, twice I have been at the point —I shudder to think of it—at the point of really marrying. I must escape as soon as possible, at any cost, from this terrible catastrophe which continually threatens me. I profit by this moment, in which, fortunately, I am not in love, and shall marry Carolinona. A flash of genius, gentlemen. A true inspiration from heaven!"

"It is necessary to see," objected Scossi, "whether Carolinona consents."

Biagio Speranza turned toward his betrothed.

"Would you do me such a wrong? To such a

good-looking young fellow as me? No, no; you see? My bride laughs, and the world laughs. It is settled, gentlemen!"

At this point Trunfo leaped to his feet, furiously tearing the napkin from his neck.

"Let us make an end to it once for all! This senseless, stupid jest gets on my nerves; this jest on a subject which you do not understand, and which I will tell you about, by Heaven!"

At thought of Trunfo's matrimonial disaster there was a moment of embarrassment. All the faces became fixed in the act of laughing, then the laughter suddenly ceased.

"Pardon me," said Biagio Speranza pacifically, "Why do you persist in believing that this is a joke of mine? I know better than you what an enormous folly it is to marry, and repeat that it is to prevent myself from committing such an act that I am marrying Carolinona."

"The reasoning could not be more logical," remarked Dario Scossi, again provoking all to mirth. "And I appeal to Cedebonis, professor of logic."

"Most logical, most logical!" the latter affirmed. "Signor Speranza is, in fact, marrying so to escape the temptation of marrying."

"Exactly!" replied Biagio Speranza. "And this is no joke. For Carolinona is seriously afraid of the poet Cocco Bertolli, and I am seriously afraid of losing my liberty some day or other. By marrying, we are both saving ourselves; she from that kind of a husband, I from a feared reality of a future wife. Married, we

are both of us absolutely free to do whatever we please.
She here, and I in my own home. In the eyes of the
law, we have but the name in common, which is not
properly a name at all, I beg you to observe, gentlemen. Speranza[1], just a common noun; I do not know
what to do with it, and I cede it voluntarily. What
do you say, Carolinona?"

"As far as I am concerned," said Pentoni, smiling
and shrugging her shoulders, "if you do not regret
it—"

New applause, new congratulations, amid bursts of
laughter.

The following day the whole city was filled with
the amazing news. Biagio Speranza, stroking his fine
blond beard with his fat, white hand, laughed with his
limpid blue eyes, and from time to time his hand passed
quickly, with a gesture habitual with him, from his
beard upward and beneath his bold nose. He was
most content with the great folly he was about to commit. Folly in the opinion of stupid people, be it understood. He was conscious of acting well. He had
thought it over all night long, and had almost died of
laughing. "Carolinona, my wife!"

Friends and acquaintances stopped him on the
streets. "You are joking, then?"—"No; I mean to
marry, really to marry. But as a precaution, you
understand? To protect myself from taking a wife,
that is all."—"What! But you *are* marrying!"—
"Why, yes! I shall stay in my own home; I shall do

---

[1] Speranza, in the Italian language, means " hope."—Transla-
tor.

as I please. I shall only go to her home as I do now, to dine. I shall not give her anything except the price of my meals, as usual. Well?"—"And your name?"— "But if she is willing, why not? It does not seem to me such a serious thing."

And he left his questioner planted there in the middle of the street.

He had an appointment with Dario Scossi at the pension, to go over Carolinona's papers together. At the pension besides Scossi, a witness for the groom, he found the timorous Martinelli, a witness for the bride, who had come purposely first of all to dissuade Signora Pentoni from lending herself to this highly scandalous proceeding.

"But do you think so?" she had replied, with a sad smile. "They are merry young fellows, let them alone. They were joking, and by this time think no more of it. I, on the other hand, have not been able to close my eyes all last night, thinking of that other in the hospital."

But at the arrival of Scossi she had been amazed.

"What is this all about? Really? Again?"

Biagio Speranza found her obstinate in her refusal.

"Oh, do not let us have any nonsense," said he to her. "Do you wish to make me lose the thousand francs of the wager?"

"What thousand francs? Nonsense, say no more about it, Signor Biagio."

"What?" said the latter. "Did we not come to an agreement yesterday evening? Have you repented? You are then no longer afraid of Cocco Bertolli? You will see that he will seriously wish to marry you then."

And once more he began to discuss the terms of the bargain, and dilate upon the reciprocal advantages of this marriage, at once serious and burlesque. "We, Carolinona, should not ascribe any importance to this our marriage, is it not so? and therefore for us it is not a serious affair."

"Now, perhaps not," remarked Signora Pentoni. "But what if later you repent it?"

"But undoubtedly I shall repent it!" admitted Biagio. "And just when I repent it I shall feel the advantage of it. Do you understand? That is why I am taking this step."

"You understand then?" said Pentoni in conclusion. "If I offer opposition it certainly is not for myself. What have I to lose by it? I have everything to gain and nothing to lose. While you—"

"Do not think of me," said Biagio Speranza, cutting short the discussion. "I know what I am doing. Come, let us get on, Scossi, it is getting late. But come then, answer, Carolinona: Name (I know that), paternity—age—place of birth—state; maid, widow, nothing; it is not necessary to tell the truth on this point. But the age, yes, be accurate; I beg of you."

"Thirty-five," replied Carolinona.

"There now!" exclaimed Biagio, shrugging his shoulders. "Do not begin at once!"

"Thirty-five, I assure you; I was born in 1865 at Caserta."

"Good gracious! So you are still young and ten-

'der? Oh, my dear! One would never have thought
it. And—well, shall we say a maid?"

"Most assuredly, yes, sir!"

"I believe you. Let us then write to Caserta for
the birth certificate. Come, Scossi, let us hasten
to the City Hall for the announcement."

III

There were two reasons for hastening this memora-
ble marriage: first, Giannatonio Cocco Bertolli was
leaving the hospital, cured; secondly, Biagio Speranza
had as usual fallen in love in the mean time with
a seductive woman. During these days, in order to
escape temptation, he walked the streets with his eyes
on the ground and his nose in the air.

But the Pentoni had wished for time at least to have
a new gown made for the ceremony. White? Oh, no
indeed. Modest, suitable to her age, but new. Could
she go to the City Hall otherwise? "And what do you
care about it?" Biagio had asked her.

"Nothing for my own sake, of course. But for you,
Signor Speranza. What would people say?"

"Let them talk. What does it matter to me? Dress
as you like. I do not want you to throw away money
needlessly."

And what pains the choice of the gown cost her!
Although so long subdued and resigned to her lot, she
felt her heart oppressed that day by a strange anguish,
which brought to her lips an unusual desire to laugh,
to her eyes a longing to weep.

Though without wishing to ascribe importance to this buffoonery, yet the mere idea, the word "marriage," instinctively awoke in her weary frame a certain sense of her real womanhood; not enough to cause her self-love to rebel against the part she was to play, yet enough to make her feel the bitterness, almost scorn, of it: and so she was to be married as a joke! And she laughed at it with the others, and still more than the others. Bah!

When the wedding day arrived, before the little procession started for the City Hall, for they would not perpetrate the joke in church, Biagio Speranza declared that he did not wish to take the thousand francs of the wager: he did not wish it to be said that this marriage had put money in his pocket; Cariolin should, therefore, buy with it a gift for the bride according to the bride's own taste.

The bride objected to this. She did not wish anything either. But they all protested, Cariolin more loudly than any, for he had lost the thousand francs, and being at a ball, as the saying goes, wished to dance. "No, no, I will attend to it! I have already thought of something; you will see, Signora Speranza, a fine present, and very useful. Let me attend to it!"

He was in full dress, as he had promised, this tiny Cariolin, and wore an elegant black velvet vest. Scossi, too, was in evening dress. Cedebonis remembering at the last moment that he was professor of philosophy and pedagogy, came in a frock coat. The most dismal of all was good Martinelli, with his shiny coat, his light trousers, and his time-yellowed white cravat. Trunfo was the only one absent from the festive group.

Although the dining-room was all decked with flowers, a present from the boarders, and the long table in the middle was splendidly arranged by two hotel waiters hired for the occasion by Cariolin, who was to pay for the wedding repast, the merriment that each one had promised himself for this great day was lacking. Laughter was forced. How could that Carolinona have chosen material of such an incredible shade for her wedding gown! And why was not Biagio Speranza in evening dress? Good gracious! Was he or was he not going to be married? Biagio Speranza felt a sinking in his stomach, listening to Cariolin's silly jests, who wished—so Biagio fancied —to avenge himself for the money he had lost, by calling Carolinona "Signora Speranza." He now wished to get through with the ceremony as soon as possible, that he might think no more of it, that he might think of other things.

"Come, come! Let us get through with it all!"

"Wait a moment," said Carolinona, her hat already on her head; "I want to take a look at the kitchen—"

There was a general exclamation of horror at so commonplace a thought thus ingenuously expressed at such a moment. Cariolin rushed forward ahead of them all, and, with the gracious bow befitting the conqueror of an Austrian archduchess, offered his arm to the bride.

The ceremony over, Cariolin rushed away to pur-

chase the gift, begging them to wait a little while for
him before sitting down to the table. He wished to
keep the secret absolutely dark.

At table they at last began to be merry. Biagio
Speranza, who could now see the end of this carnival,
was most gallant to his bride. The dinner was choice,
delicious, abundant. With the champagne, toasts began. Toasts of all shades and to every one. Among
others, one of Dario Scossi's to Martinelli's absent
wife was so positively unfortunate that it made Martino, who, contrary to custom, had buried his nose
somewhat too deeply in his glass, weep. While they
were at table Cariolin's long-expected gift arrived.

"There's a couple of porters outside," one of the
hotel waiters announced.—Everybody became interested.—"Porters? So the gift had come in a cart?"
—"And what then is the gift?"

They all rose and rushed out into the hall. There
stood a magnificent double bed of inlaid wood, with
complete furnishings. Biagio Speranza was annoyed.

"What a pity!" cried Carolinona, wringing her
hands, sorry that a thousand francs should be so
wasted.

But all the others applauded Cariolin's magnificent
idea. Cariolin himself was radiant. "Gentlemen,
help me to set up this bed."

Carolinona interposed, mortified, unhappy: "Where
do you wish to put it, Signor Cariolin?"—"Where?
In your room?"—"But it would not go in, pardon me.
And besides, what do you think I could do with it?"
—"Do you ask me?" cried Momo Cariolin.

These last words caused a fresh burst of applause and confused outcries. The pieces of the bed were taken by assault, and carried into Carolinona's room. Her own bed was quickly pulled apart, and the new one, the nuptial couch, set up in its place.

She laughed, poor thing, at sight of these inexpert men laboring so hard, first at placing the mattress, then the first sheet, the second embroidered one, then putting the pillows in their slips, and finally covering the bed with a splendid silk cover. They were all perspiring. But where was Biagio Speranza? Oh, rascal! He had quietly stolen away.

IV

It was already evening. Carolinona, although tired after the tumultuous day, must spend several hours in putting the house in order. Finally, having dismissed the waiters and cook and sent her own servant to bed, she retired to her room. And the bed? Certainly she was not going to sleep in that new bed. She went and examined it closely, and first passed her hand gently over the pink silk coverlet; but against the soft, delicate, rose-colored material she suddenly noticed how dark her fat hand looked, disfigured by hard work, with short, rough nails, and instinctively she drew it back, murmuring anew: "What a pity!" She stooped down to examine the embroidery of the sheet, but no longer noticed the beauty of the bed; she was thinking of herself, thinking that if she had been pretty this ridiculous marriage would not have occurred; if she had been pretty she would have been married long ago. And yet, how many of her former friends, certainly not prettier than she, had married, and now had homes of their own, position, while she—as a joke—married, and no wife! "Fate!"

She started, looked around; saw in a corner, rolled up, the mattress of her bed, the iron framework leaning against the wall. She stood for a moment perplexed whether or not to call the servant to help her. What should she do? She moved toward the corner where stood the mattress, but passing before the mirror of her wardrobe, she caught sight of herself and paused. From the attentive examination of herself in the mirror there arose in her a lively dislike for the task of making up her bed. No, she would not do it! She would sleep in the armchair. So much the worse for her that at her age, to amuse others, she had lent herself to such folly, ridicule, mockery.

But immediately the instinctive need for excusing herself called up the reasons that had led her to be persuaded; namely, her fear of being bound to that other crazy man, who wished to become her husband by force; the pitying promise which she had allowed her lips to utter that day in the hospital because of having listened to that fool Martinelli. "Bah!" she thought. "And when that crazy man comes out of the hospital furious, he, my husband, will defend me, recognizing the reason for which I consented to play the buffoon."

She began to unfasten her gown. Suddenly she stopped; it was useless, since she was to sleep sitting

in the chair. Another lie this, unearthed to prevent
herself from acknowledging a foolish hope which she
knew could not be realized even in a dream. She ex-
tinguished the lamp, she seated herself in the armchair. Through the silence that reigned in the street
below she listened intently, unconsciously. Where
was he at this hour? Perhaps in some café with his
friends. And she imagined the room of a café, illuminated, and saw them all, her boarders, seated there
at little tables, and he was laughing, laughing, and answering witticisms. Certainly her name was in every
one's mouth, and derided. What did it matter to her?
She waited for the noisy reunion to come to an end
that she might see him alone. Where would he go?
Home? Or would he perhaps—perhaps go else-
where? At this thought she paused, as before an
unexpected abyss, taken aback. Why, yes, yes! Was
he not absolutely free?

And she was seated there in the armchair. Oh, fool,
oh, madwoman! And she found sleep impossible.

V

No, Biagio Speranza had not gone to the café, as
Carolinona had imagined.

Annoyed by the jokes of his friends, he had gone
home, with the firm determination of setting out for
Barcellona the next day, and making an end of it.

He had begun preparing what he needed for the
journey, when he thought that he had not enough
money for this hastened departure. And then, con-

fronted with this material obstacle, he agreed that, on
the whole, flight was not worthy of him. Yes, yes;
he had really done wrong to be annoyed, to sneak
away thus. And he must not abandon to the wrath
of Cocco Bertolli that poor woman who had nothing
to do with these pranks, who would keep to her agreement, and would never annoy or molest him; of that
he was sure.

"Poor Carolinona!" he thought with a smile.
"With what a look she pronounced that 'yes' with a
glance at the official, as much as to say: 'You see what
value that can have! For my part, I do not think that
one should jest thus, but these young fellows thought
that there was no harm in it, and here I am to satisfy
them. What else could I do? I must write too?
Sign my name?' "

He went to bed, and was not long in falling asleep.
He had bad dreams! Carolinona would not listen to
reason; was she or was she not his wife? And she
wished to enjoy all her rights—ready, oh, most ready,
to take upon herself all her duties. She seized him
by the arm and did not intend to let him go. But how
about their agreement? It was all a joke! Joke?
She had really signed the contract. And therefore he
must stay here with her. Infamy, treachery! All the
doors closed? Kicks, pinches, blows at each door.
In vain! Oh, what grief, what rage, what agony!
Behind those closed, bolted doors the friends laughed
as though they would split their sides: Cariolin,
Scossi, Cedebonis, and even Martinelli. Trunfo
sneered. An infamous conspiracy! Did they then

wish his death? No, no, even if it cost him his life, no; he would not be made to sleep in that bed. Ah, they would take him by force? They were binding him? Cowards! So many against one! Softly, softly! There at the throat, no— Ah, they were suffocating him—

He rose late, and in the worst of humors. He would go to the pension as usual that day, and by his manner would make his friends understand that it was time to be done with the whole affair.

That evening all the other boarders, including Trunfo, arrived at the house. Then Biagio Speranza arrived, and was at once assailed with questions.

"Why, of course! Naturally!" he answered with a gay face. "When did I return? Exactly at midnight. The hour of fantasy. The door was closed, and she, the very one who has been denying it, threw me down the key from her window. Why deny it, my wife? We owe this satisfaction to our friends who are so interested in our conjugal felicity. And this evening you will see me remain here at my post, as master of the house; and I hope that this will satisfy you, and that from now on you will allow me to enjoy the pleasures of married life in peace. Is it agreed?"

He seated himself beside Carolinona; during the meal he ostentatiously displayed, amid general merriment, all the attentions, the manners of an enamored monkey which a newly married man should show to his bride, and Carolinona let him have his way, and laughed too.

At a certain point Trunfo gruffly asked Biagio Speranza: "Will you permit me to continue correcting my papers here?"

"No, no!" Biagio hastened to reassure him. "You, dear *maestro*, are free to suit your own convenience here by day or night. Am I not right, Carolinona?"

"The *maestro*," said she, somewhat quietly, "has never caused me the least annoyance."

"Very well then!" concluded Trunfo, rising.

He made a quick, slight bow, with his hands resting on the back of his chair, and left the room, suffocated with bile.

"My friends," remarked Biagio Speranza, a little later, "in the interest of my wife, I advise you to stop, if you do not wish to make her lose a client. A joke is all very well, but it should not be allowed to injure the pocket—"

"Oh, as for you, joking aside," declared Cariolin, rising from the table with the others, "keep your promise, and do not take this excuse. We are going, and wish you a pleasant evening."

"I," added Scossi, "shall remain with Cedebonis outside the door on guard; and you may be sure that I will not let you escape."

"You may all be sure that I shall not escape," replied Biagio Speranza, accompanying his fellow boarders to the door.

Carolinona began to feel uneasy, not knowing what this crazy fellow would do next.

"What fools, eh?" said Biagio, once more entering

the dining-room. "And they are really capable of waiting outside in the street, do you know it?"

Carolinona tried to smile and look at him, but she lowered her eyes promptly.

"Do you know that our position is actually ridiculous?" resumed Biagio, breaking out into his sonorous laughter. "But we must do this in order to have peace. Otherwise they will never have done. I will wait a half hour before I go; you must have patience."

"Oh, as for me, of course," said she, without raising her eyes, and faintly.

Biagio Speranza looked at her. He was very calm himself, and thought that she ought to be so, too. But noting Carolinona's embarrassment he laughed again. Wounded by this laugh, she raised her eyes, and, trying as best she could to hide the bitterness with a smile, said:

"You are a man, and they all know that you are only doing this to make them laugh. Although, if I am to tell the truth, I do not see that it is a joke any longer, now that it has arrived at this point— They are all laughing at you and me—"

"Let us laugh too!" concluded Biagio. "Why not?"

"Because I can not," promptly replied Carolinona. "Pardon me, but you must understand that it can not please me that you, to make an end to an annoying joke, are forced to make me play a part that does not suit me—"

"What!" exclaimed Biagio. "The rôle of wife! By heavens, you ought to thank me."

Carolinona took fire. "Pardon me, and am I to

thank you also for the words you said to Trunfo on
my account? Your wife for a joke I understand; but
since you have committed the folly of giving me your
name in the eyes of the law, it seems to me, I do not
know, but it seems to me that you ought at least to
show that you do not believe certain calumnies, and
not make a jest of them. Because they are calumnies
I would have you to know! The vilest calumnies! I
have always attended to my own business. I am poor,
yes, but honest, honest! It is well that you should
know it. And you may set your mind at rest on this
point—"

Biagio looked at her and let his arms fall. "You
alarm me, Carolinona! I did not believe you capable
of telling the truth with such insistence and such
warmth. I believe you, I believe you—but let me
look out of this window and see if those tiresome fellows are gone, and we will make an end to this at
once."

He went to the window and looked out into the
street. "No one," said he, turning away. "I am sorry
that the joke has finished really badly. Enough; the
thing is done, and we must think no more about it.
Good-by, eh?"

He held out his hand; the Pentoni hesitatingly laid
her own, fat and black, in it, murmuring: "Good-by."
Then, all vibrating with emotion, she shut herself up
in her room, and burst into tears.

Biagio Speranza, having taken a few steps, saw,
spying in the shadows of the little square opposite the
door, instead of Scossi and Cedebonis, Signor Marti-

nelli, who was rubbing his hands with the cold. The good man was quite robbed of breath at hearing his name called. Then a hand smote him sharply on the shoulder.

"What are you doing here, my fine fellow? Tell me, were you perhaps waiting until I should have gone away to—"

"May Heaven forbid! What are you saying, Signor Speranza?" stammered poor Martinelli, so tremblingly that Biagio could not keep from laughing. "I —I was just going—"

"And meanwhile you are here!" replied Biagio, recovering himself, and pretending to be severe. He took him by the arm, and added as they moved away: "Come, let us go, and explain to me—"

"But, sir—" Martinelli hastened to reply, greatly embarrassed, "I confess—since you, yes, I say—since you suspected me— (May Heaven defend me!) I confess that I remained here, not so much out of curiosity, as because—yes, I say—to congratulate myself that finally you had recognized the—the—the sacredness of the bond, because—"

"And am I really to believe you?" Biagio interrupted him, standing still. "You stood there in the shadow like a vile deceiver; you can not deny it."

"But pray do not say that even in jest!" cried Signor Martinelli, his eyes turned heavenward, and forcing himself to smile. "Pardon me, but at my age? And then she—a thoroughly virtuous woman, I would swear it— And she has always been so—so good to me, has always confided—yes, I say—confided

so many things to me, poor thing— And I stood
there, believe me, congratulating myself—that—"

"You must excuse me! Good-by!" Biagio Speranza
hastily interrupted him, withdrew his arm, and hurried
after a flashily dressed woman who at that moment
emerged from a café.

Martino Martinelli stood there, abandoned in the
middle of the street; involuntarily he raised his hand
to his hat, then his eyes followed for a time the couple
who went away together laughing loudly, perhaps at
him, perhaps at the Pentoni; and he shook his head
sorrowfully, wounded.

VI

Neither the next evening nor the following ones did
Biagio Speranza come to the pension.

Momo Cariolin and Dario Scossi ceased teasing
Carolinona after the first evening, and, truth to say,
she was somewhat distant with them. Trunfo tried
to take his revenge by reminding them how he had
warned them not to joke stupidly in a matter that had
no joke in it. Cedebonis gave himself no peace, thinking that with this marriage had been celebrated the
funeral of mirth, and for several evenings he repeated
this phrase, which seemed to him particularly felicitous. He alone, with his Calabrian obstinacy, continued fuming; he fumed because the fire would not
once more burst forth with the fine witticisms of former days. But no one paid any attention to him, and
he consoled himself after a fashion, thinking that a
renewal of this huge joke was inevitable, in one way

or another, as soon as Cocco Bertolli should leave the
hospital.

Trunfo, meanwhile, who had resumed his former
habits, between one note and another of his hissed
opera, instigated Carolinona to avenge herself.

At these vindictive exhortations of his a desire for
vengeance flamed in the heart of the Pentoni; but soon
after, suffocated, as though the flame had suddenly
become smoke—a slow, dense smoke—she buried her
face in her hands, and shook her head bitterly.

"Make good your rights," said Trunfo. "A woman
never lacks for means." But she really recognized no
rights of hers, and saw no means. He had made the
terms of the agreement plain to her in advance. It
was true, they were injurious, even shameful for her,
but had she not accepted them? And if there arose in
her heart a sentiment she had never before felt, and
which she was not capable of explaining to herself,
but which tormented her, and which she blushed for
without respite, what fault was it of his? He had
given her but a single cause for offense; he did not
wish to believe in her honesty. What vengeance could
she take for that? Possibly, if she felt herself capable
of it, she might actually deceive him— But no, never!
She inclined rather toward the advice of Martinelli, who
counseled her to win him by fair means, to soften him.

"Write to him," finally advised Martinelli. "Ask
him to come as before, to do at least—yes, I say—his
duty, now that that other—yes, I say—that example
of the wrath of God is about to leave the hospital."

"Have you news of him?" asked Carolinona.

Yes, Signor Martinelli had news, but he gave it to her with compunction, anxiously. Unfortunately, that "wrath of God" would be discharged in two or three days—the beast! One of the nurses had told him that while he was already convalescent he heard of this marriage and had had a relapse. "A dangerous fellow, dangerous!" finished Signor Martino. "So much so that I would almost advise you to go to the police without further delay." Poor Pentoni stood pondering for a moment, then smiled.

"Signor Martino, do you know what I have decided? I shall not do anything. I will not move even a finger. Let Bertolli come and beat me. Or perhaps he will wish to kill me? It would really be laughable. Let us leave it to God!"

Now that is all very well; God is great, omnipotent, watches over all, protects the good and the oppressed. Nevertheless, Martinelli thought it well to inform Scossi and Cedebonis of the violent designs with which Cocco Bertolli would leave the hospital. It was therefore decided, after a long confabulation, to send Scossi to the home of Biagio Speranza, whom no one had seen since that day he had disappeared; and if he was not at home, a note was to be left, warning him of the Pentoni's danger; if he was away, Scossi was to learn his address and telegraph him.

He was neither at home nor out of town. Dario Scossi was obliged to hire a cab and repair to a farm belonging to Speranza's old landlady, some three kilometers outside of the city gates. Yes, Biagio had been there for four days and was to remain until his departure for Barcellona; he had warned his landlady not to tell any one where he had taken refuge, and the landlady, as we have seen, had kept her promise. But it really was a question of something serious?

"Most serious! Most serious!" Scossi reassured her.

Having thus forced the citadel, Scossi began to feel the real necessity for believing in the danger that threatened Carolinona, and in the dreadfulness of Cocco Bertolli, so that he might have courage enough to face Biagio Speranza. The cab finally stopped before a rustic gate, consisting of a single bar, supported on posts not less rustic, behind which rose two tall cypress trees. A narrow path led up from the gate, between the vines, to the little knoll, on the summit of which stood the small house, amid trees. What poetry! What a dream! What quietude!

Before ringing the bell, Scossi glanced up the path for a few minutes; suddenly he heard the shrill squawks of geese, then the voice of Biagio Speranza, calling gaily: "Nannetta! Nannetta!"

Oh, wretch; Oh, renegade! A true idyl! He began to regret having come. "Shall I wait?" asked the driver.

"Yes, wait. I will ring." He rang very softly; the tongue of the bell barely touched the edge, without giving a sound. Suddenly he pulled the chain, and the bell rang furiously. "It is done! Now the deluge! By Jove!"

Up at the end of the path an old peasant shortly afterward presented himself, who, seeing the cab outside the gate, hastened to come down. "What do you wish, sir?"

"Speranza."

"What do you mean? Oh, yes, sir, you mean the young gentleman. He is here." He opened the gate, and Scossi entered. Again the geese squawked from above, and the old peasant began to laugh, shaking his head. "Biagio!" exclaimed Scossi. "What is he doing?"

"Oh, he does and thinks of a hundred things," replied the peasant. "Come and see. He has put soldiers' caps on the poor geese, and drives them thus toward the lady who stands down there by the garden fountain."

"Nannetta, Nannetta!" once more cried Biagio from above. "Look at Carolinona, who comes at a run! I have made her corporal."

"Horrible!" cried Dario Scossi, presenting himself on the level stretch of ground.

"Dario!" exclaimed Biagio Speranza, amazed. "What! You here?" And he came toward him. But Scossi drew back a step, and gazed at him severely.

"You give a goose the name of your wife?"

"Oh, be quiet!" replied Biagio, shaking himself. "Have you come even out here to annoy me? How did you know?"

Scossi then explained the reasons for his coming, told him that it was neither just nor fair for him to leave that poor woman yonder in her embarrassment, and that his presence at the pension was urgently re-

quired for three or four days at least. Biagio Speranza
grew discouraged.

Suddenly there arrived at a run, her face crimson,
a straw hat on her beautiful, ruffled. tawny hair, Nannetta, the same woman whom Signor Martinelli had
seen coming out the café that evening.

"Well, Biagio? Oh, pardon me, how do you do,
sir—"

"Good day, my dear," replied Scossi, holding out
his hand.

But Nannetta held her own in the air.

"I can not. They are dripping wet. If you like,
with his permission, you may give me a little kiss
here." And she offered her flaming cheek.

"Do you permit?" asked Scossi, moved to compunction. "Her hands are wet—"

"One only," replied Biagio gloomily. "There is
nothing to be said. I shall have to go."

"Is your wife sending for you?" asked Nannetta
sadly, her cheek still upturned, upon which Scossi was
all the while imprinting a series of soft kisses. "Oh,
that is enough, sir; one only, I beg of you. Your wife,
then?"

"Oh, do not you too annoy me!" cried Biagio, exas-
perated. "You may thank your God, Scossi, that I
have not a stick in my hand. Get out at once. I shall
return to the city to-morrow. This evening I am going
to make up for it all by staying here. I shall wring
the neck of the goose that looks so like her and eat
it all for supper, with the appetite of a cannibal. Get
out!"

But Nannetta wished to keep Scossi for dinner. At table Biagio explained to him why he had escaped.

"I do not say that she actually loves me; but it is near, do you know? Who would ever have expected it? Of course I understand that I am a very good-looking fellow, agreeable—" Nannetta protested with a laugh.

"And I assure you that she gave me a veritable lecture like a real wife."

"Poor woman!" cried Nannetta. "If what you say is true, then all of you, especially you, Biagio, have been cruel beyond comparison. Go, make up to her for it now. Believe me, it is the best thing that you can do."

Biagio Speranza did not open his lips, but opened his eyes very wide, and stared at Nannetta with such an expression that she smiled, and repeated: "Poor woman!"

"Enough, enough, my dear!" interrupted Scossi. "Or you will keep him from ever returning to the city."

"No, no," said Biagio seriously. "I have promised, and I will come. To think of it! For the diversion of humanity, Destiny had contrived a truly ideal marriage: Cocco Bertolli and Carolinona. I, fool, stupid, imbecile, go and interfere with her plans. I must pay for it. That great man loved her, his dove, and now I must show him the door. I feel remorseful, I assure you, but I have promised, and I will keep my word."

The evening of the same day Dario Scossi related to the friend of the pension what he had done, where he had found Speranza, and in whose company. Cedebonis feigned to be scandalized at such immediate infidelity; but Scossi, who, in relating the affair, had allowed this information to escape him without intending it, replied that Carolinona should not take it amiss in him. Wives were made purposely to be deceived by their husbands, and vice versa, except in the case of the Martinelli couple, of course, who were unique beneath the heavens. Finally he announced that Biagio Speranza would return without fail the evening of the following day. "The sheep will return to the fold."

VII

Biagio Speranza came somewhat late, saluted the lady of the house and his friends, and seated himself in his usual place. Some embarrassment was felt at first, but gradually conversation became more or less general. Only Martinelli kept his round, owl-like eyes fixed on Speranza as though expecting any moment some explanation of his unworthy manner of acting, some sign of repentance.

Carolinona sat with lowered eyes; but from time to time she would look about her, and if she saw that no one was looking, give a rapid side glance at Speranza, and become greatly moved. She suffered; she felt that she suffered, but still she controlled herself so that no one noticed it. She had given orders to the servant not to open the door without first looking through the peep-hole. If Cocco Bertolli came in the daytime she was to tell him that her mistress was not at home; if in the evening, while the boarders were at table, before opening the front door she was to come into the dining-room and give warning.

At every ring of the bell they all stopped to listen, and the poor woman felt her heart almost burst with agitation until they went on talking.

After an unusually loud ring, Cedebonis remarked: "You will see that that is not he. He certainly will first try to get in by day, and not succeeding in this will return in the evening." And this would undoubtedly have been the more logical method; but one thing Cedebonis did not take into account; Cocco Bertolli was mad. And so it happened that it *was* just he who rang the bell. The servant rushed into the room in alarm to announce him.

All rose in consternation, save Biagio Speranza. "I beg you," said he calmly, "to remain seated. I alone must go. You go on chatting here quietly. You will see; two peaceful words, and I shall make him reasonable."

He rose and moved toward the door; but before leaving the dining-room he turned and added, raising one hand: "I beg you, then." But the Pentoni, who until then had controlled herself with difficulty, burst into tears. Some surrounded her, trying to comfort her; others went on tiptoe to listen outside the drawing-room door.

Biagio Speranza himself went to open the door, resolutely; but at sight of Cocco Bertolli he stood as though turned to stone. The unfortunate fellow seemed to have scarcely an ounce of flesh on his bones, and his enormous ox-like eyes in his wasted, cadaverous face were positively terrifying. He paused at sight of Biagio Speranza, and twisted his mouth into a ferocious sneer. "Ah, you!" he murmured.

"Pardon me, what do you want?" asked Biagio.

"Now!" Cocco Bertolli clenched his fist, his eyes almost bursting from their sockets, "I merely wish to say two words to the lady in yonder, and to cut off her ears and nose."

"Good Heavens! You would spoil her for *me!*" cried Biagio, laughing. "Come, come, my dear poet; you must know that I am now master of this house, and you shall enter it neither now nor at any other time."

Cocco Bertolli, all of a tremor, drew down his loosely hanging vest, and said: "Very good. We will see about that. I merely wished to remind that good lady of a certain promise."

"But pardon me, do you not understand," Speranza tried to persuade him, "that the lady of whom you speak hoped, or rather was sure, that you—pardon me —that you were dying?"

"But I am not dead!" cried Cocco Bertolli, with fierce joy. "And I would have you understand that for her I have defied death!"

"Too bad!" exclaimed Biagio. "Too bad! Come now, if you will permit me to say so, do you really think that was worth while?"

"Ah, do you too know," sneered Cocco Bertolli, "that your wife is a shameless woman?"

Biagio Speranza spread out his hands. "A stout

woman, pardon, let us rather say a stout woman, so
as not to offend her."

"But I wish to offend her!" replied Cocco Bertolli,
raising his arms, terrible in his wrath. "I wish to
offend her before you, her worthy husband. Buffoon!"

Biagio Speranza paled, closed his eyes, then said
mildly: "Listen, Cocco. Go away peaceably, or I will
kick you out."

"Me?"

"You. Or rather, see; I shut the door in your
face to keep myself from kicking a poor madman, for
you are nothing more than that." And he closed the
door.

"Vile clown!" roared Cocco Bertolli outside the
door. "But I shall wait in the street for you, do you
hear? I will make you pay for this!"

Biagio Speranza returned to the dining-room, still
pale and trembling with the effort he had made to
control himself. "Well?" asked all anxiously.

"Nothing," he replied, with a nervous smile. "I
have sent him away."

"And he is waiting outside for you!" added Cariolin, who had heard in the hall the madman's threat.

"Oh, Heavens!" moaned Carolinona, her face hidden in her handkerchief. "For my sake!" This weeping irritated Biagio Speranza; he felt an aversion for
the part he was about to play, and shrugged his shoulders angrily. "Let him wait. I will go and give him
what he deserves now!" And he looked for his hat
and stick.

Then the Pentoni, as though impelled by a force

stronger than her nature, started to her feet. "I implore you! For pity's sake! Do not have anything to do with that madman. Let the others go first! Listen to me!"

All save Martinelli, who was shaking like a leaf, and the scornful Trunfo, echoed Carolinona's words, and offered to go. But Biagio Speranza made way for himself violently, and crying, "Pray, what do you take me for?" he went out. The others followed him. At the foot of the stairs he turned, and again begged them to be good enough to remain behind.

"You make me lose my patience by acting thus," he called to them. "Do you seriously believe that I will lift my hand against that poor unfortunate who has just left the hospital, unless he actually drives me to the wall? So stay where you are, I beg of you! Do not let him see you, for if he does he will begin haranguing. Do not aggravate the ridiculousness of my position."

Dario Scossi then made a sign to the others to stop, and let Speranza go on alone. Shortly after they continued downstairs and paused in the hall to spy. Cariolin, who was slightly in advance, put his head a little way out of the front door. Biagio and Cocco Bertolli were talking vigorously, a slight distance apart; but suddenly Cariolin saw Cocco Bertolli raise one hand and solemnly administer a blow upon Speranza. At that they all rushed forward. Carolinona, who was standing at a window, gave a scream and fell back fainting in the trembling arms of Martinelli, while Trunfo, attracted by the cries from the street, rushed to the entrance, repeating scornfully: "This is too much! A fight! Clowns!"

Biagio Speranza, tearful with rage, and struggling to free himself, cried out to the friends who were holding him: "Let me go! Let me go!"

"At your disposal!" roared Cocco Bertolli as they dragged him away, amid the crowd which was flocking from every direction. "At your disposal! The Caffè della Svizzero!"

Dario Scossi, Cedebonis, and Cariolin finally succeeded in leading Biagio Speranza away, while he cried furiously: "I must kill him! I must kill him! Two of you, you, Scossi, and you, Cariolin, go at once to find him. Ridiculous as it is, atrociously ridiculous, a duel with that wretch, because of that woman in yonder, I must fight, for otherwise when I see him I should kill him like a dog. Go, go, I will await you at my home."

The three friends sought to dissuade him, to persuade him not to attach any importance to what had occurred. After all it was but the onset of a madman. But Biagio Speranza would not listen to reason. "He has struck me, do you understand?" And he sprang into a cab to go home, while Scossi and Cariolin, followed by Cedebonis, serious, placid, and curious, repaired to the Caffè della Svizzero.

They found Cocco Bertolli there, swelling with pride, while he narrated the adventure amid the laughter of the crowd that had followed him.

"At once! At your service!" he called, coming toward them. "Pistols, swords, daggers; what you

please, at your choice! Or even with hands and feet;
but at once!"

Scossi made him understand that two more men
were needed, with whom they could discuss the details
of the meeting.

"I know no one," protested Cocco Bertolli. "I
would like to send Signor Speranza my two friends,
Nero and Erostratus, but unfortunately they are both
dead. So, pray, find me two living wretches; I do not
wish to trouble myself with such paltry details."

"I would assist in my quality of physician," said
Cedebonis. "But what can I do? I have lessons at
the *liceo*."

So Dario Scossi and Cariolin, together with Cocco
Bertolli, set out in search of two seconds other than
Erostratus and Nero.

Biagio Speranza, trembling with impatience, waited
in his home for almost an hour. Then the doorbell
rang; but instead of Scossi and Cariolin appeared Nannetta, who, having heard at the café about the quarrel,
had come for news.

"Why, yes, I have been struck!" said Biagio. "Come
in, Nannetta. We were *so* comfortable in the country, we two, were we not? I have acted foolishly, but
what will you? I must pay for it, as I told you—"

"A duel?" Nannetta asked him, terrified.

"Of course. Struck, I tell you."

"Where?"

"Here."

Nannetta kissed his cheek. "Dear, and if they kill
you? Have you thought of that?"

"No, really I have not!" said Biagio, shrugging his shoulders, and he continued staring impatiently out of the window.

Nannetta followed him, but instead of staring down into the street she began gazing up at the stars, which glowed thickly in the moonless sky. She sighed, and said: "Do you know, Biagio, that I really wish you would not fight this duel?"

Struck by the strange tone of her voice, Biagio asked her with a forced smile: "Are you so fond of me?"

Nannetta shrugged her shoulders, smiling mournfully; she closed her eyes, and replied: "How do I know?—I do not want—"

"Come!" cried Biagio, with a start, "no melancholy! I have here some *marsala;* let us drink it! I must have some biscuits too—then you shall help me pack my valises. To-morrow, after giving that dog a good lesson, I shall be off!"

"For always?"

"For always!" He took the bottle of *marsala,* the biscuits, and invited Nannetta to sit down and drink. There was another ring at the door. It was Signor Martino Martinelli, reduced to the very shadow of himself, as though a breath could blow him away like a feather. "Come in, come in, my very dear Signor Martino!" cried Biagio, slapping him on the back. "Who sent you, eh? I bet you I can guess. My wife!" Nannetta burst out laughing at seeing the man with his huge nose standing there, petrified at sight of her.

"Do not laugh, Nannetta," said Biagio. "Allow me

to present to you the prototype of faithful husbands, Signor Martino Martinelli, famed for the biggest nose in the world. Signor Martinelli, tell my esteemed wife that you found me safe and sound, with a good bottle of wine in front of me, and a charming little lady at my side. Do not sneeze! Will you have something to drink?"

"Par—pardon me," stammered Signor Martinelli thickly and indignantly; "permit me to tell—to tell you that you—yes, sir—that—you—misjudge, yes, I say, unworthily—yes, sir—a heart—a heart of gold, which at this moment beats—yes, I say—beats for you. Good evening."

The laughter of Biagio and Nannetta followed him to the door. Signor Martinelli felt relieved after this outburst, and, elevated to a sphere of heroism, went away with his nose high in the air, like a war trumpet.

VIII

Giannantonio Cocco Bertolli arrived first at the place appointed for the meeting, accompanied by the physician and two artillery officers, friends of Cariolin, who had volunteered to act as seconds. He was most calm. Like a true poet, he praised the mild April morning. "The zephyr returns, bearing with it fair weather—" He praised the trilling of the birds, saluting the sun; inhaled voluptuously the resinous odor which the pine trees gave out, and the cypresses of the handsome villa nearby; recited an ode of Anacreon which he had translated, and finally told the two officers that they were enjoying the apologue of the geese and the migrating crane. He was the crane; that is to say, according to the geese, a madman. "For I have neither overeaten nor drunk too much, you must know. Since yesterday, gentlemen, food has not entered my disheartened stomach. Water; I have drunk water at the public fountain. Diogenes, gentlemen, had a cup, but when he saw a boy drinking out of his own hand, he broke his own cup and he too drank out of his own hand. I do the same. I do not know whether I shall eat to-day, or where I shall sleep. Perhaps I will present myself to some farmer in the country. I will dig. Then I shall eat; but free from all ties in this absolute, sublime liberty which intoxicates me, and which must naturally seem like madness to the slaves of the law, of necessity, of social conventions. In a short time I shall break the head of the imbecile who has tried to cross my path, and then I shall work on my great poem, 'Erostratus.' "

A little later Biagio Speranza, Dario Scossi, and Momo Cariolin arrived with another physician. Biagio Speranza was very nervous; the thought of fighting with this madman, who had struck him, seemed to degrade him. But he tried to appear hilarious, so as not to lend too much importance to this duel, the grotesque epilogue of a silly prank. His valises and everything for his departure were ready, prepared at home. Now he would either give or receive a scratch, and all would be over. And by Jove, it was time!

The direction of the duel fell by lot to the young officer who acted as first second. But already it appeared that everything was being arranged most amicably. The ground being chosen and measured, the adversaries were then invited to take their places opposite each other. "If you please," said the officer to Cocco Bertolli, "you must remove your coat." Cocco took it off furiously and flung it far from him. At sight of his ragged and soiled shirt, torn at the elbows, all received a most painful impression; repulsion, disgust, and pity, all in one; they looked in each other's eyes, questioning if this were not a case that should be brought to an end at once. But Cocco Bertolli, who already had his sword in hand, and quivered with impatience, demanded with proud indignation: "Well?"

"On guard!" said the officer.

Immediately Cocco Bertolli leaped forward like a tiger with terrible fury, flourishing his sword, and howling, upon his adversary. Thus attacked, Biagio Speranza, still under that painful impression, started back, parrying the storm of blows as well as he could. He might easily have run Cocco through the body simply by holding his sword stiff, straight out, with a sudden lunge; but he banished the temptation, and continued parrying the attacks. Suddenly, in his fury, the sword fell from Cocco Bertolli's hand. "Enough!" cried the officer who was directing the encounter.

"What do you mean by enough?" cried Cocco Bertolli, out of breath. "Do you wish to profit by my misfortune? I appeal to my adversary, who surely can not consider such paltry satisfaction 'enough.'"

Biagio Speranza stooped and picked up the fallen

sword, and offered it courteously to Cocco Bertolli.
"Here it is. On guard!" Then he glanced at his
friends, as much as to say: "You see to what you
have brought me?" And his nervous irritation increased. "If the other evening, after that blow, you
had allowed me to give him a sound beating, I should
not now have found myself under the hard necessity
of killing this poor madman, so forlorn and miserable,
or of letting him kill me."

At the second command for attack, Speranza was
resolved to oppose his adversary seriously. But without warning Cocco Bertolli was upon him again with
redoubled fury. "Stop!" cried the officer.

But already, in this lightning-like assault, Biagio
Speranza had been wounded, for he suddenly fell to
the ground, his hands clenched to his breast. A sneer
choked in his throat. He looked at the four seconds
and the physicians, tried to say: "It is nothing!" but
instead of words blood gushed from his mouth, and he
sank back, terrified.

Having recovered from their first feeling of horror,
the others bent over him, lifted him cautiously, and
carried him with the greatest care into the house of
the keeper of the villa, where they deposited him on
a bed. The doctors thought at first that he had but a
few minutes to live; nevertheless, they administered
the first remedies, and waited, anxious, terrified. An
hour passed, two, and one of the physicians proposed
to send some one to the city for a stretcher. So,
toward evening, Biagio Speranza was carried home,
between life and death. The Pentoni, his old land-

lady, and Nannetta were waiting for him, all bathed in tears. But the latter, shortly after, when the first confusion was over, was politely sent away by Scossi. "It is not proper for you to stay here, my dear." She made no reply, but under Carolinona's very eyes wished to imprint a kiss upon the brow of the wounded man, who lay unconscious, flushed with fever.

"Ah," she then said weeping to Scossi, "if you had only left us there in the country! Poor Biagio! My heart told me this would happen. But at least take away this unfortunate woman from his side; if he opens his eyes he will die of despair at seeing her beside him." Then she went away.

While Nannetta was saying this, Carolinona had left the head of his bed, understanding herself that the sight of her in these first moments would not be acceptable to the wounded man. She had desired so ardently that he might return to the pension, but she had not said even a word to that effect, nor taken a single step to urge him to return. It would be most unjust to hold her responsible for the misfortune that had happened; and he should be the first to admit it, he who had forced her, actually forced her, to commit this folly. So he ought not to feel horror at sight of her there by his bed, nor cherish any rancor. But Carolinona at heart felt the positive necessity, almost instinct, to ascribe to others the fault of our own misfortunes; so she drew back into the shadow to watch, to give him the most passionate care, without any flattering hope of recompense. She merely wished, longed, and prayed that he might recover; she wished nothing for herself, not even gratitude, not even that he should know that she had secretly nursed him.

Dario Scossi, Cariolin, and Cedebonis, after the first few days, seeing that the wound began to improve, began to insist that she should take some hours of rest. But they insisted in vain. "It will do me no harm; I am accustomed to it," Carolinona would reply.

One day Dario Scossi looked at her, and she no longer appeared so ugly to him. Grief and love, both despairing, seemed to have transfigured her. Those eyes, for instance, so intense with passion; she did not know it, but they were actually beautiful at that moment. Seeing herself gazed at kindly, Carolinona smiled faintly at him, while her eyes filled with tears. And to Dario Scossi that smile seemed sublime.

The vigils continued heroically for about a month, during which time Carolinona, like mother and sweetheart in one, watched anxiously at the sick man's bedside while he slept, ready to retire into shadow as soon as he awoke. She actually lost flesh, but, illuminated from within by the joy of knowing him safe at last, she became beautful—really beautiful? No, but—in the opinion of all—more than possible as a wife. "And then," they added, "if she has won out, that is saying very little. Has she not actually restored him to the world? Biagio is her own from now on."

But she could not believe in her own happiness until one day Biagio, still in bed, but already convalescent, called her to him, and said in a voice trembling with tenderness, gazing into her eyes, and pressing her hand: "My good Carolina!"

TWO MEN AND A WOMAN

BY GRAZIA DELEDDA

Grazia Deledda was born at Nuoro, Sardinia, in 1872. Until her marriage in 1900 she lived in her native province. At scarcely twenty years of age she published a volume of Sardinian tales, and in 1900 obtained her first great success with "Elias Portolù," which gave her fame throughout Europe. Besides these two volumes, her works consist so far of two collections of short stories, eight romances, and an exquisite drama. Her chief characteristics as a writer are spontaneity of inspiration, truth of observation, and a simplicity of style most refreshing after the labored subtleties of the psychologists. Her characters, all drawn from the surroundings of her early youth, are generally simple souls, living next to nature and full of violent passions.

TWO MEN AND A WOMAN

A STORY OF ITALIAN PRISON LIFE

BY GRAZIA DELEDDA

AMONG the prisoners who arrived at the Penitentiary on the 23d of March, as the setting sun was flooding with crimson its cold, grim walls, was a young man of distinguished appearance; he was dressed in gray, and the folds of his large, soft gray hat, adorned with a knot of gray ribbon, quite hid his pale, thin face, with its aquiline nose and carefully kept pointed beard. During the journey he had not spoken once, but sat with bent head and knitted brows, his eyes intently fastened upon his thin, nervous hands with their long, polished nails, enclosed in the shining bands of the steel handcuffs. On reaching the Penitentiary he had for an instant raised his head and fixed his shining, burning eyes upon the countenance of the Direttore, who on his side returned the gaze coldly and at length. By a queer coincidence, the prisoner and the Direttore had the same name— Cassio Longino! And they both knew it; and the prisoner, who in his distant country across the sea where "Cassio" means "a white petticoat," had often been the subject of many a caricature, experienced now a sort of bitter satisfaction, on seeing himself on

Translated by Florence MacIntyre Tyson. Copyright, 1903, by The Current Literature Publishing Company.

that account sought by the cold, scornful glance of the
Signore Direttore. With the first glance, the two men
hated each other. The Direttore was approaching
middle life, was small and stooped a little. His feet
and hands were small, and the latter were always
plunged in the pockets of his long, black overcoat.
His clean-shaven face bore the marks of physical suffering, which was accentuated in deep lines about the
pale, thin lips; his eyes were small and green and full
of an almost cruel indifference; his hair was blond
and short, and his ears large and prominent. For all
these reasons, but chiefly because he was the com-
mandant of the prison, he was exceedingly displeasing
to No. 245; and No. 245 was displeasing to the com-
mandant on account of his haughty manner, the fiery
look with which he observed him, and especially on
account of his vigorous, superb youth.

While the prisoners were being consigned to their
quarters, the Direttore did not open his mouth, and
for several days Cassio, shut up in a private cell, did
not again see him. His cell faced the east, and
through the tiny aperture pierced in the great stone
rampart he could see the distant Apennines, still covered with snow, and the Tuscan landscape, over which
the early spring was scattering a vivid green sward,
and the pale, tender coloring of bursting twig and
blossom. In the Penitentiary garden, which was cultivated by prisoners clad in white linen suits and red
caps, Cassio, who by especial permission of the Gov-
ment retained his gentleman's clothes, watched the
peach trees burst into a glory of intensest pink, and

the apple trees toss their delicate bloom in rich masses through the balmy fragrant air.

A prey to keen anguish and despair, he never wandered far from his cell. The long, silent evenings overwhelmed him with despair; often he did not sleep at night, but tossed feverishly upon his hard straw pallet. When, in the morning, the guard, a great, tall fellow, whose red head brushed against the ceiling of the cell, would come in to make up the bed, Cassio was always dressed and standing before his tiny, barred window.

Outside the swallows were wheeling and fluttering about, their wings and breasts flashing in the sunshine. The prisoner did not deign to speak a word to the guard, nor did he take the slightest notice of the continual complaints, whistles, or gestures of his neighbor on the right; but when the exercise hour arrived and he was allowed to walk in the courtyard, he paced in haughty indifference, without even a glance at his companions, up and down the sad, dew-covered pavement.

The rumor spread through the prison that he was a very rich lord from Sardinia, a relation of the Direttore, and since the Direttore was feared and hated (though none of the prisoners knew the reason of this hate and fear, for the poor man had never done them any evil, except with his look of icy indifference), No. 245, within a week after his arrival, was hated, and strange to say, was feared.

Having requested permission to write, the first of April he was sent for into the office; through the barred window there penetrated a ray of pale sun-

shine, in whose light danced the shadows of a distant
treetop. The Direttore, bent more than usual, was
working at a gray table; he neither moved nor spoke
for a long time, during which Cassio, standing upright
and stiff, his eyes fixed on the branches trembling in
the sunshine, grew hot with humiliation.

Ah! in the presence of the others, of that crowd of
criminals, and the vile guards, he could at least give
himself the satisfaction of taking refuge in a certain,
scornful dignity; he was stronger than those who
bound him, greater than those whom he would not
even deign to call companions in misfortune, but in
the presence of this little man, so ill and full of
disdain, he must bow, must reply, must humiliate
himself.

"You," said the Direttore bruskly, turning around,
but not rising, "are condemned to three years of simple
detention for forgery; and you may write only once
a month."

His voice was rather weary, but the tone was pure
Tuscan.

"I know it," replied Cassio, "but I have not asked
to be allowed to write to my own home, but on my
own account, in my own cell."

"It is not possible. Why do you not ask to be
placed in the office of the clerks?"

"Is there chance of being allowed to do so?"

"Yes, there is every chance."

That very day Cassio proffered his request, and on
the next was placed in the office, where a great quan-
tity of work was badly executed by three other pris-

ers. The room, which was next to that of the Direttore, was even more desolate and gloomy, and the three
clerks, the first, fat and bald, with small, bleared eyes;
the second, fair, pale, and with a transparent look,
and the third a tall muscular young man, with black
curly hair, and the face of a Roman emperor, made a
bad impression on the new arrival.

They appeared resigned to, and even contented
with, their melancholy fate. Cassio, on the other hand,
experienced a profound disgust, which was but accentuated by the stupid resignation of his companions in
misfortune—a very anguish of impotent desperation,
and regretted his request. Better to have remained
alone in his cell, with his hands clasping the bars of
the little window, and before him the distant Apennines, that brought to him memories of his own native
mountains, resounding with the neighing of his black
charger, dashing in pursuit of the straying sheep—
alone with his sentence and his sorrow!

He of the curly head, bolder than the other two, who
contented themselves with casting stealthly glances at
him, sought promptly, though respectfully, to make
his acquaintance. (They knew that he had the same
name as the Direttore, and so it was told among the
other prisoners.)

"Are you a Sardinian?"

"Yes," replied he coldly.

"Since Fate has sent you to this place, allow me—"

"A beautiful Fate!" interrupted Cassio bitterly, and
cut off sharply the compliment the unfortunate man
was about to present to the presumed great Sardinian

signore. But he said nothing more himself, nor asked anything of the others.

Three days later, there arrived for him from Sardinia a letter bearing an air of indefinable elegance. The handwriting was large and firm, while a delicious, almost imperceptible fragrance escaped from the sheets.

The Direttore opened it, and read it with a certain hesitation and half feeling that he had been expecting it.

After all, he was a man who was still young; he had suffered much and loved much, and if his own sufferings had produced that profound indifference which passed for cruelty among the unhappiness it was his fate to control, there still remained in his heart something of sympathy and compassion. Had No. 245 been a poor devil, like almost all the other prisoners, instead of a most interesting personality, the Direttore, after the first day, would never have given him another thought. But this handsome young stranger, with his haughty, distinguished air, who had arrived surrounded by a romantic mystery, had attracted the attention of every one, as well as his own.

The queer stories current in the gloomy cells and dark corridors had also reached his ears.

The thought that there might be something of truth in them had even begun to pierce his customary indifference with a faint interest, which was augmented as ne perused the letter.

Not that it contained anything of especial interest. It was written by a half-sister of Cassio.

An intense affection manifested itself through all the four sheets, a certain nameless sweetness, and exquisite suggestion of comfort and resignation.

"Have courage, Cassio, do not despair nor suffer too much; remember that we two are alone in the world, alone to love and believe in one another. The time will pass, and when God reunites us I will know how to recompense thee for the immense sacrifice thou hast made for me. Do not feel humiliated nor cast down; the good know that thy fault was an act of heroism—"

"Indeed," thought the Direttore, "prisoners are always innocent, generally are victims, but that they should be heroes!"

This letter, so different from the vulgar epistles that were accustomed to come to the Penitentiary; so good, delicate, and loving, gave him food for reflection.

A sort of morbid curiosity took possession of him, against which he struggled in vain, to find out, to know everything. So that in spite of himself, though not contrary to the regulations of the establishment, which he scrupulously observed, he sent for No. 245, and on his arrival, he opened the conversation by explaining some difficult work to be done in the office, and then, fixing a look of close scrutiny upon him, said:

"Here is a letter for you."

Cassio proffered never a word, but raised his head, and his face turned red to the tips of his ears.

And for the second time a wonderful thing happened. The Direttore of the Penitentiary envied

488   GRAZIA DELEDDA

his prisoner. For to the prisoner in his profound
wretchedness had come a voice of comfort and affection, illuminating his dark horizon with a glory that
was mirrored on his countenance, and to him, free and
powerful, alone and lost in the infinite sadness of deep
suffering, there never came one word of tenderness,
one ray of light.

In spite of his emotion, Cassio perceived something
abnormal was passing in the mind of the Direttore,
and, astute Sardinian that he was, he took advantage
to ask eagerly if he might not have the letter at once
and read it there in the office.

Better there, under the badly concealed indifference
of the little green eyes, than in the repulsive surroundings of his workroom, subject to the vulgar curiosity
of the three clerks.

From that day he became more sociable, more resigned, and the Signore Direttore showed him a certain deference which did not escape the eyes of the
others, and but confirmed the report of an assumed
relationship.

But still he did not receive permission to write until
he had been there a month, though on the very day
he was given two sheets. And his letter was not less
affectionate than had been his sister's, though less
sweet and delicate; in every line was displayed the
agony of helplessness:

"I have been here but a month, though it seems
thirty years. I am beginning to be more resigned.
They have put me in the clerk's office, with three terrible strangers [this the Direttore erased], the work

is hard, but it helps to pass the time. At first I could not accustom myself to it, now I am less desperate. The Signore Direttore is very kind to me. Yes, I know the time will pass somehow or other, but still I feel as if my sentence would be eternal; that the 987 days yet remaining are as boundless as the waves; but most of all do I suffer when I think of thee; and yet the thought brings me much comfort. Thou art so good. Please do not forget me and get married when I am away! But I am ashamed, my dear Paola, such a thing I well know is impossible. How could a good sister forget her unhappy brother? But all the same, when I am tossing sleeplessly on my narrow bed, the thought fills me with terror. Who could believe such a thing possible?

"Though I am now resigned to all, I did once believe in the justice of men. But what have they done to me? Write very soon and do not forget me. If that were to happen I would soon find a termination to my sufferings."

Not a word nor thought for any one else, only for her! The answer arrived by return mail, together with clothes, books, and money.

The Signore Direttore felt anew the strange fascination of envy and longing, as he read the delightful, tender letter of Paola. She had not a word of reproach for the lack of confidence the unhappy man had shown in her, but said how grieved she was that he should be so sad, and assured him she would never marry until his return. She had, too, a good word for the Signore Direttore. "Love and respect him;

he can do much for thee; can be like a father to thee"
["a brother, young lady," thought the Direttore]. "I
pray for thee and for him."

"Thanks," he murmured rather bitterly.

In the third letter, Cassio having asked what she
was doing and how she passed the days:

"The days pass sadly in thy absence. I look after
my affairs as well as I can, and often go into the
country with my foster-parents. Poor things, they
are a great comfort to me! We go on horseback,
and these trips are my only diversion. In the house
nothing new has happened. I am embroidering the
tapestry I began at school, when my dreams were so
different from the present reality. I am working into
it certain rich Sardinian embroideries ferreted out by
the foster-mother.

"I never see any one, but am always thinking of
thee and counting the days."

"Why in the world do not these people, who seem
rich and cultivated, think of asking for a pardon?" the
Direttore asked himself, and, rising, he went into the
garden—where the Tuscan spring was rioting amid
a very glory of roses, crimson, white, and yellow;
while gleaming among the deep green of the shrub-
bery, like brilliant butterflies, moved about the little
red caps of the prisoner gardeners—and fell into a
strangely sweet strain of thought of which the tender,
strong sister of No. 245 was the subject. In fancy
he saw her, tall and dark, like her brother, with the
pallor and distinguished appearance so marked in the
prisoner; or bending patiently over her embroidery;

or else trotting on her little Sardinian horse, her eyes half closed as she faced the ardent beams of the midday sun. Then, lost in wonder, he took himself to task for such boyish romance, till he worked himself into quite a frenzy of anger at his foolishness, which left him exhausted and more indifferent even than was his wont.

And so the months rolled by, bringing three or four more letters from Paola. In the last she promised to send her picture, if Cassio was quite sure he would be allowed to receive it.

"It is allowed," wrote the Direttore at the bottom of the page before sending it to the prisoner.

For one, two, three weeks, in that great pile, under the overarching blue sky and ardent sunshine that turned it into a very furnace, two souls were awaiting with passionate eagerness, though under different aspects, that picture of a woman.

The waiting of Cassio was sweet and full of peace, amid the passive resignation that habit and hope had begun to plant in his heart. The pleasure of anticipation brought him almost a sentiment of happiness; he would rise up early in the morning with the thought that perhaps to-day he would receive it, and as he waited for the guard who came to conduct him to the office, he would turn to his little window and reach out his hands as if striving to gather in some of the freshness of the morning; and he was always thinking of the picture.

Outside the swallows were flitting and wheeling as they sang, their wings and tails gleaming in the sunshine; the yellow corn surrounded with its golden glory the shining green of the distant vineyards, while farther away, the watching Apennines shone in the luminous morning air. The prisoner called to mind the crimson dawns of his native mountains, brilliant with flowering yellow broom, then his thoughts turned to the expected picture, till he felt a vague feeling that was almost happiness.

The Direttore quitted his bed with a face even paler than was its wont, and he, too, thought of the picture; but his waiting was made up of a strange mingling of restlessness, bitterness, and anger against himself, because he could not overcome his foolish curiosity, his foolish sentimentalism, the foolish interest "these people" awakened in him.

He went into the garden, and then into his bureau, and did his duty, performing all his tiresome work, and with cold eyes, and hands in his pockets, inspected those men clad in their prison garb of shame, but all the time he was waiting for the picture. In the bottom of his heart, under his anger and cruel indifference, there glimmered a spark of joy, from which a tiny ray sprang into his eyes and stayed there. And this spark, this hidden ray of light, burst into brilliant flame on the arrival of the picture, so instinct with life and loveliness and charm. She was not in the least as his fancy had pictured her; for hers was a blond and delicate loveliness. The beautiful dark eyes, and the delicately curved lips and dimpled chin were suffused with an infinite sweetness. It was the same ineffable sweetness as filled her letters, a fra-

grance exhaled from every word, and this mysterious
and suggestive fascination it was which had conquered
the soul of this silent man, who was thought cruel and
was feared and hated only because he was a poor
dreamer.

The letter accompanying the photograph was, as
usual, full of sweetness and charm.

"I was thinking of thee and smiling when the picture was taken; may it bring thee a little joy and comfort in hoping for better days. Read in my eyes all
that I would fain say to thee."

Just here, the Direttore, too, looked into the eyes of
the picture, then finished reading the letter, only to
return to gaze on the picture, turning it so the full
light should fall upon it, until the face seemed to as-
sume a sort of reality, the lovely eyes to shine, the lips
to smile.

"Oh, Dio! What a fool I am!" said Signore Longino to himself; but in his heart he was thinking:
"How would this exquisite creature write to her lover,
if she writes thus to her brother!" And then he fell
to thinking sadly, that he was small, ugly, almost old,
hated and feared by all those unfortunates whom his
cold eyes dominated.

Once more he read the letter and gazed at the glowing picture, and—and that day neither the one nor the
other were given to the prisoner.

That night the Signore Direttore had a queer
dream; he thought a mutiny had broken out among
the prisoners and they yelled and shook their chains
and rushed upon him. He held Paola's picture in his

hands and could neither move nor defend himself, for
then the picture would fall to the ground and No. 245
would know that he had stolen it. But just as he was
about to be killed by the prisoners, Cassio threw himself between, crying: "Leave him alone, for he is to
marry my sister, and then he will become good because
she is so good."

He waked up bathed in perspiration, and passed the
rest of the night sleeplessly tossing about his bed.

Cassio, in the meanwhile, was waiting patiently,
though as the days passed a vague anxiety disposed
his new-found repose. A week went by and still no
picture came, and he had waited so long! so long!
What could be happening over yonder, beyond the
sunlit sea among the purple solitudes of the fragrant
thyme-scented mountains? Paola must be ill—or had
she forgotten him? Cassio fell back into the agonized
despair of his first days. He asked, but was refused,
permission to telegraph. With difficulty he got permission to write two days sooner than his allotted
month.

His letter was so sad and full of despair that the
Direttore felt more than ever ashamed of his deed;
for two weeks he had lived in torment, and while he
seemed more cruel and hard than ever, his little, green
eyes fell sadly upon the prisoners, for at last he understood how, against his will, a man might be led into
crime. As he read the sad letter of No. 245, he murmured again: "But why do not they ask for pardon?"
And he became aware that with the new-found pity
awakened for No. 245 mingled a certain egotism of

hope, that then he could speak frankly to the prisoner
—one no longer—and say: "Signore, I may be a
fool, but all the same I have fallen desperately in love
with your sister, whom I have never seen. Will you
give her to me for my wife?"

Paola telegraphed at once that she had sent another
photograph by registered mail. In the eagerness for
the peace of her poor prisoner, she pretended she had
not sent a picture, and had been unable to write on
account of a lot of reasons, which she detailed at
length, principally she had been unable to be photo-
graphed before.

"How good she is!" thought the Direttore in admiration, and he felt inclined to write and tell her everything.

But of course he did not do so. "She will think I
am mad, and will fear for her brother."

And so the summer passed and autumn approached;
prisoners came and went. In the office the three clerks
were not only resigned, but even happy, but showed an
ill-concealed dislike for the haughty Sardinian, who,
to an extent, was himself resigned. Only amid the
sweetness of the autumn, when the dawn flooded the
pure sky with crimson and gold or the setting sun
threw his red beams on the sad walls, he was tortured with longing for freedom and home; and he
fretted like a horse taken from his free pastures and
shut up in confinement; but he was learning to control
these rebellions and to immerse himself to the lips in
hope and dreams of the future, till the present seemed
scarcely a reality. But when winter came and the

Apennines were black with storm clouds, and the angry rain pelted incessantly the grim fortress, Cassio felt his nerves snap like cords stretched too far. During the day the three heads of the clerks, pinched with cold, the blear blue eyes, the transparent profile, the head like the Roman emperor, appeared to him as in some tortured vision, awakening within him a brutal desire to seize some object and crush them to pieces. This desire increased from day to day, and was at times so intense that Cassio experienced the strange sensation of having realized it. Once in his cell he would come to himself and understand that he hated the three unfortunate clerks because they represented during those terrible winter days all the human power that was torturing him, against which his inmost soul revolted. His nights were almost sleepless. Outside the wind was roaring with a suggestion of distant torrents. Amid the darkness and roar of elements Cassio lost all perception of time, and as he tossed on his narrow bed, blessed visions came at last to his storm-tossed heart. The sighing of the wind in his distant well-loved mountains; the prints of the wild boar among the green ferns; the noisy stream bounding from rock to rock; the partridges flitting among the flowering oleanders; the joyful neighing of his black horse, and, above all else, the smile of Paola.

But with the gray dawn the sweetness of dreams was turned into bitter reality, and no one knows what might have happened to the three clerks had he not been one day providentially summoned to the Direttore's office.

The Signore Direttore deigned to ask a favor. He had been sent a little fragrant plant with a few slender, dry branches; it had come from Sardinia, and he wanted to know if the prisoner could tell him anything about it.

Cassio took the slender branches in his long, delicate hands, and inhaled its fragrance with closed eyes. The perfume brought him a vision of the green mountains of Gennargentu. An intense homesickness thrilled him.

"It is the tirtillo."

"The tirtillo. I thought so. The precious secret of the Sardinian shepherds that gives its especial aroma to the Sardinian cheese."

Cassio bowed in assent.

"The famous tirtillo," continued the Direttore, "the new cure for epizootic."

"In Sardinia it has been used for centuries," replied Cassio humbly. "Many things that on the continent pass for discoveries are well known on the island."

The Direttore did not reply, but turned his back and resumed his writing, and apparently all was over, when, suddenly turning around, he addressed Cassio without looking at him.

"Has a pardon been asked for you?"

"Yes; after the sentence in the Court of Cassation I appealed in the Giudiziarie of Cagliari."

"To whom did you appeal?"

"To the Ministry."

"That was unfortunate. The Ministry when appealed to never decides. Often the prisoner has finished his term before they arrive at any conclusion."

Cassio looked very grave.

"It would be better to send your request to the Queen; it would sooner be obtained."

"Pardon me," returned Cassio, bowing his head, "but is there a chance that it would be obtained?"

"If the request should be made by your sister, it would be granted," answered the other bruskly, and again he turned his back so that he should not see the prisoner's emotion, and the latter should not see the Direttore's confusion.

This time the conversation was really over, and Cassio was reconducted to his office. But he was really another man; the presence of his three unhappy companions aroused his compassion, but no longer his hatred. Around his thin fingers still lingered the fragrance of the tirtillo, and, raising them to his mouth, he inhaled the fresh sweetness of his distant meadows.

And probably for the first time, the Direttore was sincerely loved by one of his prisoners.

Cassio wrote to Paola begging her to ask the Queen for a pardon.

"You can make the request for yourself, without having recourse to the formal process of the law. Explain things as they are. I hope and bless him who has counseled it."

And so the winter passed. In the limpid dawn of a February day, Cassio was standing before his grated window; his face was pale and bloodless, but his eyes were shining with hope. From the Apennines, which

raised their lofty, white crests into the crystal azure
of the sky, there came a delicious odor of snow; long
strips of vivid green were scattered over the valley,
and already in the garden the apricot trees were displaying their rosy blossoms.

Cassio felt his blood dance through his veins with
the mysterious expectation of coming happiness; all
the glories of the opening spring seemed reflected in
his soul.

Another man, free, in his cold and melancholy
rooms, felt the same tumultuous, though sweet sensation; his green eyes reflected the tender splendor of
the budding season, his heart enclosed a precious
shrine.

There came a day when the inquiry of the Ministry
into the conduct of the prisoner, Cassio Longino de
Isidoro, reached him. The Direttore's reply was of
the best. He did not know why No. 245 had been
guilty of forgery, but he believed him to be an honest
young man, of fine morals and excellent education.
By the same mail he also sent to an intimate in the
Bureau a letter that, coming from such a person as
Signore Longino, could not fail to effect.

Whether it was instrumental in bringing about the
result or not, the decree of pardon and order for freedom arrived very soon after—when Cassio had been
there just a year.

Once more he was summoned to the Direttore's
office. Outside, the air was balmy and fragrant, and
the sky of deepest blue. Inside, the shadows of distant branches trembled in the sunshine that poured in

through the barred window. The Direttore was seated at his table, but this time he rose as Cassio entered. The youth noticed it, but did not dare to give words to the wild hope that sprung up within him, but he felt his heart beat with a violence that well-nigh choked him.

"The decree has arrived," said the Direttore, and he was holding something in his hand.

"The decree?"

"The decree of pardon?"

"For whom?" asked Cassio eagerly.

The Direttore began to lose patience.

"For whom but for you?" And he rejoiced in the deep emotion shown by the young man. So much the better; if the thing was so great as to seem impossible, so much the greater would be his gratitude. But then he thought sadly: Suppose his efforts should result in failure! If in the excess of his gratitude Cassio should give him false hopes!

"For me! for me!" stammered the poor youth. "For me! For how long?"

"For all the rest of your sentence. You are free— that is, not at once, but after a few formalities, in a week at most."

Gradually Cassio pulled himself together. At first he had gazed at the Direttore without seeing him. Now he began to look at him. He observed his pale face was flushed, that the air of physical suffering had disappeared, that the small, green eyes were shining.

He, on the other hand, was trembling violently, his

face was ashy, his hands cold, and a mist floated before his eyes.

"This man is fine, when he is rejoicing in the happiness of another. How I have misjudged him," he thought. Then he asked himself: "But why did he do it?"

He was to know very soon.

The Direttore begged him to be seated; he showed him the decree, and profited by the moment in which Cassio was looking at the King's signature to begin:

"Now, I have something else to tell you. Listen and do not judge hastily. I have long been awaiting this moment, and the thing seemed easy, but now I see I need great courage and you great indulgence if we are to understand each other."

He smiled sadly, and the old expression of suffering returned once more.

Cassio looked at him stupidly, still confused with the weight of his happiness, but beginning to gain his self-control. The other understood that his opportunity was slipping away and hastened to speak, though, in spite of every effort, his voice trembled.

"I scarcely know how to express myself so you may understand everything; but I have confidence in your intelligence. Listen. I have done everything in my power to obtain that piece of paper there"—and he pointed to the decree, and Cassio, following his gesture, sat gazing at the sheet—"and, above all, I did so because I felt you deserved it." ("Does he know my story?" Cassio asked himself, feeling that his deserts in prison had been very few.) "I do not ask for gratitude, indeed I will be thankful if you will not allow that sentiment to influence you at all. I wish to speak to you as one gentleman to another." ("Heavens! does he think me a grand Signore and wish to ask me for money?" thought Cassio. "I am not ungrateful, but what *can* he want of me?") "Now you are free and are at liberty to act as seems good to you."

"Speak," returned the other, with a sad impatience, "whatever lies in my power—"

"I do not know if it lies in your power."

"Speak! Speak!"

"Listen, but do not ill-judge me, nor think me insane. While reading your sister's letters, I have learned to appreciate so good and noble a soul, and—" ("Oh, Dio mio! he has fallen in love with her!" cried Cassio to himself, and the world grew suddenly dark.) "I have learned to love her. Do not laugh at me. I am still young!"

But Cassio felt small inclination to laugh.

"Have you written to her?" he asked bruskly.

"No, certainly not. Pray do not be offended. I have not allowed myself so great a privilege. Only to you—"

"But it is impossible, not to be thought of—impossible!" interrupted Cassio, striking as he spoke the paper which was lying on his knees, till it rustled.

"It seems impossible, but it is true; and though it may be strange, it is not the first time it has happened. My demand is serious, Signore Longino. Can your sister accept it?"

"What demand?"

The other thought a moment. "This young man is laboring under too much excitement; I was wrong to speak to him so suddenly. He is not in a state to hear it."

"My proposal of marriage."

Cassio did not reply at once. By a terrible effort he controlled himself. When the mist cleared from his eyes he turned and looked at the Direttore, and beheld him as in the past, pale, suffering, and ugly, and into his terrible pain there fell one drop of comfort—she would not accept him, he felt sure.

"But," he asked, "have you reflected what you are doing? Have you written to my country and obtained information? In such cases—"

"I have not written. What would be the good? I know your sister, that she is good and noble, I desire nothing more. I, too, am all alone."

"You are too good. I do not know how to properly express my gratitude. Do not fear you are not understood. I both understand and admire you. I feel myself greatly honored by your offer, and if it remained with me—but let me assure you I will do all in my power. Do not despair."

He rose and rolled up the pardon, looking at it with ill-concealed bitterness as he towered over the small person of the Direttore, who approached with extended hand to express his thanks. He asked permission to return to his cell and unroll his bed. Everything was granted him. As he threw himself on his comfortless cot he groaned in agony. Paola was not his sister, but his fiancée. For her he had soiled his honor, compromised his future, and broken with his family. She alone remained to him. She had feigned to be his sister in order that she might write to him. And must he lose her now? That other possessed a splendid position, was good and noble. Had he a right to snatch such a brilliant future from Paola? He had sacrificed to her his honor and well-nigh two years of liberty, but she had not asked the sacrifice of him, and was it right that in exchange he should ask for her whole life? In any case she must decide for herself, and at the bottom of his heart he felt secure of her—but it made him wretched to think he had deceived and was still deceiving so noble and excellent a man.

"I will tell him everything, come what may," he decided after an hour of anxious thought, then uncertainty took possession of him once more. "No, I will say nothing. After all he has no right to know, and I will write when I reach home. After all he did it only because he wanted to on his own account. His cat-like eyes fill me with distrust; perhaps he would do me some harm."

Later he grew ashamed of his distrust, and cried out loud in his lonely cell, "Am I indeed vile?"

Approaching the grating, he stood gazing at the white, diaphanous clouds piled up on the horizon; they had assumed the shape and coloring of an alabaster staircase whose luminous steps disappeared into the unscaled heights. Cassio, as he looked, was overwhelmed with an intense homesickness, and suddenly he felt good and pure, as if he had indeed mounted to

the last step of those silver stairs and caught from that
height a glimpse of his beloved native land. He
murmured:

"Had it not been for him I should have languished
here for yet a weary time. I might have died or committed some madness. I will tell everything, let the
result be what it may."

He waited anxiously the hour when it would be possible for him to see the Direttore, then addressed him
in clear tones:

"See, Signore Direttore, I have been thinking of
what you were very good enough to tell me this
morning."

"Very well," answered the other, though he feared
for the result.

"Before entering upon the subject, please allow me
to tell you in a few words of the strange circumstances
of my condemnation, for," he added, smiling sadly,
"I am bold enough to believe you do not think me
guilty."

The other man said never a word.

"Listen. For ten years I have loved a maiden of
my own country. She was rich, but an orphan living
with her guardian. I was sent away to college and
was absent many years. On my return I learned that
the poor girl, although she had attained her majority,
was kept in subjection and badly treated by her guardian, who had possessed himself of all her property.
He gave her nothing, but kept her shut up and frightened with terrible threats. I succeeded in communi-
cating with her, and, finding that she loved me, I

vowed to free her and restore her property. 'Let us be married,' she said, 'and I will fly with you.' But as my intentions might involve me in many difficulties, I would not accept her offer. I assisted her to take refuge with friends, and when she was in safety I began my operations.

"And can you guess what I did? I almost think so. I forged the name of her guardian, and since he was very rich and well known at home and abroad, and his credit was illimitable, I obtained a good deal of money. I placed all in the name of the young girl and waited. When the notes fell due, all became known. I had foolishly hoped I should be considered a hero. Instead I was seized, vilified, condemned. My little property was taken, my family disowned me. She, alone of all the world, remains to me, and she, Signore Direttore, is Paola."

The Signore Direttore remained absolutely silent. What, indeed could he say? He only felt that Cassio's story and his own seemed impossible, though he knew but too well it was but too true. Cassio understood him perfectly.

"It is strange, impossible, is it not? Had I been told it, I would not have believed it."

"Life is strange," said the other at last, and he clenched his hands till the nails penetrated the flesh. "The ways of destiny are indeed mysterious."

"He is resigned," thought Cassio, and he hazarded another remark.

"Life is often a terrible romance." But looking the Direttore in the face he saw an expression of such

agony imprinted as caused him to retract his thought of
a moment before.

"But see," he continued, "in spite of everything I
will do all in my power to prove my gratitude."

"What do you mean?"

"Let me speak. It was my duty to let you know
the exact truth, but you have been so good to me that
I give you my word of honor, as a gentleman, that I
will do everything—"

"What are you saying? What are you saying?"
repeated the other in a strange tone, as if he were
listening to distant voices, and not to Cassio's words.

"After all, Paola alone can decide. I will tell her
everything, as if I were indeed her brother and nothing
more."

"Oh, no! No! What are you saying?"

"Nay, if you will allow it I will write this very day,
and we will await her reply. Perhaps when it comes
I will not need to return to my own country."

"What are you saying?" repeated the Direttore;
but now his voice had regained its strength, and, raising his eyes, he looked Cassio full in the face. "You
must not write, but return at once to your home, where,
I prophesy, every happiness awaits you. From the
bottom of my heart I hope so. And yet, who would
ever have imagined it! You are right. Life *is* a
terrible romance."

"But," Cassio persisted, "let me write. I beg it of
you as a personal favor. You will see the debt I owe
you can never be canceled, and duty should be stronger
than love. Paola will be much more fortunate with

the Direttore than with me, and above all things I desire her happiness and well-being."

The other listened patiently; once his eyes flashed with a vivid light, but he remained immovable.

"See," he concluded, after having expressed his appreciation of Cassio's generosity, "if your duty is to prove yourself grateful and generous toward the signorina, her duty is no less to make you happy and recompense you for all you have suffered."

"But—" interrupted Cassio.

"One moment—let me finish, please. If the signorina were to act otherwise, she would not be the noble, lofty being I have imagined her, and then my offer would no longer exist. Do you understand? Am I not right?"

But Cassio answered never a word, and the Direttore turned toward the window. And the soul of each was full to overflowing. Cassio thought but of his happiness, and the Direttore reminded himself with bitterness that in any case his dream was lost to him forever.

RAILROAD AND CHURCHYARD

BY BJÖRNSTJERNE BJÖRNSON

*Björnson, said to be the first great figure
in Norway to teach the bourgeoisie to rise by
their own efforts, was born in 1832. In 1860
appeared his epoch-making story of peasant
life, "Arne," and the trilogy, "Sigurd Slembe,"
and other plays. Declaring for the separation
of Norway and Sweden, he became chief of
the Republican Party. The critic Brandes says:
"The mention of his name among his country-
men is like running up the national flag."*

*Two sharply marked periods appear in
Björnson's literary career—the first, romantic, religious, in which he wrote, among other
things, Norway's national hymn; the second,
from 1874 on, being realistic, critical, aggressive.
His vigorous imagination, love of truth, excessive yet sincere enthusiasm, are in a style
so compressed as to be at times almost obscure.
Björnson has been called the "Creator of the
National Drama in Norway," the "Great Rival
of Ibsen," the "Victor Hugo of Norway."*

RAILROAD AND CHURCHYARD

BY BJÖRNSTJERNE BJÖRNSON

I

KNUD AAKRE belonged to an old family in
the parish, where it had always been renowned
for its intelligence and its devotion to the public welfare. His father had worked his way up to
the priesthood, but had died early, and as the widow
came from a peasant stock the children were brought
up as peasants. Knud had, therefore, received only
the education afforded by the public schools of his day;
but his father's library had early inspired him with a
love of knowledge. This was further stimulated by
his friend Henrik Wergeland, who frequently visited
him, sent him books, seeds, and much valuable counsel.
Following some of the latter, Knud early founded a
club, which in the beginning had a very miscellaneous
object, for instance: "to give the members practise in
debating and to study the constitution," but which later
was turned into a practical agricultural society for the
entire bailiwick. According to Wergeland's advice, he
also founded a parish library, giving his father's books
as its first endowment. A suggestion from the same
quarter led him to start a Sunday-school on his gard,
for those who might wish to learn writing, arithmetic,

and history. All this drew attention to him, so that he
was elected member of the parish board of supervisors,
of which he soon became chairman. In this capacity
he took a deep interest in the schools, which he brought
into a remarkably good condition.

Knud Aakre was a short man, brisk in his movements, with small, restless eyes and very disorderly
hair. He had large lips, which were in constant motion, and a row of splendid teeth which always seemed
to be working with them, for they glistened while his
words were snapped out, crisp and clear, crackling like
sparks from a great fire.

Foremost among the many he had helped to gain
an education was his neighbor Lars Högstad. Lars
was not much younger than Knud, but he had developed more slowly. Knud liked to talk about what he
read and thought, and he found in Lars, whose manner was quiet and grave, a good listener, who by
degrees grew to be a man of excellent judgment. The
relations between them soon became such that Knud
was never willing to take any important step without
first consulting Lars Högstad, and the matter on hand
was thus likely to gain some practical amendment. So
Knud drew his neighbor into the board of supervisors,
and gradually into everything in which he himself took
part. They always drove together to the meetings of
the board, where Lars never spoke; but on the way
back and forth Knud learned his opinions. The two
were looked upon as inseparable.

One fine autumn day the board of supervisors con-

vened to consider, among other things, a proposal from
the bailiff to sell the parish grain magazine and with
the proceeds establish a small savings-bank. Knud
Aakre, the chairman, would undoubtedly have ap-
proved this measure had he relied on his unbiased
judgment. But he was prejudiced, partly because the
proposal came from the bailiff, whom Wergeland did
not like, and who was consequently no favorite of
Knud's either, and partly because the grain magazine
had been built by his influential paternal grandfather
and by him presented to the parish. Indeed, Knud
was rather inclined to view the proposition as a personal insult, therefore he had not spoken of it to any
one, not even to Lars, and the latter never entered on a
topic that had not first been set afloat by some one else.

As chairman, Knud Aakre read the proposal without adding any comments; but, as was his wont, his
eyes sought Lars, who usually sat or stood a little
aside, holding a straw between his teeth—he always
had one when he took part in a conversation; he either
used it as a toothpick or he let it hang loosely in one
corner of his mouth, turning it more rapidly or more
slowly, according to the mood he was in. To his surprise Knud saw that the straw was moving very fast.

"Do you think we should agree to this?" he asked.

Lars answered dryly:

"Yes, I do."

The whole board, feeling that Knud held quite a
different opinion, looked in astonishment at Lars, but
the latter said no more, nor was he further questioned.
Knud turned to another matter, as though nothing had

transpired. Not until the close of the meeting did he
resume the subject, and then asked, with apparent indifference, if it would not be well to send the proposal back to the bailiff for further consideration, as it
certainly did not meet the views of the people, for the
parish valued the grain magazine. No one replied.
Knud asked whether he should enter the resolution in
the register, the measure did not seem to be a wise one.
"Against one vote," added Lars. "Against two,"
cried another, promptly. "Against three," came from
a third; and before the chairman could realize what
was taking place, a majority had voted in favor of the
proposal.

Knud was so surprised that he forgot to offer
any opposition. He recorded the proceedings, and
read, in a low voice: "The measure is recommended
—adjourned."

His face was fiery red as he rose and put up the
minute-book; but he determined to bring forward the
question once more at the meeting of the representatives. Out in the yard, he put his horse to the wagon,
and Lars came and took his seat at his side. They
discussed various topics on their way home, but not
the one they had nearest at heart.

The next day Knud's wife sought Lars's wife to
inquire if there was anything wrong between the two
men, for Knud had acted so strangely when he came
home. A short distance above the gard buildings she
met Lars's wife, who was on her way to ask the same
question, for her husband, too, had been out of sorts
the day before. Lars's wife was a quiet, bashful per-

son, somewhat cowed, not by harsh words, but by silence, for Lars never spoke to her unless she had done something amiss, or he feared that she might do wrong. Knud Aakre's wife, on the other hand, talked more with her husband, and particularly about the board, for lately it had taken his thoughts, work, and affection away from her and the children. She was as jealous of it as of a woman; she wept at night over the board and quarreled with her husband about it during the day. But for that very reason she could say nothing about it now when for once he had returned home unhappy; for she immediately became more wretched than he, and for her life she could not rest until she had discovered what was the matter. Consequently, when Lars's wife could not give her the desired information, she had to go out in the parish to seek it. Here she obtained it, and of course was at once of her husband's opinion; she found Lars incomprehensible, not to say wicked. When, however, she let her husband perceive this, she felt that as yet there was no breach between Lars and him; that, on the contrary, he clung warmly to him.

The representatives met. Lars Högstad drove over to Aakre in the morning; Knud came out of the house and took his seat beside him. They exchanged the usual greetings, spoke perhaps rather less than was their wont on the way, and not of the proposal. All the members of the board were present; some, too, had found their way in as spectators, which Knud did not like, for it showed that there was a stir in town about the matter. Lars was armed with his straw,

and he stood by the stove warming himself, for the
autumn was beginning to be cold. The chairman read
the proposal, in a subdued, cautious manner, remarking when he was through that it must be remembered
this came from the bailiff, who was not apt to be very
felicitous in his proposals. The building, it was well
known, was a gift, and it was not usual to part with
gifts, especially when there was no need of doing so.

Lars, who never before had spoken at the meetings,
now took the floor, to the astonishment of all. His
voice trembled, but whether it did so out of regard
for Knud, or from anxiety lest his own cause should
be lost, shall remain unsaid. But his arguments were
good and clear, and full of a logic and confidence
which had scarcely been heard at these meetings before. And when he had gone over all the ground, he
added, in conclusion:

"What does it matter if the proposal does come
from the bailiff? This affects the question as little
as who erected the building, or in what way it came
into the public possession."

Knud Aakre had grown very red in the face (he
blushed easily), and he shifted uneasily from side to
side, as was his wont when he was impatient, but none
the less did he exert himself to be circumspect and to
speak in a low voice. There were savings-banks
enough in the country, he thought, and quite near at
hand, he might almost say too near. But if, after all,
it was deemed expedient to have one, there were surely
other ways of reaching it than those leading over the
gifts of the dead and the love of the living. His voice

Björnson

was a little unsteady when he said this, but quickly
recovered as he proceeded to speak of the grain magazine in itself, and to show what its advantages were.

Lars answered him thoroughly on the last point,
and then added:

"However, one thing and another lead me to doubt
whether this parish is managed for the sake of the living or the dead; furthermore, whether it is the love
and hatred of a single family which controls matters
here, or the good of the whole."

Knud answered quickly: "I do not know whether he
who has just spoken has been least benefited by this
family—both by the dead and by him who now lives."

The first shot was aimed at the fact that Knud's
powerful grandfather had saved the gard for Lars's
paternal grandfather, when the latter, on his part, was
absent on a little excursion to the penitentiary.

The straw which long had been in brisk motion
suddenly became still.

"It is not my way to keep talking everywhere about
myself and my family," said Lars, then turned again
with calm superiority to the subject under discussion,
briefly reviewing all the points with one definite object.
Knud had to admit to himself that he had never viewed
the matter from such a broad standpoint; involuntarily
he raised his eyes and looked at Lars, who stood before him, tall, heavily built, with clearness on the vigorous brow and in the deep eyes. The lips were tightly
compressed, the straw still played in the corner of his
mouth; all the surrounding lines indicated vigor. He
kept his hands behind him, and stood rigidly erect,

while his voice was as deep and as hollow as if it proceeded from the depths of the earth. For the first time
in his life Knud saw him as he was, and in his inmost
soul he was afraid of him; for this man must always
have been his superior. He had taken all Knud himself knew and could impart; he had rejected the tares
and kept what produced this strong, hidden growth.

He had been fostered and loved by Knud, but had
now become a giant who hated Knud deeply, terribly.
Knud could not explain to himself why, but as he
looked at Lars he instinctively felt this to be so, and
all else becoming swallowed up in this thought he
started up, exclaiming:

"But Lars! Lars! what in Heaven's name is the
matter with you?" His agitation overcame him—
"you, whom I have—you who have—"

Powerless to utter another word, he sat down; but
in his effort to gain the mastery over the emotion he
deemed Lars unworthy of seeing, he brought his fist
down with violence on the table, while his eyes flashed
beneath his stiff, disorderly hair, which always hung
over them. Lars acted as if he had not been interrupted, and turning toward the others he asked if this
was to be the decisive blow; for if such were the case
there was no need for further remarks.

This calmness was more than Knud could endure.
"What is it that has come among us?" cried he.
"We who have, until to-day, been actuated by love
and zeal alone, are now stirred up against each other,
as though goaded on by some evil spirit," and he cast
a fiery glance at Lars, who replied:

"It must be you yourself who bring in this spirit, Knud; for I have kept strictly to the matter before us. But you never can see the advantage of anything you do not want yourself; now we shall learn what becomes of the love and the zeal when once this matter is decided as we wish."

"Have I then illy served the interests of the parish?"

There was no reply. This grieved Knud, and he continued: "I really did persuade myself that I had accomplished various things—various things which have been of advantage to the parish; but perhaps I have deceived myself."

He was again overcome by his feelings; for his was a fiery nature, ever variable in its moods, and the breach with Lars pained him so deeply that he could scarcely control himself. Lars answered:

"Yes, I know you appropriate the credit for all that is done here, and if one should judge by the amount of speaking at these meetings, you certainly have accomplished the most."

"Is that the way of it?" shouted Knud, looking sharply at Lars. "Is it you who deserve the entire honor?"

"Since we must finally talk about ourselves," said Lars, "I am free to admit that every question has been carefully considered by both of us before it was introduced here."

Here little Knud Aakre regained his ready speech:

"Take the honor, in God's name; I am able to live without it; there are other things harder to lose!"

Involuntarily Lars evaded his gaze, but said, as he set the straw in very rapid motion:

"If I were to express *my* opinion, I should say that there is not very much to take credit for. No doubt the priest and the schoolmasters are content with what has been done; but certainly the common people say that up to the present time the taxes of this parish have grown heavier and heavier."

Here arose a murmur in the crowd, and the people grew very restless. Lars continued:

"Finally, to-day we have a matter brought before us that might make the parish some little amends for all it has paid out; this is perhaps the reason why it encounters such opposition. This is a question which concerns the parish; it's for the good of all; it is our duty to guard it from becoming a mere family matter."

People exchanged glances, and spoke in half-audible tones; one of them remarked, as he rose to go for his dinner-pail, that these were the truest words he had heard in these meetings for many years. Now all rose from their seats, the conversation became general, and Knud Aakre, who alone remained sitting, felt that all was lost, fearfully lost, and made no further effort to save it. The truth was, he possessed something of the temperament attributed to Frenchmen: he was very good at a first, second, or even third attack, but poor at self-defense, for his sensibilities overwhelmed his thoughts. He was unable to comprehend this, nor could he sit still any longer, and so resigning his place to the vice-chairman, he left. The others could not refrain from a smile.

He had come to the meeting in company with Lars, but went home alone, although the way was long. It was a cold autumn day, the forest was jagged and bare, the meadow gray-yellow, frost was beginning here and there to remain on the roadside. Disappointment is a terrible companion. Knud felt so small, so desolate, as he walked along; but Lars appeared everywhere before him, towering up to the sky, in the dusk of the evening, like a giant. It vexed him to think it was his own fault that this had been the decisive battle; he had staked too much on one single little issue. But surprise, pain, anger, had mastered him; they still burned, tingled, moaned, and stormed within him. He heard the rumbling of cart-wheels behind him; it was Lars driving his superb horse past him, in a brisk trot, making the hard road resound like distant thunder. Knud watched the broad-shouldered form that sat erect in the cart, while the horse, eager for home, sped onward, without any effort on the part of Lars, who merely gave him a loose rein. It was but a picture of this man's power: he was driving onward to the goal! Knud felt himself cast out of his cart, to stagger on alone in the chill autumn air.

In his home at Aakre, Knud's wife was waiting for him. She knew that a battle was inevitable; she had never in her life trusted Lars, and now she was positively afraid of him. It had been no comfort to her that he and her husband had driven away together; it would not have consoled her had they returned in the same way. But darkness had fallen and they had not come. She stood in the doorway, gazing out on

the road in front of the house; she walked down the
hill and back again, but no cart appeared.

Finally she hears a rattling on the hard road, her
heart throbs as the wheels go round, she clings to the
casement, peering out into the night; the cart draws
near; only one is in it; she recognizes Lars, who sees
and recognizes her, but drives past without stopping.
Now she became thoroughly alarmed. Her limbs gave
way under her, she tottered in and sank down on the
bench by the window. The children gathered anxiously about her, the youngest one asked for papa; she
never spoke with them except of him. He had such a
noble disposition, and this was what made her love
him; but now his heart was not with his family, it
was engrossed in all sorts of business which brought
him only unhappiness, and so they were all unhappy.

If only no misfortune had befallen him! Knud was
so hot-tempered. Why had Lars come home alone?
Why did he not stop? Should she run after him, or
down the road after her husband? She was in an
agony of distress, and the children pressed around her,
asking what was the matter. But this she would not
tell them, so rising she said they must eat supper alone,
then got everything ready and helped them. All the
while she kept glancing out on the road. He did not
come. She undressed the children and put them to
bed, and the youngest repeated the evening prayer
while she bowed over him. She herself prayed with
such fervor in the words which the infant lips so soothingly uttered that she did not heed the steps outside.

Knud stood upon the threshold, gazing at his little

company at prayer. The mother drew herself up; all the children shouted: "Papa!" but he seated himself at once, and said, softly: "Oh, let him say it once more!"

The mother turned again to the bedside, that he, meanwhile, should not see her face, for it would have seemed like intruding on his grief before he felt the need of revealing it. The little one folded its hands over its breast, all the rest did likewise, and it repeated:

> "I, a little child, pray Heaven
> That my sins may be forgiven;
> With time, I'll larger, wiser grow,
> And my father and mother joy shall know,
> If only Thou, dearest, dearest Lord,
> Will help me to keep Thy precious word!
> And now to our Heavenly Father's merciful keeping
> Our souls let us trust while we're sleeping."

What peace now fell upon the room! Not a minute had elapsed ere all the children were sleeping as in the arms of God; but the mother moved softly away and placed supper before the father, who was, however, unable to eat. But after he had gone to bed, he said: "Henceforth I shall be at home."

And his wife lay at his side trembling with joy which she dared not betray; and she thanked God for all that had happened, for whatever it might be it had resulted in good!

II

In the course of a year Lars had become chairman of the parish board of supervisors, president of the savings-bank, and leading commissioner in the court of reconciliation; in short, he held every office to which his election had been possible. In the board of supervisors for the amt (county) he was silent during the first year, but the second year he created the same sensation when he spoke as in the parish board; for here, too, coming forward in opposition to him who had previously been the guiding power, he became victorious over the entire rank and file, and was from that time himself the leader. From this his path led him to the storthing (parliament), where his fame had preceded him, and where consequently there was no lack of challenges. But here, although steady and firm, he always remained retiring. He did not care for power except where he was well known, nor would he risk leadership at home by a possible defeat abroad.

For he had a pleasant life at home. When he stood by the church wall on Sundays, and the congregation walked slowly past, saluting him and stealing side glances at him, and one after another paused in order to exchange a few words with him—then truly it might be said that he controlled the entire parish with a straw, for of course this hung in the corner of his mouth.

He deserved his honors. The road leading to the church, he had opened; the new church they were standing beside, he had built; this and much more was the fruit of the savings-bank which he had founded and now managed himself. For its resources were further made fruitful, and the parish was constantly held up as an example to all others of self-management and good order.

Knud Aakre had entirely withdrawn from the field,

although at first he attended a few of the meetings of the board, because he had promised himself that he would continue to offer his services, even if it were not altogether pleasing to his pride. In the first proposal he had made he became so greatly perplexed by Lars, who insisted upon having it represented in all its details, that, somewhat hurt, he said: "When Columbus discovered America he did not have it divided into parishes and deaneries: this came gradually;" whereupon Lars, in his reply, compared the discovery of America with Knud's proposal—it so happened that this treated of stable improvements—and afterward Knud was known by no other name in the board than "Discovery of America." So Knud thought that as his usefulness had ceased, so too had his obligations to work, and he refused to accept further reelections.

But he continued to be industrious; and in order that he might still have a field for usefulness, he enlarged his Sunday-school, and placed it, by means of small contributions from the attendants, in communication with the mission cause, of which he soon became the centre and leader in his own and the surrounding counties. Thereupon Lars Högstad remarked, that if ever Knud undertook to collect money for any purpose, he must know beforehand that it was to do good thousands of miles from home.

There was, be it observed, no more strife between them. To be sure, they no longer associated with each other, but they bowed and spoke when they met. Knud always felt a little pain at the mere thought of Lars, but strove to suppress it, and persuade himself that matters could not have been otherwise. At a large wedding-party, many years afterward, where both were present and both were in good spirits, Knud mounted a chair and proposed a toast for the chairman of the parish board, and the first representative their amt had sent to the storthing! He spoke until he became deeply moved, and, as usual, expressed himself in an exceedingly handsome way. Every one thought it was honorably done, and Lars came up to him, and his gaze was unsteady as he said that for much of what he knew and was he was indebted to him.

At the next election of the board of supervisors Knud was again made chairman!

But had Lars Högstad foreseen what now followed, he would certainly not have used his influence for this. "Every event happens in its own time," says an old proverb, and just as Knud Aakre again entered the board, the best men of the parish were threatened with ruin, as the result of a speculation craze which had long been raging, but which now first began to demand its victims. It was said that Lars Högstad was the cause of this great disaster, for he had taught the parish to speculate. This penny fever had originated in the parish board of supervisors, for the board itself was the greatest speculator of all. Every one down to the laboring youth of twenty years desired in his transactions to make ten dollars out of one; a beginning of extreme avarice in the efforts to hoard, was followed by an excessive extravagance, and as all minds were bent only on money, there had at the same time developed a spirit of suspicion, of intolerance, of caviling, which resulted in lawsuits and hatred. This also was due to the example of the board, it was said, for among the first things Lars had done as chairman was to sue the venerable old priest for holding doubtful titles. The priest had lost, but had also immediately resigned. At that time some had praised, some censured this suit; but it had proved a bad example. Now came the consequences of Lars's management, in the form of loss to every single man of property in the parish, consequently public opinion underwent a sharp change! The opposing force, too, soon found a leader, for Knud Aakre had come into the board, introduced by Lars.

The struggle began forthwith. All those youths to whom Knud in his time had given instructions, were now grown up and were the most enlightened men in the parish, thoroughly at home in all its transactions and public affairs. It was against these men that Lars now had to contend, and they had borne him a grudge from their childhood up. When of an evening after one of these stormy proceedings he stood on the steps in front of his house, gazing over the parish, he could hear a sound as of distant rumbling thunder rising toward him from the large gards, now lying in the storm. He knew that the day they met their ruin, the savings-bank and himself would be overthrown, and all his long efforts would culminate in imprecations on his own head.

In these days of conflict and despair, a party of railroad commissioners, who were to survey the route for a new road, made their appearance one evening at Högstad, the first gard at the entrance to the parish.

In the course of conversation during the evening, Lars learned that there was a question whether the road should run through this valley or another parallel to it.

Like a flash of lightning it darted through his mind that if he could succeed in having it laid here, all property would rise in value, and not only would he himself be saved but his fame would be transmitted to the latest posterity! He could not sleep that night, for his eyes were dazzled by a glowing light, and sometimes he could even hear the sound of the cars. The next day he went himself with the commissioners while they examined the locality; his horse took them, and to his gard they returned. The next day they drove through the other valley; he was still with them, and he drove them back again to his house. They found a brilliant illumination at Högstad; the first men of the parish had been invited to be present at a magnificent party given in honor of the commissioners; it lasted until morning. But to no avail, for the nearer they came to a final issue, the more plainly it appeared that the road could not pass through this locality without undue expense. The entrance to the valley lay through a narrow gorge, and just as it swung into the parish, the swollen river swung in also, so that the railroad would either have to take the same curve along the mountain that the highway now made, thus running at a needlessly high altitude and crossing the river twice, or it would have to run straight forward, and thus through the old, now unused churchyard. Now the church had but recently been removed, and it was not long since the last burial had taken place there.

If it only depended on a bit of old churchyard, thought Lars, whether or not this great blessing came into the parish, then he must use his name and his energy for the removal of this obstacle! He at once set forth on a visit to the priest and the dean, and furthermore to the diocese council; he talked and he negotiated, for he was armed with all possible facts concerning the immense advantage of the railroad on one hand, and the sentiments of the parish on the other, and actually succeeded in winning all parties. It was promised him that by a removal of part of the bodies to the new churchyard the objections might be set aside, and the royal permission obtained for the churchyard to be taken for the line of railroad. It was told him that nothing was now needed but for him to set the question afloat in the board of supervisors.

The parish had grown as excited as himself: the spirit of speculation which for many years had been the only one prevailing in the parish, now became madly jubilant. There was nothing spoken or thought of but Lars's journey and its possible results. When he returned with the most magnificent promises, they made much of him; songs were sung in his praise; indeed, if at that time the largest gards had gone to destruction, one after another, no one would have paid the slightest attention to it: the speculation craze had given way to the railroad craze.

The board of supervisors assembled: there was presented for approval a respectful petition, that the old churchyard might be appropriated as the route of the railroad. This was unanimously adopted; there was even mention of giving Lars a vote of thanks and a coffee-pot in the form of a locomotive. But it was finally thought best to wait until the whole plan was carried into execution. The petition came back from the diocese council, with a demand for a list of all bodies that would have to be removed. The priest made out such a list, but instead of sending it direct, he had his own reasons for sending it through the parish board. One of the members carried it to the next meeting. Here it fell to the lot of Lars, as chairman, to open the envelope and read the list.

Now it chanced that the first body to be disinterred was that of Lars's own grandfather! A little shudder ran through the assembly! Lars himself was startled, but nevertheless continued to read. Then it furthermore chanced that the second body was that of Knud Aakre's grandfather, for these two men had died within a short time of each other. Knud Aakre sprang from his seat; Lars paused; every one looked up in consternation, for old Knud Aakre had been the benefactor of the parish and its best beloved man, time out of mind. There was a dead silence, which lasted for some minutes. At last Lars cleared his throat and went on reading. But the further he proceeded the worse the matter grew; for the nearer they came to their own time, the dearer were the dead. When he had finished, Knud Aakre asked quietly whether the others did not agree with him in thinking that the air about them was filled with spirits. It was just beginning to grow dark in the room, and although they were mature men, sitting in numbers together, they could not refrain from feeling alarmed. Lars produced a bundle of matches from his pocket and struck a light, dryly remarking that this was no more than they knew before.

"Yes, it is," said Knud pacing the floor, "it is more than I knew before. Now I begin to think that even railroads can be purchased too dearly."

These words sent a quiver through the audience, and, observing that they had better further consider the matter, Knud made a motion to that effect.

In the excitement which had prevailed, he said, the benefit likely to be derived from the road had been overestimated. Even if the railroad did not pass through this parish, there would have to be stations at both ends of the valley; true, it would always be a little more troublesome to drive to them than to a station right in our midst, yet the difficulty would not be so very great that it would be necessary because of it to violate the repose of the dead.

Knud was one of those who when his thoughts were once in rapid motion could present the most convincing arguments; a moment before what he now said had not occurred to his mind, nevertheless it struck home to all. Lars felt the danger of his position, and concluding that it was best to be cautious, apparently acquiesced in Knud's proposition to reconsider. Such emotions are always worse in the beginning, he thought; it is wisest to temporize with them.

But he had miscalculated. In ever-increasing waves the dread of touching the dead of their own families swept over the inhabitants of the parish; what none of them had thought of as long as the matter existed

merely in the abstract, now became a serious question
when it was brought home to themselves. The women
especially were excited, and the road near the courthouse was black with people the day of the next meeting. It was a warm summer day, the windows were
removed, and there were as many without the house
as within. All felt that a battle was to be fought.

Lars came driving up with his handsome horse, and
was greeted by all; he looked calmly and confidently
around, not seeming to be surprised at anything. He
took a seat near the window, found his straw, and a
suspicion of a smile played over his keen face as he
saw Knud Aakre rise to his feet to act as spokesman
for all the dead in the old Högstad churchyard.

But Knud Aakre did not begin with the churchyard.
He began with an accurate exposition of how greatly
the profits likely to accrue from having the railroad
run through the parish had been overestimated in all
this turmoil. He had positive proofs for every state-
ment he made; he had calculated the distance of each
gard from the nearest station. Finally he asked:

"Why has there been so much ado about this railroad, if not in behalf of the parish?"

This he could easily explain to them. There were
those who had occasioned so great a disturbance that
a still greater one was required to conceal it. Moreover, there were those who in the first outburst of
excitement could sell their gards and belongings to
strangers who were foolish enough to purchase. It
was a shameful speculation which not only the living
but the dead must serve to promote!

The effect of his address was very considerable. But Lars had once for all resolved to preserve his composure let come what would. He replied, therefore, with a smile, that he had been under the impression that Knud himself was eager for the railroad, and certainly no one would accuse him of having any knowledge of speculation. (Here followed a little laugh.) Knud had not evinced the slightest objection to the removal of the bodies of common people for the sake of the railroad; but when his own grandfather's body was in question then it suddenly affected the welfare of the whole community! He said no more, but looked with a faint smile at Knud, as did also several others. Meanwhile, Knud Aakre surprised both him and them by replying:

"I confess it; I did not comprehend the matter until it touched my own family feelings; it is possible that this may be a shame, but it would have been a far greater one not to have realized it at last—as is the case with Lars! Never," he concluded, "could this raillery have been more out of place; for to people with common decency the whole affair is revolting."

"This feeling is something that has come up quite recently," replied Lars; "we may, therefore, hope that it will soon pass over again. May it not perhaps help the matter a little to think what the priest, dean, diocese council, engineers, and government will all say if we first unanimously set the ball in motion, then come and beg to have it stopped? If we first are jubilant and sing songs, then weep and deliver funeral orations? If they do not say that we have gone mad in this parish, they must at all events say that we have acted rather strangely of late."

"Yes, God knows, they may well think so!" replied Knud. "We have, indeed, acted very strangely of late, and it is high time for us to mend our ways. Things have come to a serious pass when we can each disinter his own grandfather to make way for a railroad; when we can disturb the resting-place of the dead in order that our own burdens may the more easily be carried. For is not this rooting in our churchyard in order to make it yield us food the same thing? What is buried there in the name of Jesus, we take up in Moloch's name—this is but little better than eating the bones of our ancestors."

"Such is the course of nature," said Lars, dryly.

"Yes, of plants and of animals."

"And are not we animals?"

"We are, but also the children of the living God, who have buried our dead in faith in Him: it is He who shall rouse them and not we."

"Oh, you are talking idly! Are we not obliged to have the graves dug up at any rate, when their turn comes? What harm if it happen now?"

"I will tell you. What was born of them still draws the breath of life; what they built up yet remains; what they loved, taught, and suffered for, lives about us and within us; and should we not allow them to rest in peace?"

"Your warmth shows me that you are thinking of your own grandfather again," replied Lars, "and I must say it seems to me high time the parish should be rid of *him*. He monopolized too much space while he lived; and so it is scarcely worth while to have him lie in the way now that he is dead. Should his corpse prevent a blessing to this parish that would extend through a hundred generations, we may truly say that of all who have been born here, *he* has done us the greatest harm."

Knud Aakre tossed back his disorderly hair, his eyes flashed, his whole person looked like a bent steel spring.

"How much of a blessing what you are speaking about may be, I have already shown. It has the same character as all the other blessings with which you have supplied the parish, namely, a doubtful one. It is true, you have provided us with a new church, but you have also filled it with a new spirit—and it is not that of love. True, you have furnished us with new roads, but also with new roads to destruction, as is now plainly manifest in the misfortunes of many. True, you have diminished our public taxes, but you have increased our private ones; lawsuits, promissory notes, and bankruptcies are no fruitful gifts to a community. And *you* dare to dishonor in his grave the man whom the whole parish blesses? You dare assert that he lies in our way; ay, no doubt he does lie in your way, this is plain enough now, for his grave will be the cause of your downfall! The spirit which has reigned over you, and until to-day over us all, was not born to rule but to enter into servitude. The church-yard will surely be allowed to remain in peace; but to-day it shall have one grave added to it, namely, that of your popularity, which is now to be buried there."

Lars Högstad rose, white as a sheet; his lips parted, but he was unable to utter a word, and the straw fell. After a few vain efforts to find and recover his powers of speech, he burst forth like a volcano with:

"And so these are the thanks I get for all my toil and drudgery! If such a woman-preacher is to be allowed to rule—why, then, may the devil be your chairman if ever I set my foot here again! I have kept things together until this day, and after me your trash will fall into a thousand pieces, but let it tumble down now—here is the register!" And he flung it on the table. "Shame on such an assembly of old women and brats!" Here he struck the table with great violence. "Shame on the whole parish that it can see a man rewarded as I am now."

He brought down his fist once more with such force that the great courthouse table shook, and the inkstand with its entire contents tumbled to the floor, marking for all future generations the spot where Lars Högstad fell in spite of all his prudence, his long rule, and his patience.

He rushed to the door and in a few moments had left the place. The entire assembly remained motionless; for the might of his voice and of his wrath had frightened them, until Knud Aakre, remembering the taunt he had received at the time of *his* fall, with beaming countenance and imitating Lars's voice, exclaimed:

"Is *this* to be the decisive blow in the matter?"

The whole assembly burst into peals of merriment at these words! The solemn meeting ended in laughter, talk, and high glee; only a few left the place, those remaining behind called for drink to add to their food, and a night of thunder succeeded a day of lightning. Every one felt as happy and independent as of yore, ere the commanding spirit of Lars had cowed their souls into dumb obedience. They drank toasts to their freedom; they sang, indeed, finally they danced, Knud Aakre and the vice-chairman taking the lead and all the rest following, while boys and girls joined in, and the young folks outside shouted "Hurrah!" for such a jollification they had never before seen!

III

Lars moved about in the large rooms at Högstad without speaking a word. His wife, who loved him, but always in fear and trembling, dared not come into his presence. The management of the gard and of the house might be carried on as best it could, while on the other hand there kept growing a multitude of letters, which passed back and forth between Högstad and the parish, and Högstad and the post-office; for Lars had claims against the parish board, and these not being satisfied he prosecuted; against the savings-bank, which were also unsatisfied, and so resulted in another suit. He took offense at expressions in the letters he received and went to law again, now against the chairman of the parish board, now against the president of the savings-bank. At the same time there were dreadful articles in the newspapers, which report attributed to him, and which were the cause of great dissension in the parish, inciting neighbor against neighbor. Sometimes he was absent whole weeks, no one knew where, and when he returned he lived as secluded as before. At church he had not been seen after the great scene at the representatives' meeting.

Then one Saturday evening the priest brought tidings that the railroad was to run through the parish after all, and across the old churchyard! It struck like lightning into every home. The unanimous opposition of the parish board had been in vain, Lars Högstad's influence had been stronger. This was the meaning of his journeys, this was his work! Involuntary admiration of the man and his stubborn persistence tended to suppress the dissatisfaction of the people at their own defeat, and the more they discussed the matter the more reconciled they became; for a fact accomplished always contains within itself reasons why it is so, which gradually force themselves upon us after there is no longer possibility of change. The people assembled about the church the next day, and they could not help laughing as they met one another. And just as the whole congregation, young and old, men and women, ay, even children, were all talking about Lars Högstad, his ability, his rigorous will, his immense influence, he himself with his whole household came driving up in four conveyances, one after the other. It was two years since his last visit there! He alighted and passed through the crowd, while all, as by one impulse, unhesitatingly greeted him, but he did not deign to bestow a glance on either side, nor to return a single salutation. His little wife, pale as death, followed him. Inside of the church the astonishment grew to such a pitch that as one after another caught sight of him they stopped singing and only stared at him. Knud Aakre, who sat in his pew in front of Lars, noticed that there was something the matter, and as he saw nothing remarkable in front of him, he turned round. He saw Lars bowed over his hymn-book, searching for the place.

He had not seen him since that evening at the meeting, and such a complete change he had not believed possible. For this was no victor! The thin, soft hair was thinner than ever, the face was haggard and emaciated, the eyes hollow and bloodshot, the giant neck had dwindled into wrinkles and cords. Knud comprehended at a glance what this man had gone through; he was seized with a feeling of strong sympathy, indeed, he felt something of the old love stirring within his breast. He prayed for Lars to his God, and made a resolute vow that he would seek him after service; but Lars had started on ahead. Knud resolved to call on him that evening. His wife, however, held him back.

"Lars is one of those," said she, "who can scarcely bear a debt of gratitude: keep away from him until he has an opportunity to do you some favor, and then perhaps he will come to you!"

But he did not come. He appeared now and then at church, but nowhere else, and he associated with no one. On the other hand, he now devoted himself to his gard and other business with the passionate zeal of one who had determined to make amends in one year for the neglect of many; and, indeed, there were those who said that this was imperative.

Railroad operations in the valley began very soon.

As the line was to go directly past Lars's gard, he tore down the portion of his house that faced the road, in order to build a large and handsome balcony, for he was determined that his gard should attract attention. This work was just being done when the temporary rails for the conveyance of gravel and timber to the road were laid and a small locomotive was sent to the spot. It was a beautiful autumn evening that the first gravel car was to pass over the road. Lars stood on his front steps, to hear the first signal and to see the first column of smoke; all the people of the gard were gathered about him. He gazed over the parish, illumined by the setting sun, and he felt that he would be remembered as long as a train should come roaring through this fertile valley. A sense of forgiveness glided into his soul. He looked toward the churchyard, a part of which still remained, with crosses bowed down to the ground, but a part of it was now the railroad. He was just endeavoring to define his own feeling when the first signal whistled, and presently the train came slowly working its way along, attended by a cloud of smoke, mingled with sparks, for the locomotive was fed with pine wood. The wind blew toward the house so that those standing without were soon enveloped in a dense smoke, but as this cleared away Lars saw the train working its way down through the valley like a strong will.

He was content, and entered his house like one who has come from a long day's work. The image of his grandfather stood before him at this moment. This grandfather had raised the family from poverty to prosperity; true, a portion of his honor as a citizen was consumed in the act, but he had advanced nevertheless! His faults were the prevailing ones of his time: they were based on the uncertain boundary lines of the moral conceptions of his day. Every age has its uncertain moral distinctions and its victims.

Honor be to him in his grave, for he had suffered and toiled! Peace be with him! It must be good to rest in the end. But he was not allowed to rest because of his grandson's vast ambition; his ashes were thrown up with the stones and the gravel. Nonsense! he would only smile at his grandson's work.

Amid thoughts like these Lars had undressed and gone to bed. Once more his grandfather's image glided before him. It was sterner now than the first time. Weariness enfeebles us, and Lars began to reproach himself. But he defended himself also. What did his grandfather want? Surely he ought to be satisfied now, for the family honor was proclaimed in loud tones above his grave. Who else had such a monument? And yet what is this? These two monstrous eyes of fire and this hissing, roaring sound belong no longer to the locomotive, for they turn away from the railroad track. And from the churchyard straight toward the house comes an immense procession. The eyes of fire are his grandfather's, and the long line of followers are all the dead. The train advances steadily toward the gard, roaring, crackling, flashing. The windows blaze in the reflection of the dead men's eyes. Lars made a mighty effort to control himself, for this was a dream, unquestionably.

There, now I am awake. Come on, poor ghosts!

And lo! they really did come from the churchyard, overthrowing road, rails, locomotive, and train, so that these fell with a mighty crash to the ground, and the green sod appeared in their stead, dotted with graves and crosses as before. Like mighty champions they advanced, and the hymn, "Let the dead repose in peace!" preceded them. Lars knew it; for through all these years it had been sighing within his soul, and now it had become his requiem; for this was death and death's visions. The cold sweat started out over his whole body, for nearer and nearer—and behold, on the window pane! there they are now, and he heard some one speak his name. Overpowered with dread he struggled to scream; for he was being strangled, a cold hand was clenching his throat, and he regained his voice in an agonized "Help me!" and awoke. The window had been broken in from the outside; the pieces flew all about his head. He sprang up. A man stood at the window, surrounded by smoke and flames.

"The gard is on fire, Lars! We will help you out!"

It was Knud Aakre.

When Lars regained his consciousness, he was lying outside in a bleak wind, which chilled his limbs. There was not a soul with him; he saw the flaming gard to the left; around him his cattle were grazing and making their voices heard; the sheep were huddled together in a frightened flock; the household goods were scattered about, and when he looked again he saw some one sitting on a knoll close by, weeping. It was his wife. He called her by name. She started.

"The Lord Jesus be praised that you are alive!" cried she, coming forward and seating herself, or rather throwing herself down in front of him. "O God! O God! We surely have had enough of this railroad now!"

"The railroad?" asked he, but ere the words had escaped his lips a clear comprehension of the case passed like a shudder over him; for, of course, sparks from the locomotive that had fallen among the shavings of the new side wall had been the cause of the fire. Lars sat there brooding in silence; his wife, not daring to utter another word, began to search for his clothes. He accepted her attentions in silence, but as she knelt before him to cover his feet, he laid his hand on her head. Falling forward she buried her face in his lap and wept aloud. Many eyed her curiously. But Lars understood her and said: "You are the only friend I have."

Even though it had cost the gard to hear these words, it mattered not to her; she felt so happy that she gained courage, and rising up and looking humbly into her husband's face, she said:

"Because there is no one else who understands you." Then a hard heart melted, and tears rolled down the man's cheeks as he clung to his wife's hand.

Now he talked to her as to his own soul. Now too she opened her mind to him. They also talked about how all this had happened, or rather he listened while she told about it. Knud Aakre had been the first to see the fire, had roused his people, sent the girls out over his parish, while he had hastened himself with men and horses to the scene of the conflagration, where all were sleeping. He had engineered the extinguishing of the flames and the rescuing of the household goods, and had himself dragged Lars from the burning room, and carried him to the left side of the house from whence the wind was blowing and had laid him out here in the churchyard.

And while they were talking of this, some one came driving rapidly up the road and turned into the churchyard, where he alighted. It was Knud, who had been home after his church-cart—the one in which they had so many times ridden together to and from the meetings of the parish board. Now he requested Lars to get in and ride home with him. They grasped each other by the hand, the one sitting, the other standing.

"Come with me now," said Knud.

Without a word of reply, Lars rose. Side by side they walked to the cart. Lars was helped in; Knud sat down beside him. What they talked about as they drove along, or afterward in the little chamber at Aakre, where they remained until late in the morning, has never been known. But from that day they were inseparable as before.

As soon as misfortune overtakes a man, every one learns what he is worth. And so the parish undertook to rebuild Lars Högstad's houses, and to make them larger and handsomer than any others in the valley. He was reelected chairman, but with Knud Aakre at his side; he never again failed to take counsel of Knud's intelligence and heart — and from that day forth nothing went to ruin.

BJÖRN SIVERTSEN'S WEDDING TRIP

BY HOLGER DRACHMANN

By general consent Drachmann fills a niche in the temple of fame as introducer of the modern "short story" into Denmark. He was born at Copenhagen in 1846, and is a man of extraordinary versatility both in accomplishment and temperament. Besides being a marine painter of some note, and, before he joined with the conservative party of thinkers in 1880, the most conspicuous of the new realistic school of writers in Denmark, he has been at various times royalist, socialist, realist, romanticist, radical, orthodox, national, cosmopolitan.

With his volume of poems, published in 1872, followed by skilful, realistic tales of fisherman life, the revolutionary march in Danish literature began, with Brandes as drum-major.

Drachmann's stories are marked by sudden outbursts of real inspiration—by impulses rather than by principles—curiously combined with a strong feeling for form.

BJÖRN SIVERTSEN'S WEDDING TRIP

BY HOLGER DRACHMANN

THE "strong Björn," was about to be married. The usual signs of such an occurrence had come to pass, even to the most important of them all, he had become engaged.

Exactly how this happened, however, history does not state. After the death of the head fisher-master he had inherited the house, and had paid off his brother Niels for his share with a good sum of money, so that the latter could build his own home farther off in the village. There sat Björn then with his house and innkeeper's outfit, very lonely in all his new glory. He got into the habit of sauntering more frequently than usual down to the inn, to get his short pipe filled, to drink a glass and spin a yarn. The jolly innkeeper had been married about a year, and was as busy as could be, running in at the door of the inner room every few minutes, "to look after something."

"What is the matter there?" asked Björn. "Can't you let the women attend to the child?"

The innkeeper explained it was the "teeth," that he was so interested in.

"Teeth?"

"Yes, Björn. When the teeth come the crying stops."

"Is that so? Say, tell me, could I see the child?"

BJÖRN SIVERTSEN'S WEDDING TRIP

BY HOLGER DRACHMANN

THE "strong Björn" was about to be married. The usual signs of such an occurrence had come to pass, even to the most important of them all; he had become engaged.

Exactly how this happened, however, history does not state. After the death of the head fisher-master he had inherited the house, and had paid off his brother Niels for his share with a good sum of money, so that the latter could build his own home farther off in the village. There sat Björn then with his house and his sail-maker's outfit, very lonely in all his new glory.

He got into the habit of sauntering more frequently than usual down to the inn, to get his short pipe filled, to drink a glass and spin a yarn. The jolly innkeeper had been married about a year, and was as busy as could be, running in at the door of the inner room every few minutes "to look after something."

"What is the matter there?" asked Björn. "Can't you let the women attend to the child?"

The innkeeper explained it was the "teeth" that he was so interested in.

"Teeth?"

"Yes, Björn. When the teeth come the crying stops."

"Is that so? Say, tell me, could I see the child?"

Translated by Grace Isabel Colbron.   Copyright, 1907, by P. F. Collier & Son.

The father escorted him proudly into the nursery where the young wife sat at a window with the child on her lap. She was bending over it, and was also looking for "the teeth."

Björn saluted and came slowly nearer.

"Come and look at him," she said, smiling.

The giant bent his head, but the child became frightened at the heavy hair and beard and screamed. Björn drew back in alarm, but during his retreat he turned several times and looked back at the window.

When he and the innkeeper were alone in the latter's private room Björn stood a while in thought, scratching with his thick finger in his mane.

"Say, innkeeper, what a wonderful thing such a little fellow is! He had real nails on his fingers, and he looked at me."

The young father grew knock-kneed with pleasure, and, rubbing his hands, answered: "You ought to have just such a one yourself. You have a house and money."

"Yes. But it is not so easy to find a wife, friend."

Björn sat down, lost in thought, and when the innkeeper touched his glass with his own, he looked up absently. "Do you know what I am thinking of, innkeeper?"

"No. Let us hear it."

"I was wondering if at any time I could really have been as small as that."

"I hope, for your mother's sake," said the innkeeper, laughing, "that when you were born you were a good deal smaller than my baby now is."

Then there was no more talk on that subject.

Several days later Björn set out in his good old boat with a load of potatoes for the nearest town.

The boat was known as "The Pail."

Heaven knows where it got the name; probably from some nickname given in mockery—people are so wicked. But, as it often happens, the nickname had become a pet name, and the boat was always called "The Pail." Red Anders, a relative, went along with him, and after having sold their potatoes—and sold them well at that—they were now lying alongside the wharf waiting for a little more wind. Then it happened that an old skipper of the town, who had retired, but could not altogether keep away from the water, came sauntering down to the dock, his hands in his pockets and his little twinkling eyes on the lookout for something of interest. He stopped on the dock, blinking still more, and seemed to be taking the measure of "The Pail."

"Heh, boys, where are you from?"

Björn looked up, surprised at this question about anything so well known.

"From Fiskebäk, of course."

"Are you the owner?"

Björn looked up at the skipper, with his hand behind his ear.

"I am a little deaf; but if you are speaking of the boat, it is 'The Pail,' and I am the owner."

"Why do you call her 'The Pail'?"

"That is her name."

"Has she any faults?"

"We all have faults ourselves, and so do boats."

"She is not very new?"

Björn began to get somewhat impatient.

"See here, my man, how old are you yourself?"

The skipper laughed and took his hands from his pockets.

"Will you sell your boat?"

Björn looked at Red Anders, and Red Anders looked at Björn. Then they both looked up at the questioner, and at last they looked around at the boat.

"What do you say, Anders?" asked Björn.

Björn was in good humor. The potato transaction had gone off famously, and the buyer had, over and above, treated them well. Finally he slapped his leg and said, with a broad grin:

"My soul. Why shouldn't I sell her?"

"Yes, why not? Then you can buy a new one."

"That's so," said Björn, and nodded to the skipper.

"How much do you want for her?" asked the latter.

"Two hundred dollars as she swims now."

"One hundred and eighty," was bidden.

Björn did not answer, but prepared to let go the mooring.

"Who made her sails?" was asked.

"The man with the rudder," answered Björn, and cut the after-ropes loose.

"All right. Tie up again and let me come aboard."

Then came a turning upside down and a ransacking of everything inside "The Pail." The bulkheads, the flooring, the combing, the seats, nails, cleats, and painting, masts and oars were examined, and about an hour later Björn and Anders stood outside the tavern, where the bargain had been sealed with a drink. The summer sun shone down on their burning faces and beaming eyes, but when Björn looked toward the harbor and saw "The Pail" being taken away from its place his expression changed, and, turning to Anders, he asked: "What do you think they will say when we come home without 'The Pail'?"

Anders put on a thoughtful mien. "I don't know. But, anyway, it was your boat, and the skipper promised to be good to her, and keep her scraped and tarred and painted when she needs it."

"You are right," said Björn. "But are we to *walk* home?"

It was very hot and the sun burned. It was a good twelve miles to the fishing village, and the road was for the most part flat, sandy, and open.

"Do you want to ride?" asked Anders. "I am afraid the most of the wagons have gone home, unless you want to hire one."

Björn stood a moment without answering. It was perhaps not such a bad idea to postpone the home-coming and the explanations for a little.

"I propose we go to the capital."

"Do you treat?" asked Anders, cautiously.

"Certainly," answered Björn, and slapped his pocket where the money lay. They went through the town to the railway station, where a train was just about to start. The two were like two big children. They had been to the capital already, but neither of them had ever ridden on the railroad.

Some one showed them the way to the ticket office.

Björn planted himself in front of the opening, with his pocketbook in his hands.

"Can I get a cabin for two men to the capital?" he asked, in a tone which he took for a whisper, but which could be heard throughout the hall. "Return?" was asked.

"What's that he says?" asked Björn of his comrade.

"Second or third?" came again from the office, in rather an angry tone.

"Take what you can get," whispered Anders, who, as his expenses were paid for him, saw no reason for being economical.

"All right, give me the whole thing," said Björn, and pushed a bill in at the impatient voice.

"Two excursions, second. You can come back on the evening train, do you hear?" said the voice.

Björn received a number of silver coins for his bill. He took it all but one piece. "We can afford to tip to-day," he said to his cousin, in the same loud voice.

The ticket seller put his head out of the opening. "Take your money!" he called angrily.

"All right," said Björn, crestfallen. He put the coin in his pocket, and as they walked through the waiting rooms to the platform he muttered: "That villain of an innkeeper at home told me that if you want to ride comfortably on the railroad you must tip the conductors. But it doesn't seem to go here."

They entered the compartment, where sat a stout man, with close cropped hair, white neckband, and long black coat. His face was red and good-natured.

"Whew, it's warm here," said Björn, and opened

a window. The stout man coughed. The engine whistled, and the train began to move.

"There she goes, d—— me," said Anders.

"Some speed in her," answered Björn with a similar oath as the car began to lurch.

"Open the other porthole," cried Björn, after a while. "I'll suffocate in this box. This is a new sort of sailing on dry land." The stout man coughed still more.

"Does it trouble you, sir?" asked Björn, politely.

"Yes."

Björn gave orders for Anders to close the porthole. The stout gentleman eyed him sharply.

They came to a sharp curve in the road, the car swung round, and Björn nearly fell off his seat.

"Well, I'll be blasted eternally," he cried, half surprised and half in sly cunning. "Do you think they'll send us to hell in this hurry, Anders?"

"Do you always swear like this, my man?" asked the stout gentleman. Björn looked at him with a wink.

"That's as it happens, my good sir, but I generally do when on shore. Meat goes with bread, as the baker's dog said when he stole the steak."

"I do not think it is quite necessary," said the stout gentleman. "I know, for I am a clergyman."

"A clergyman?" repeated Björn, looking at him. "Beg pardon, but will you swear to that?"

The stout gentleman looked severely at him at first. But the big child was in such a good humor that day that he was quite irresistible, with his half-simple, half-roguish smile, and his good-nature, from which all severity ran off like water from a duck's back.

In five minutes they were the best of friends. Björn told, in his own style, his story of "The Pail," and the jolly priest laughed until his asthma nearly choked him, and before they reached the capital he had Björn's promise to visit him next day in his little village rectory near the city.

Anders went home that night on his excursion ticket, and Björn set out alone next day for the country. Then it happened that after that day Björn undertook several excursions to Copenhagen with corresponding journeyings to the rectory, until, according to his own version, he was "caught by a petticoat."

But this was all he would say about it. He went around wearing a broad, shining gold ring, which pinched his fat finger. How the ring was ever squeezed on that finger in the beginning was a mystery, but there it sat, and there sat Björn.

All winter long he pondered over his thoughts of marriage. The innkeeper and his wife teased him, at which he grew angry in jest and then in earnest. And then, when his anger had passed, he showed them first the photograph of a girl with a very dark face and two bright pink hat ribbons. The picture appeared to need much polishing of Björn's coat sleeve, to give it, as he said, "the proper point of view." He did not at all like any sport being made of this picture, but was honest enough to acknowledge that it looked more like "the portrait of a nigger than of a respectable country girl."

During the winter he bought himself a new boat. With all necessary ceremonies this boat was christened the "Flying Fish." But during the christening feast there was considerable of a row. The otherwise so good-natured Björn fired up about some chance teasing words, some mocking nickname given the boat. Without knowing just why the matter excited him so, he became first sarcastic, and then rude and threatening. Next day, however, he was much dissatisfied with himself, and went to consult with his friend the innkeeper, accusing himself of having forgotten his duties as host. But the innkeeper comforted him, and told him that was all the fault of his approaching marriage. A man in that condition can't keep the right balance, and is liable to slop over either way on the slightest provocation. That was always so. The thing to do was to close the matter as soon as possible.

Björn did not answer. He muttered something about spring, and sheets and linen, etc., and then went for a sail in his new boat. She was a flyer and no mistake, he could prove that to the scoffers on shore any day!

Then spring came at last, and now "this nonsense should have an end." He had a good new boat; all he wanted was a wife, so Björn swore to himself.

Thus the marriage came about.

The ceremony, naturally, was to be held in the little country church. A relative of Stine—Stine was the bride—had suggested that as Stine's parents were both dead, and he himself was an innkeeper in Copenhagen, he should give the wedding feast in his house. Björn protested vigorously against this. He and his brother were to sail to the city, and lay up the boat at

Kroyer's Wharf. Niels would take care of the boat,
and he himself would "play monkey just long enough
for the splice"; then back to the city, and on board the
boat to take his wife home.

Stine and her party protested against this arrange-
ment with equal energy, if not with equal warmth of
expression. A wedding without a feast was an im-
possibility, and there would always be time enough for
the sail, thought Stine to herself. So she clung to her
decision, supported by her cousin of the Gilded Tarpot, and for the first time in his life, even before the
"splice," Björn learned what unlooked-for obstacles
can be put in our way by the so-called weaker sex. At
least, so the old poets call it.

Björn grumbled, but was clever enough to hold his
peace. In all secrecy he laid a counter-mine, telling
his brother to take the "Flying Fish" out as far as the
custom-house and lay her up in the ferry harbor, with
all ropes clear for sailing, and when that was done to
come himself to the Gilded Tarpot, which was a favorite place of refreshment for country people, soldiers,
and petty officials.

In this way each party felt sure of the eventual victory, and the marriage could come off. The minister
tied the knot in his little country church and gave them
a glass of sherry and a silver soup-ladle in the rectory.
Björn put both "inside his vest," and then the innkeeper drove them into town. The village people gave
them a hurrah, and finally the merry company sat
down in the Gilded Tarpot's basement rooms to a
board laden with roasts of lamb and pork, ham and

vegetables, and all manner of other good things. Sweet cordials were there for the ladies, and French wines, while for the men there was brandy and punch.

Through the basement window one could see a high brick wall, gleaming in the strong sunlight, and if one laid one's self over the table, with one's head in the neighbor's lap, 'way high up one could see a tiny piece of blue sky as large as a handkerchief perhaps, with feathery clouds driving over it.

Some of Stine's female relatives were there, and the innkeeper's family and best friends. Among the family was a ship's-joiner, who proved his sympathetic comprehension of the importance of the occasion by getting drunk at once and making pathetic speeches. And among the good friends was a "former officer of justice," as he called himself, a man with a decoration in his buttonhole; also a drunken-looking jailer, who wore a stiff collar and his service medal to remind the world that he had once been a non-commissioned officer. He looked as if he had his serious doubts about the company, and expected the one or the other of them to make away with the spoons. Probably because of this doubt therefore he kept a distance between himself and the rest of the company, and poured out an endless series of small whiskies for himself, "on the top of the glass," as he expressed it, without any appreciable effect. He laughed a sudden and ferocious-sounding laugh, drank half his glass, cleared his throat, poked his elbows in the host's ribs, and said: "Old comrade, here's to the good old times." This for him was the height of sociability.

He called Björn "Captain," but after a few repetitions of the word the bridegroom laid down his fork, with a large slice of beet on it, and remarked:

"Port your helm, friend, and let up on that 'Captain,' if you don't want to make me angry."

After this admonition he compromised on "Boatsman."

Björn was decidedly out of sorts. He had the impression of being left out in the cold, which was probably due to his deafness. He certainly filled his place in the literal sense, but Niels did not come, and Stine, the bride—well, Stine sat there at his side in a black merino gown, with wreath and veil, her red hands in her lap, as straight up and down in her chair as if she had swallowed a yardstick.

That was probably the correct thing to do, for a northern bride should not be too vivacious. But there seemed to be in her nature a certain dignity, which would be a good thing in a home no doubt, but which seemed out of place here between roast and cordial.

"One certainly could not call her too affectionate," Björn said afterward, when describing the occasion.

He sat alone and she sat alone. She ate very little; he ate enough for two. The ship's-joiner made one speech after another, the sun shone down on the brick wall, and Björn leaned over on Stine and looked up out of the window.

Stine pulled her veil aside, smoothed her dress, and asked: "What are you looking at?"

"Fine opportunity that," said Björn. Her eyes followed his.

"You mean that fourth story to let up there? Yes,
I would rather like to live there. Then one would not
have to be on the water so much."

"A fine opportunity to sail home, I mean," explained
Björn. "The wind is strong from the south."

Stine glanced at him uneasily, and then at the innkeeper.

"A stiff south breeze," continued Björn. "It has
been a north wind for some time, and will be to-night
again. We don't have a chance like this every day."

At a glance from Stine the innkeeper proposed a
"good, old-time Danish cheer" for Björn, in the at-
tempt to change the train of his thoughts, and the
ship's-joiner made his fifth speech.

Then mine host proposed a song, in which all
joined, even the jailer, who held second voice and
tooted like a clarinet.

After that, in spite of some objection, the ship's-
joiner rose, and, supporting himself by his neighbors'
shoulders, began, with tears in his eyes:

"Good friends and hearers, we are all that, I
think—"

"Yes, yes," they answered.

"We will now—something must be said to them before they leave father and mother—I mean before
they leave the circle of these kind friends—"

"They don't go until to-morrow," said mine host.

"No," said Björn, banging the table with his fist.

"He's right," said Niels, coming in just then. "The
wind is fresh from the south, Björn."

"I know," said Björn, getting up.

"Hush!" whispered the innkeeper. "Let the joiner finish his speech."

"Listen, dear friends," continued the joiner, reeling from side to side. "We are all mortal, and we all love our native country. I do not say fatherland; I say native country. We do not know where our fathers came from, but we know where we were born ourselves—"

"What nonsense is this?" whispered Niels, who grasped the situation and was ready to fight.

"Who is that man?" asked the joiner, trying to fix his bleary gaze on Niels and holding fast to his neighbor's shoulder. "Is that a man who will not drink to his native country? If he is, then I say: 'Fie, for shame,' say I."

Niels looked meaningly at Björn.

"Shall we clear the place and take Stine with us?"

Björn motioned to him. But one of the guests who supported the joiner heard what Niels said. He drew away his shoulder, the joiner fell to the floor, and in a minute the place was in an uproar. Every one spoke or screamed at once. Niels had already collared the jailer. Then, at this highly critical moment, the sense of duty of the women of the old days awoke in Stine. She placed herself by the side of her chosen lord and master and announced that "she would sail to Jutland with him rather than have a fight on her wedding day." That settled the matter. The joiner was carried into the next room and put to bed, the guests shook hands cordially and drank one another's health. Niels and Björn became most amiable at once, and

Niels ordered more punch. The innkeeper made the
best of a bad business, and peace settled down on the
spirits of the company.

Then the party broke up.

In his delight at his victory Björn invited the entire
party, even to the jailer, to take a sail on the "Flying
Fish." He would put them ashore at the limekilns
when they had had enough, he said.

The invitation was accepted, probably in the desire not to disturb the nearly sealed peace. But when
they all came up out of the Gilded Tarpot, the fresh
air and the sunshine, or the joy of his own victory,
or the feelings of a bridegroom, or all of them at once,
so overcame Björn that he took Stine round the waist
and swore he would dance a waltz with her then and
there. Which he did, in spite of her obstinate pro-
test, to the great delight of the passers-by. Then he
dropped Stine, and, seizing the jailer, danced a polka
with him. He next insisted upon carrying off a sen-
try-box to try the sentry's gun on the Amalienplads.
But this last was too much for the military feelings of
the jailer. He declared it "scandalous" and walked
away as red in the face as a lobster, and took the innkeeper with him. At the next corner was a flaring
menagerie poster, with pictures of elephants, monkeys,
and bears. These last caught Björn's attention; he
declared that he must go and see his cousins perform,
and the wedding guests had difficulty in getting him
away safely. By this time quite a crowd had collected,
which listened with interest to the lively remarks made
by the big fisherman, and when at last, to the immense

delight of the crowd, he gave a plastic imitation of a dancing bear, the rest of the invited guests fled, and an assemblage of those not invited followed Björn, Neils, and Stine down to the harbor.

"Come, now, Björn, keep quiet," said Neils, soothingly, as a policeman appeared interested in their movements.

"Shouldn't I be merry on my wedding day?" queried Björn, looking around beamingly.

Stine was ready to cry, but held out heroically. She had chosen her lot in life, and was ready to take whatever came.

"It will be better later," was her consoling thought.

They got down to the harbor somehow and into the boat.

"You'll have to reef," said the ferry-keeper.

"Full sail!" called Björn. "This is my wedding trip."

"All right," said the ferryman. But he whispered aside to Niels: "Can he sail a boat?"

"Well, rather," laughed Niels.

"All ready, Niels?" asked Björn.

"Yes."

"Stine stowed away safely?"

"Yes."

"All off then; let go!"

"Hurrah!" called the ferrymen, but shook their heads nevertheless.

"That will be a wet wedding trip if he doesn't take in some of that sail," they commented.

And it certainly was wet.

Stine will never forget it, and Björn tells the story himself in this wise:

"We just skipped through the water. I must say the 'Flying Fish' did fly that day. As we went past the ferry-boats and the pilot-boats they called out to us, but I waved my hat and asked if they could see the color of her bottom.

" 'I hope she will stand it,' said Niels.

" 'She'll have to,' I answered.

"Stine lay in the bottom of the boat and gave up all the good dinner they served us in the inn. It was a good thing she had not eaten more.

"I tried to cheer her up, but I don't think she heard me.

"Niels and I were dripping wet, the sails were dripping wet, and so was Stine. I haven't sailed like that before or since.

"I didn't dare sail all the way home with her like that, so put up at the dock of the town.

"The old skipper who bought 'The Pail' came down to the water. 'What sort of weather is that for full sail?' he asked. 'Have you a cargo?'

" 'A wedding cargo,' I answered, 'but it's more dead than alive, I guess. Come, help us get the old woman ashore, or she will give up the ghost right here.' We handed Stine up. She couldn't stand on her legs at all, and we had to leave her at the house of a good friend in the town. She stayed there three days and nights, and I had to go round with dry mouth, couldn't get even so much as a kiss.

"It was all right afterward, but she was angry at

me for some time because I had 'made a fool of her in that way.' What can one expect from such land lubbers, who have never seen more water than a pool in a village street in all their lives?

"Whenever I speak of that day Stine gets cross, but I rub my nose with the back of my hand and say: 'Well, anyway, that was the most wonderful wedding trip I ever heard of.'

"And that is why I haven't made any more like it"

JALO THE TROTTER

BY JOHANN JACOB AHRENBERG

Among Scandinavians it seems to be a common thing for the artistic impulse to drive in many directions at once. The Swedish-Finnish novelist Ahrenberg is architect as well as writer. He was born in 1847 at Wiborg, and studied in Helsingfors and at the Art Academy in Stockholm. He is now chief Government architect for his state. The first novels and tales that brought him into literary prominence were published in 1880, followed since then by many other East Finland pictures. Among these, "Jalo the Trotter," the story of a superb horse and his two masters, is characteristic not only of the author's style, but of his country as well.

JALO THE TROTTER

A FINNISH TALE

BY JACOB AHRENBERG

IT was late in the afternoon of an August day, but the sun was still pouring its hot slanting rays into Christian's sitting-room. The flies were buzzing merrily around the head of the landlord, who sat by the window, apparently watching the two balsams blooming in broken china pots on the sill. Christian had been there a long time, staring between the leaves and flowers of the plants at the little gate of the fence, as if he was expecting some one.

He had already reached middle life, but looked considerably older. His eyes were sunk deep in their sockets, and wrinkles seamed his face. His wife, who was working busily at the loom, did not seem to have her mind wholly on her task; for, whenever Christian made the slightest movement, she glanced anxiously toward the door as if she, too, was expecting somebody.

Suddenly Laurikamen, the assessor of the district court, entered, greeted the couple, and shook hands ceremoniously with them. This guest, whose visit seemed to afford neither pleasure nor surprise, sat down at the table, and, after a short silence, lighted his pipe, and finally remarked that it really was far too hot for five o'clock in the afternoon, to which

Translated by Mary J. Safford. Copyright, 1901, by The Current Literature Publishing Company.

undeniably truthful remark Christian replied that
the heat would at least do the oats good. Gradually the conversation grew more fluent; they discussed
the questions of the day, the fall of stocks, the price
of grain at home and in Russia, and the sessions of
the court. Then the assessor had reached the point
at which he was aiming. Rising deliberately, he went
to the hearth, knocked the ashes from his pipe, and
remarked, as if casually:

"By the way, you are summoned there."

"I? To the court? By whom?"

"By Jegor Timofitsch Ivanov, your neighbor."

"H'm! What is he after? Is it about the beating
I gave him last spring?"

"Not at all; he must put up with that. It's the
affair of Jalo, his trotter, you know."

"Well, what's that to me?"

"I don't know. Come to-morrow, and you'll find
out."

The assessor uttered a sigh of relief, rose, took his
leave, and went away.

Christian scratched himself behind the ear, and went
out thoughtfully. Sighing heavily, he wandered rest-
lessly over the pastures and meadows until late in the
evening.

As it was still too warm in the room, he sat down
on the steps to enjoy the cool evening air. It was a
damp, hot night; the stars shone dimly through the
air, which lay like a thin veil on the horizon. The
full moon was rising in majesty above the moor, loom-
ing in a large, reddish gold disk through the firwood,

which grew sparse and stunted upon the moss-covered hill. The last birds were twittering sleepily, and the night-jar flew clumsily, as if drunk, first to the right, and then to the left, sometimes vanishing in the gloom. Country folk hate the night-jar, and this aversion probably made Christian's whole surroundings suddenly seem unspeakably desolate. His mood was transmitted to the scene about him. He could not possibly drive that business of Jalo the trotter out of his head. All the memories of his life were associated with the name. Everything he had dreamed and hoped, everything which had disturbed and alarmed him, had revolved wholly around Jalo. How well he recollected the day Jegor Timofitsch Ivanov opened his shop in the village of Tervola. Everything that previously was brought from the city could now be bought at Jegor Timofitsch's. How humble and cringing the fellow had been then; how well he understood how to ingratiate himself with everybody.

At that time Jalo was nearly three years old.

Jegor had been everybody's most humble servant. Doubling up like a pocket-knife in his obsequiousness, he had treated his customers to tobacco and sbitin,[1] promised them unlimited credit, and thereby won all hearts. "You haven't any money? Oh, that makes no difference—we'll charge it; you can pay another time." It was all so easy and simple, but when a year had gone by, Jegor's account book was full,

_____
[1] A Russian national drink, very popular among the lower classes, made of sirup, thin beer, and water.

and all the insignificant entries were found to amount
to an enormous sum.

If anybody needed a loan, who but Jegor had the
money? True, he asked twelve per cent, but then
there was no bothering with lawyers, judges, assessors,
and such people. And who did not need money in
these times? Everybody wanted it, and Christian,
perhaps, most of all.

But when four years had passed, Jegor Timofitsch
from being everybody's servant had become everybody's master. Now he carried his back as stiff as
a ramrod; now he used a very different tone: "Lout,
do you mean to sow rye? No, you must sow oats;
I can't sell rye in these times. You want money to
buy a cow? You have scarcely enough feed for the
one you own. No, that won't do."

He sold the peasant's grain from the fields before
it was mowed. He felled their woods for fuel and
lumber, without any further ceremony than to notify
them of his intention. And yet, how the terrible debt
grew! It was as insatiable as the Moloch of the Phil-
istines. Everything disappeared in its mighty jaws.
It was never settled, in spite of all the sacrifices and
payments in the shape of tar, wood, tallow, sheep,
crabs, game-birds, and oats.

If any one had cause to suffer from this neighbor
it was Christian. Their farms adjoined, and he knew
better than all the rest what it means to be a debtor.
It seemed as though the flesh was being gnawed from
his body and the marrow sucked out of his bones. He
often felt utterly defenseless against the cruel foe, and

thought seriously of going out to beg his way from door to door, if only he could be a free man once more.

But in the hour of his sorest need help came. And his deliverer was Jalo, who had reached his sixth year at Michaelmas.

Oh, what an animal this Jalo was! His black coat shone like silk. Looking at his side, darker and lighter circles appeared on his back and thighs. What a tail, and what a mane he had, both so thick and long! His hoofs were like steel, his broad breast inhaled the air like bellows. His eyes were those of a sea-eagle. He not only saw at a distance, but in the mist, in the whirling snow, and in the dark. But of even greater worth than his strength and his beauty was his noble nature. He was proud. A blow from a whip was an insult that drove him nearly frantic. He was docile with all his strength, loving with all his spirit. And what a grateful heart he had! How he would rub his velvety muzzle on Christian's arm when he offered him salt and bread, oats, or a bit of sugar. This animal was better than many a human being, certainly better than his disobedient daughter and his ungrateful son-in-law. Had anybody ever seen Jalo shy? Never—he would not fear Satan himself. Had he ever stumbled? Never, no matter how steep might be the descent of the hill. Everybody was obliged to admit that Jalo was the finest animal in all Finland. His equal could scarcely be found in Russia. When Christian's debts weighed heavily upon him, when Moloch opened his jaws and demanded fresh sacrifices,

Christian went to the stable, curried his Jalo, blackened his hoofs, braided his mane, and patted his back. And he always felt lighter-hearted.

When Jegor Timofitsch's demands had gone far beyond Christian's powers to meet, and he saw no way of shaking off this vampire, he harnessed Jalo into a light sleigh and set off for Wiborg, to consult a distinguished lawyer. He could not believe that Jegor had written things down correctly. His poor little purchases, some tobacco and grain, coffee and sugar, could never amount to so large a sum. Something was surely wrong, and there was Jegor's usurious interest into the bargain!

How vividly he remembered that journey. It was a clear, cold day in January. The snow lay on the fields and meadows as smooth and level as the surface of the lake. The shadows of the fences, hayricks, and rollers lay like blue spots upon the white surface. The snow-birds hopped across the road, and the magpies chattered joyously as they ran up and down the fences. Sipi, the bear-dog, with pointed ears and woolly tail, dashed at full gallop before Jalo, who with a dainty movement of his hoofs, as if it were mere play, rushed forward at lightning speed. It was all so cheering that Christian's depression began to pass away. He had almost reached the Papula quarter, when suddenly he heard some one calling and shouting. Taking the pipe from his mouth, he leaned out of the sleigh and looked behind him. A man in a little racing sleigh was following at full gallop, waving his hand in its fur-edged gauntlet glove. Chris-

tian stopped, and the traveler, a short, stout man
dressed in furs, driving a mouse-colored horse, soon
reached him.

"Good morning, Landlord. That *is* a trotter you
have!" he said eagerly, biting his frozen mustache.
"To tell the truth, I've been driving behind you at
least a quarter of an hour without being able to over-
take you. Where did you get the animal? What is
his pedigree? How old is he? Just look at that chest
and those thighs!"

The stranger left his sleigh as he spoke to examine
Jalo more closely. Christian was pleased and proud,
answered to the best of his ability, and praised the
horse to the newcomer, who seemed to be perfectly
delighted with him.

"Well, of course, you'll come to the trotting races
day after to-morrow. As the owner of an animal like
yours, it's your duty to do it. I am Captain T., one
of the judges. Remember the first prize is a thousand
marks."

Christian had already heard of the races and even
thought of them; but in the country people usually
learn facts only after they have occurred. But now
—why not, since he was already in the city?

Christian promised to come, and the men clasped
hands on the agreement. Jalo, who was already impatient to go on, vanished from the Captain's admiring
gaze beyond the next hill like a streak of lightning.

Christian entered his horse for the races. What
glorious days, what a season of triumph and honor
for Jalo and his master! There was not a newspaper

in the whole country which did not mention Jalo and
his owner.   Telegrams announcing the horse's wonderful deeds flew from city to city.   His victory was
extraordinary; he carried off the first prize, outstrip-
ping famous old trotters.   Even now, as Christian
sat depressed and sorrowful in his entry, a bright
smile flitted over his face as he recalled that glorious
time.   How distinctly everything rose before his mind:
the golden sunlight, the blue sky, the light snow-
flakes carried by the winter wind, the music and the
cheering, the heating drinks, and Jalo, the hero of the
day.   It had undoubtedly been the brightest and hap-
piest of his life.   But as the highest surges sink the
lowest, and the tallest pine trees cast the longest shadows, it also happened that the day when Jalo and his
master reached the giddy heights of joy was followed
by very sad consequences.

Nothing favorable was obtained from the lawyer.
Instead of encouraging counsel he informed Christian
that Jegor had already obtained the final judgment
from the Governor.   Christian's debt must be paid,
principal and interest.   There was no resource except
to sell Jalo, and even that would not completely cover
the amount.   Christian drank till he was completely
dazed, wept, sobered up again, and, during all these
varying moods, constantly tried to raise the price.   At
last the bargain had to be closed.   Jalo was sold to
a Russian merchant, and Christian returned home,
deeply saddened and frantic with rage, driving a mare
which he detested from the first moment.   It was small
consolation that his pocketbook was stuffed with hun-

dred-mark notes, the farewell gift Jalo's victory had brought to his master.

Christian was inconsolable, and it seemed downright madness to pay Jegor so much good money. It was just like throwing it into the sea. But at last he was obliged to make up his mind to it, and went to Jegor's shop at an hour when he was sure of finding him alone, paid his debt, and received his note and other papers. Jegor was incautious enough to let some offensive words escape his lips, and nothing more was required to bring Christian's repressed fury to utterance. If the former had never known before what a drubbing means, he understood it when his neighbor left the shop. From that day there was the bitterest enmity between the two men.

Christian was free; but though he bragged of it in Jegor's hearing, his heart bled. What did he care for liberty without Jalo? True, he had escaped an impending danger, but in exchange had sacrificed all the happiness of his life. Existence had lost all charm for him; he had no more debts to trouble him, but also no Jalo to love. The occasional notices of the animal which he read in the newspapers were like salt in an open wound. "The famous trotter Jalo, that won the first prize at Wiborg, has again covered himself with glory," or "the well-known trotter Jalo has again carried off a prize at the races at Savastehus." On such days Christian was like a madman. Either he sat sullen and silent like a chaffinch in the rain, or he was angry and irritable, blazing out at the least provocation like Juniper in the flames.

Gradually the resolution to get possession of Jalo again at any cost became fixed in his mind. What was the use of saving and gathering to spend his life in joyless longing? His daughter and son-in-law were waiting impatiently for his death, that they might inherit his property. He had no grandchildren, so, as matters stood, the best thing he could do would be to try to get possession of Jalo once more.

After much difficulty, he found bondsmen, and pledged his land. Now he need only secure the money, and then set off to bargain for the horse. Even in the worst case, it could not be "dearer than gold."[2] His present owner in Wiborg had many horses, and would surely be willing to give up Jalo for a satisfactory price. The day of his departure was already fixed when one beautiful morning in July, just as Christian was in the act of removing a few stubbly gray hairs from his chin, he heard a familiar neigh. There was no mistake; it must be Jalo, that was just the way he always called his master when he went into his stable late in the morning. Christian threw down the razor and rushed out. There behind the corner of his own stable, to which Jegor's pasture extended, stood Jalo with dilated nostrils, tossing his head up and down. In a second he flew over the fence, and stood upon the ground of his former owner. Christian felt as though he was paralyzed in every limb. He could only utter a gasp of astonishment. A joyful smile flitted over his face like sunshine over the moorland, while all the tales of witchcraft he had overheard

---

[2] A Finnish proverb.

flashed through his excited brain. While he still stood there, rubbing his eyes, to convince himself that he was not dreaming, Jegor, his enemy, entered the yard, bridle and whip in hand. "The horse belongs to me," he said; "beware of luring him here."

Jegor seized Jalo by the lock of hair on his forehead, put on the bridle, and, swearing violently, protested that he would cure him of leaping the fence. Poor Jalo was roughly dragged away to his own barn, and after a time Christian heard the horse snorting and stamping under the blows of Jegor's whip. To beat Jalo, to abuse such an animal—who ever heard of such a thing?

From that day Christian's life was a hell. To be compelled to do without the horse was torture enough, but to know that it was in the hands of his worst enemy, that he could never own it again, to see it daily without being able to go near it, was far worse. Everything that Jegor could think of to do to the horse in Christian's presence to torment him he conscientiously did. Every blow he had himself received he returned to Jalo. And when, as sometimes happened, the horse came dashing at a gallop to his old master, as if seeking protection, Christian could be certain that thick wales on Jalo's sides would show how Jegor Timofitsch rewarded faithful friendship.

Several weeks passed in this way. It was a hot August day when the baked clods of earth cracked with the heat, and the air quivered and shimmered under the burning sunshine. Even the village dogs had stopped barking and fled to the shade under steps and outbuildings. The cows stood knee-deep in the water beneath the shelter of the dark alders. Only the gnats enjoyed the fierce heat of the sun; the dragon-flies flew through the air in shimmering circles. Christian lay stretched on the wooden bench in his house watching Jalo with burning eyes as he stood opposite to him in Jegor's meadow in the shade of a gnarled old elm. Christian was dreaming of the happy days when Jalo still belonged to him. How insignificant appeared the troubles of those times, and how great their joys. He was just falling into a light slumber when he was roused by three huntsmen from Wiborg inquiring eagerly for the landlord. They had been in pursuit of hares when they unexpectedly encountered a lynx engaged in the same chase. For two days they had followed the trail of the wild beast, which became greatly exhausted, when unluckily their dog hurt its paw and had to be left behind. The hunters now asked where they could borrow one to continue the chase. Christian owned such a dog. His Sipi could be used to track sea-fowl, hares, and bears. The gen-tlemen, accompanied by Christian and Sipi, hurried back to the moor where they had last seen the trail of the lynx. Within fifteen minutes Sipi found it and, amid joyous barking and waving of his bushy tail, ran toward the woods. Soon furious baying an-nounced that the lynx was either caught or had climbed a tree. When the hunters reached the spot, Sipi was executing a wild war-dance around a pine tree, on whose boughs lay the wild beast, gnashing its teeth at its enemy. With ears laid back smoothly against its head, and eyes glittering with rage, it seemed on the point of leaping down on its shaggy foe. But before determining to commence the fray, it fell under the bullet of the first of the approaching hunters. Its paws were bound together, a pole thrust through them, and it was carried in triumph back to Christian's farm. There the weary men ate a country luncheon, and celebrated their luck thoroughly by consuming plenty of brandy and rum. The heating drinks went to their heads, and by twilight Christian and his guests had become very excited and garrulous.

"Listen to me, Christian," said his wife, who was made somewhat anxious by the noisy company, "I won't have any loaded guns in the house; go and fire the bullets out of those barrels."

Christian rose slowly, remarking that women were always great cowards; took the guns from the bench, and went out. Daylight was failing, but darkness had not yet closed in; the perfume of new-mown clover drifted in on the breeze. From the distance echoed the notes of the cowherds' horns, and the crickets were chirping loudly in the courtyard.

Christian staggered down the steps. Suddenly he stopped. There by the corner of the stable again stood the dream of his nights and the longings of his days. Jalo raised his delicately formed head, shook his floating mane, and uttered a low, mysterious neigh, as if calling his former master.

Christian went to him and patted his neck. The animal put his velvety nozle over the low fence into Christian's pocket. The latter, deeply moved, threw

his arm over the horse's neck. It was so long since
he had caressed Jalo, stroked his soft skin, and spoken
to him. While thus passing his hand along the beautiful creature's back, he suddenly felt the wales of
Jegor's lashes. The blood surged hotly in his veins.
"Miserable brute," he muttered, shaking his fist sav-
agely at Jegor's house. "My poor friend, I'll free you
forever from his whip, his cruelty, and tyranny."
Almost before he himself was aware what he was
doing, he had snatched the gun from his shoulder—
one shot, and the noble creature fell moaning; one
sorrowful glance from the glazing eyes, and Jalo lay
lifeless behind the fence which separated him from his
former owner. Christian fled into the forest like a
murderer. Half an hour later he returned to his home
perfectly sober. The hunters had gone to look for
their dog. He was alone with his wife. Deeply agitated, he told her what he had done.

"Well, what do you mean to do?" asked Christian's
wife when her husband returned late in the evening
from Laurikamen's. "There are no witnesses."

"No, there are no witnesses; but whatever they may
do to me, I will tell them at any rate the whole story
of Jalo."

THE PLAGUE AT BERGAMO

BY JENS PETER JACOBSEN

Jacobsen is now considered to be the supreme Danish exponent of the artistic creed of the great critic Brandes, and next to Brandes the most potent influence among his country's writers of fiction. He was born in 1847 and died in 1885. In his youth he followed the methods and style of Hans Andersen. In later years he studied natural science with conspicuous success and became absorbed in the theories of Darwin. Later still he found his permanent way into literature with that wonderful story "Mogens," said to be the first specimen of realistic fiction in Denmark. Jacobsen's great aim seems to be the reconciliation of man's psychological sensations with his psychological surroundings. He is a true scientist and a true poet.

THE PLAGUE AT BERGAMO

BY JENS PETER JACOBSEN

OLD BERGAMO lay up there at the top of a steeply mountain encircled by walls and towers. New Bergamo lay below at the foot of the mountain, exposed to every wind that blows.

In the new town the plague broke out and wrought havoc indescribable. Many died, and the rest fled across the plains to every point of the compass. The men of Old Bergamo set fire to the deserted town, to disinfect the air. In vain. Men began to die on the mountain, also; at first one a day, then five, then ten, then a dozen.

There were many who sought to escape, but they could not flee as those in the new town had done; they lived like hunted beasts, hiding in tombs, under bridges, behind hedges, and in the tall grass of the green fields. For the peasants stoned all strangers from their hearths, or beat them as they would mad dogs, cruelly, pitilessly — in self-protection, as they thought, for the first fugitives had brought with them the pestilence into their houses.

So the people of Old Bergamo were as prisoners in their own town. Day by day the sun blazed hotter, and day by day the terrible infection carried off more victims.

In the very beginning, when the plague came among

THE PLAGUE AT BERGAMO

BY JENS PETER JACOBSEN

OLD BERGAMO lay up there at the top of a squatty mountain encircled by walls and towers. New Bergamo lay below at the foot of the mountain, exposed to every wind that blows.

In the new town the plague broke out and wrought havoc indescribable. Many died, and the rest fled across the plains to every point of the compass. The men of Old Bergamo set fire to the deserted town, to disinfect the air. In vain. Men began to die on the mountain, also; at first one a day, then five, then ten, then a dozen.

There were many who sought to escape, but they could not flee as those in the new town had done; they lived like hunted beasts, hiding in tombs, under bridges, behind hedges, and in the tall grass of the green fields. For the peasants stoned all strangers from their hearths, or beat them as they would mad dogs, cruelly, pitilessly — in self-protection, as they thought, for the first fugitives had brought with them the pestilence into their houses.

So the people of Old Bergamo were as prisoners in their own town. Day by day the sun blazed hotter, and day by day the terrible infection carried off more victims.

In the very beginning, when the plague came among

(583)

them, they bound themselves together in unity and peace, and had taken care to decently bury the dead, and had kindled great fires in the markets and open places, so that the purging fumes might be blown through the streets. Juniper and vinegar had been given to the poor. Above all they had gone to church, early and late, singly and in processions; each day they lifted their voices in prayer. As the sun sank behind the mountains the church bells tolled their dirge from a hundred hanging mouths. Days were set aside for fasting, and the relics were placed upon the altars.

At last, in their extremity, amid the blare of trumpets and tubas, they proclaimed the Holy Virgin forevermore Podesta of the city.

All this was of no help. And when the people saw that nothing could aid them, that Heaven either would not or could not send them relief, they did not fold their hands together and say, "God's will be done." It was as if sin, growing by a secret, stealthy sickness, had flared into an evil, open, raging pestilence, stalking hand in hand with the body's disease, the one to kill their souls, even as the other defiled their flesh —so incredible were their deeds, so monstrous their cruelty.

"Let us eat to-day, for to-morrow we die!" It was as if this theme, set to music, were played in an endless, devilish symphony on instruments without number. The most unnatural vices flourished among them. Even such rare arts as necromancy, sorcery, and devil worship became familiar to them; for there were many who sought from the powers of hell that protection which Providence had not been willing to accord them. Everything that suggested charity and sympathy had vanished; each thought only of himself. If a beggar, faint with the first delirium of the plague, fell in the street, he was driven from door to door with sharp weapons and with stones. From the dead that lay rotting in the houses, and from the bodies hastily buried in the earth, arose a sickening stench that mingled with the heavy air of the streets, and drew ravens and crows hither in swarms and in clouds, so that the walls and housetops were black with them. And about the town walls great strange birds perched here and there—birds that came from afar, with rapacious beaks and talons expectantly curved; and they sat and stared with their quiet, hungry eyes as if awaiting the moment when the doomed town would be reduced to a heap of carrion.

Eleven weeks had passed since the plague had first broken out. Then the tower watchman and others who chanced to be on high ground perceived a singular procession winding from the plains into the narrow streets of the new town, between the smoke-blackened stone walls and the charred frames of houses. A great throng! Assuredly six hundred and more, men and women, young and old. Some among them bore large, black crosses, and some held above their heads broad banners, red as blood and fire. They sang as they marched, and strange, despairingly plaintive melodies rose in the still, oppressively hot air.

Brown, gray, black, were the colors these people wore. Yet all had a red sign on their breasts. As they came nearer and nearer this was seen to be the sign of the cross. They crowded up the steep, stone-girt space that led to the old town. Their faces were as waves of white sea; they bore scourges in their hands; a rain of fire was painted on their banners. And in the surging mass the black crosses swung from side to side. Face after face plunged into the gloom of the tower gate and emerged into the light on the other side with blinking eyes.

Then the chant was taken up anew—a *miserere*. They grasped their scourges and marched even more sturdily than if their chant had been a battle song. Their aspect was that of a people who had come from a starving town. Their cheeks were sunken; their cheek-bones protruded; their lips were bloodless, and dark rings encircled their eyes. All the scourges were stained with blood.

With astonishment and uneasiness all Bergamo flocked together to gaze upon them. Red, bloated faces stood out against those that were pale; heavy, lust-weary eyes were lowered before the keen, flashing glances of the pilgrims; grinning, blasphemous mouths were struck dumb by these chants. The townspeople were spellbound.

But it was not long before the pall was shaken off. Some recognized among the cross-bearers a half-crazed cobbler of Brescia, and in a moment the procession became a butt of ridicule. Moreover, this was something new, a diversion from the monotony of every-day life, and as the strangers marched on to the cathedral, they were followed as a band of jugglers might be or as a tame bear is followed.

But soon anger seized the jostling crowd. It was clear that these cobblers and tailors had come to convert them, to pray, and to speak words that none wished to hear. Two gaunt, grizzled philosophers who had formulated blasphemy into a system incited the populace out of sheer wickedness of heart, so that the mob grew more threatening as the procession marched to the church, and more fiercely enraged. Bergamo was about to lay hands on these singular, scourge-bearing tailors. Not a hundred paces from the portal of the church a tavern opened its doors and a whole band of roisterers poured out, one on the shoulders of another. And they took their places at the head of the procession, singing and howling, assuming a mock-religious mien—all save one, who jerked his thumbs contemptuously toward the grass-grown steps of the church. Rough laughter then arose, and pilgrims and blasphemers entered the sanctuary in peace.

It was strange to be in that place again, to roam through the great cool nave, in air heavy with the stale fumes of snuffed wax tapers, over sunken flagstones so familiar to the foot, and over stones with their worn ornaments and polished inscriptions, in contemplation of which the mind had often grown so weary. And while the eye, half curiously, half involuntarily rested in the dim half-light of the vaults or strayed over the mellow gaudiness of dusty gold and grimy colors, or began to lose itself in the grotesque shadows of the apse, a kind of longing arose, not to be suppressed.

Meanwhile the tavern roisterers played their pranks

on the main altar itself.   A tall, strong young butcher
removed his white apron and wound it about his neck
so that it hung at his back like a cloak.   Thus arrayed,
he celebrated mass, with the wildest and most shocking words of sacrilege.   A small, elderly, round-bellied
fellow, lively and agile in spite of his fat, with the
face of a peeled pumpkin, played sexton and responded
with ribald songs; he made his genuflexions and turned
his back upon the altar, and rang his bell like a clown;
and the other tipplers, as they made their genuflexions, threw themselves flat on the ground and roared
with laughter, hiccuping drunkenly.

All within the church laughed, hooted, and jeered
at the strangers, and bade them notice how God was
esteemed in Old Bergamo.   Yet they wished not so
much to mock God as to rack the souls of these peni-
tents with their impiety.

In the centre of the nave the pilgrims halted and
groaned, such was their anguish.   Their blood boiled
with hate, and they thirsted for vengeance.   They
prayed to God, with hands and eyes uplifted, that He
might smite His blasphemers for the mockery offered
Him in His house.   Gladly would they perish with the
presumptuous infidels, if He would but show His
might; blissfully would they be crushed beneath His
feet, if He would but triumph, and if these godless
throats might be made to shriek in agony and despair.

They lifted up their voices in a *miserere*, each note
of which rang like a prayer for that rain of fire that
once swept over Sodom, for the strength that was
Samson's when he grasped the pillars of the Philistine

temple. They prayed with words and with song; they bared their shoulders and prayed with their scourges. Kneeling, row on row, stripped to the waist they whirled stinging, knotted cords over their backs.

Frantically they scourged, until the blood spurted under their hissing lashes. Each stroke was an offering to God. Stroke on stroke came down, until arms sank or were cramped into knots. Thus they lay, row on row, with frenzied look and foaming mouth, blood dripping from their bodies.

And those that saw this of a sudden felt their hearts beat, felt the blood mount to their temples, their breathing grow hard. Their knees shook. To be the slave of a powerful, stern divinity, to fling one's self at the feet of the Lord, to be His own, not in mute devotion, not in the mild inefficacy of prayer, but in a fury of passion, in the intoxication of self-humiliation, in blood and lamentation, and smitten with the moist, glistening tongues of scourges—this they could understand. Even the butcher held his peace; and the toothless philosophers bowed their grizzled heads.

Silence reigned in the church; only a gentle breathing passed through the multitude.

Then one of the strangers, a young friar, rose and spoke. His was the pallor of bloodless flesh; his black eyes glowed; and the sad lines of his mouth were as if cut with a knife in wood, and not mere furrows in a human face.

He lifted up his thin, suffering hands in prayer to Heaven, and the black sleeves of his gown slipped back from his lean arms.

Then he spoke—of hell, of its eternity, of the eternity of Heaven, of the solitary world of pain which each of the damned must suffer and must fill with his cries of agony. In that world were seas of sulphur, meadows of wasps, flames to be wrapped about them like a cloak, and hard flames that would pierce them like a probe twisting in a wound.

Breathlessly all listened to his words; for he spoke as if he had seen these things with his own eyes. And they asked themselves: "Is this man not one of the damned, sent to us from the mouth of hell, to testify?"

Then he preached long of the commandments and their rigor, of the need of obeying them to the very letter, and of the dire punishment that awaited him who sinned against them. " 'But Christ died for our sins,' ye say. 'We are no longer bound by the Word.' But I say that hell will not be cheated of one of you, and not one of the iron teeth of hell's wheel will your flesh escape. Ye build upon Calvary's cross? Come! Come and see it! I will lead you to its foot. It was on a Friday, as ye know, when they cast Him from their gates and laid the heavier end of a cross upon His shoulders and suffered Him to bear it to a barren and naked hill without the city; and they walked beside Him and stirred up the dust with their feet, so that it rested over them like a red cloud. And they tore His garments from Him, even as the lords of justice strip a criminal before all eyes, that all might see His body. And they threw Him down upon His cross, and stretched Him upon it, and drove an iron nail through each of His unresistant hands and a nail through His crossed feet. And they raised the cross in a hole dug in the earth; but it would stand neither firm nor upright. So they shook it and drove wedges and blocks around it. And those that did this turned down the brims of their hats so that the blood of His hands might not drip into their eyes.

"And He from on high looked down upon the soldiers casting dice for His seamless coat, and down upon all the howling mob for whose salvation He suffered. Not one tearful eye was there in all the multitude. And those who were below looked up at Him, hanging from the cross, suffering, and faint. They read the inscription above His head: 'King of the Jews,' and they mocked Him and called up to Him: 'Thou that destroyest the temple, and buildest it in three days, save Thyself. If Thou be the Son of God, come down from the cross.'

"Then God's noble Son waxed wroth and saw that these were unworthy of salvation, this mob that swarmed over the earth; and He wrenched His feet from the nail, and He clenched His fingers and tore His hands away, so that the arms of the cross bent as a bow. And He leaped to the earth and caught up His garment, so that the dice rolled over the precipice of Golgotha, and threw it about His person with the righteous wrath of a king, and ascended into heaven. And the cross stood bare; and the great work of atonement remained unfulfilled. No mediator stands between us and God. No Jesus died for us on the cross! No Jesus died for us on the cross!"

He ceased.

As he uttered the last words he bent toward the multitude and with his lips and hands flung his words, as it were, upon their heads. A groan of fear ran through the church. Sobs could be heard.

Then the butcher with uplifted, threatening hands, pallid as a corpse, stepped forward and commanded:

"Monk, nail Him to the cross again, nail Him—!"

And from all lips, pleadingly, threateningly, a storm of voices rolled to the vault above: "Crucify Him!"

But the monk looked down upon these fluttering, uplifted hands, upon these distorted faces with the dark openings of their screaming mouths, from which the teeth flashed like those of tormented beasts of prey; and in the ecstasy of the moment he extended his arms toward Heaven, and laughed. Then he descended; and his people raised the banners of the fiery rain and their plain, black crosses and pushed out of the church. Once more they marched, singing, across the marketplace, and once more they passed through the mouth of the tower gate.

And the people of Old Bergamo stared after them, as they proceeded down the mountain. The steep, wall-girt road was obscured in the uncertain light of the setting sun, and the procession could be only half seen in the glare. Their huge crosses, swaying in the crowd from side to side, cast sharp, black shadows on the glowing walls of the town.

In the distance a chant could be heard. A banner or two gleamed red from the charred site of the new town, and the pilgrims vanished into the bright plain.

KAREN

BY ALEXANDER LANGE KIELLAND

Kielland, son of a rich and aristocratic merchant, was born at Stavanger, Norway, in 1849. He studied law in Christiania, but preferred the management of a brick and tile kiln. His appointment as burgomaster of Stavanger in 1891 cut short a brilliant poetical career, and he turned to prose. The autobiographical "Garman and Worse" soon gave the public such a series of Norwegian peasant pictures that he was acclaimed one of the four great Norwegians, with Ibsen, Björnson, and Lie.

Kielland's "novelettes," or short stories, pictures of prince and peasant, are universally acknowledged to be his best work. They are modeled after the French realists, especially Daudet, as may be seen in "Karen." He is always protesting against the conventional religion and smug optimism of the conservative class. His style, though frequently lacking in force, is graceful in form and full of biting satire and fresh humor, and his subjects are always well chosen and artistically worked out.

KAREN

BY ALEXANDER KIELLAND

THERE was once upon a time in Krarup, an Inn a maiden named Karen. She attended to the serving of the guests herself, for the landlady lived among her pots and pans in the kitchen. And many people came to Krarup Inn—neighbors who collected there when the autumn evenings began to darken and sat in the warm room, and drank unlimited quantities of coffee punch. Travelers and wanderers, too, who came in blue with cold, stamping their feet and calling for something hot, that would enable them to reach the next station.

Karen went about silently, without haste, serving each in his turn. She was small and delicate, only a child, earnest and reserved, and the young fellows did not notice her. But she was very dear to the older customers, to whom a visit to the Inn was an event of importance. She prepared their coffee quickly, and served it seven times hot. When she moved about among the guests with her water, the burly, coarsely dressed men stood aside and made place for her, and every one looked admiringly after her. Karen had great, gray eyes that took in everything, and seemed to look far, far away, and her eyebrows were arched in surprise and wonder. Strangers—

Translated by Leonora Tallor. Copyright, 1896, by The Current Literature Publishing Company.

KAREN

BY ALEXANDER KIELLAND

THERE was once upon a time in Kraruper Inn a maiden named Karen. She attended to the serving of the guests herself, for the landlady lived among her pots and pans in the kitchen. And many people came to Kraruper Inn—neighbors who collected there when the autumn evenings began to darken and sat in the warm room, and drank unlimited quantities of coffee punch. Travelers and wanderers, too, who came in blue with cold, stamping their feet and calling for something hot, that would enable them to reach the next station.

Karen went about silently, without haste, serving each in his turn. She was small and delicate, only a child, earnest and reserved, and the young fellows did not notice her. But she was very dear to the older customers, to whom a visit to the Inn was an event of importance. She prepared their coffee quickly, and served it seven times hot. When she moved about among the guests with her waiter the burly, coarsely dressed men stood aside and made place for her, and every one looked admiringly after her. Karen had great, gray eyes that took in everything, and seemed to look far, far away, and her eyebrows were arched in surprise and wonder. Strangers

Translated by Leonora Teller. Copyright, 1898, by The Current Literature Publishing Company.

thought she did not understand their orders; but Karen heard it all, and made never a mistake. She had a way all her own, whether she gazed off into the distance, or listened, or waited, or dreamed. The west wind blew strong; it threw up long, heavy waves from the west sea. Salt and damp, with froth and foam it threw them on the sands. But when the wind reached Kraruper Inn it had only strength enough left to tear open the stable door, and then that which connected the kitchen with the stable. It burst in, filled the space, swung the lantern that hung from the roof back and forth; tore off the hostler's cap and rolled it out into the darkness; threw the horses' blankets over their heads, and finally blew a white hen from her perch into the water trough. The hen squawked frightfully, the hostler swore, the chickens cackled. The kitchen was full of smoke; the horses grew restless and beat sparks of fire from the stones with their hoofs. Even the ducks which were gathered quacking together near the manger to be at hand when the oats were scattered, began to chatter, and through it all the wind roared fearfully. At last two men came out of the inn parlor and, putting their broad backs against the door, pushed it shut, while a shower of sparks rained from their pipes over their dark beards. Having done all the mischief possible the wind fled back over the plain, crossed the great pond, and shook the mail coach that rolled majestically along about half a mile from the inn.

"What terrible haste he always makes to reach Kraruper Inn," muttered the postilion, Anders, crack-

ing his whip over the smoking horses. For the twen-
tieth time the conductor had let down the window to
call to him. At first it had been a friendly invitation
to take a coffee punch with him, then little by little
the good-nature disappeared. Finally the window
went down with a bang, and remarks far from con-
ciliating were showered on driver and horses.

The wind swept low on the ground, and long, mysterious sighs murmured through the heather bushes.
The moon was full, but thick clouds obscured its light.
Behind Kraruper Inn lay the gloomy moor, covered
by black heaps of peat and deep, treacherous holes.
And between the heather bushes wound a strip of
grass that looked like a path, but it was no path, for
it came to a sudden end at the brink of a hole deeper
than the others, and filled with water. In the grass
a sleek fox crouched and waited, and a hare hopped
softly over the plain. The fox could reckon with certainty that the hare would not make a long circuit
so late in the evening. He stretched out a cautious
nose, and, as he sniffed in the direction of the wind
and sought a secure post of observation, he thought
how wise foxes always were and how stupid the hares.

Yonder in the inn there was an unusual commotion.
A couple of traveling men had ordered roast hare.
The landlord had gone to an auction at Thisted, and
his wife was used only to the responsibilities of her
kitchen. Now it happened unfortunately that the Advocate would speak with the host on business, and
because he was not at home the good woman must
listen to a long speech and take charge of an impor-

tant letter, a proceeding that sadly disturbed her composure. A stranger, who was waiting for a bottle of soda water, stood by the stove in greasy sailor clothes. Two fish pedlers had three times ordered brandy for their coffee. The stable boy stood with an empty lantern and waited for a candle, and a tall, rough farmer followed Karen with longing eyes—she owed him change for a crown he had just given her. Karen came and went without haste, without error. One would hardly imagine she could attend to so many things at once. The great eyes and the high arched brows were full of wonder and expectation. The fine little head was held straight and still. If she would make no mistakes she must keep her thoughts collected. Her blue woolen dress was too small for her. The tight neckband wrinkled her flesh just under the hair. "The maiden from Agger has a white skin," said one fish pedler to the other. They were young people and spoke of Karen as connoisseurs.

Some one stood near the window, and looking at the clock said: "The post is early to-night." It rattled over the pavement, the doors were thrown open, and the wind blew the smoke from the stove. Karen entered from the kitchen just as the conductor stepped into the door and greeted the company with a hearty "Good evening!" He was a tall, handsome man, with dark eyes, a crisp brown beard framed his face, and curly brown hair covered his small head. His long heavy mantle of beautiful red royal Danish cloth was trimmed with black fur, and hung from his shoulders. The entire light of the two dim paraffin lamps that were suspended from the wall over the table centred itself on this spot of glorious crimson, as if it loved it, and left all the black and gray of the room to grow still grayer and blacker. And the tall figure with the fine, dark curly head, the long folds of the crimson cloak shone like a very marvel of splendor and color.

Karen came in quickly from the kitchen with her waiter. She bent her head so no one could see her face, as she hastened from one guest to the other. She set the roast hare before the fish pedlers, and brought the commercial traveler, who sat in an adjacent room, the bottle of soda water. She gave the anxious farmer a tallow candle, and, slipping to the stranger by the stove, she thrust the change from the crown in his hand.

The hostess was in the deepest despair. Everything had gone wrong in her kitchen. She had lost the advocate's letter, and boundless confusion filled the inn. The traveler pounded the table with the bell loudly; the fish pedlers laughed until they were half dead over the hares spread before them; the bewildered farmer tapped the landlady on the shoulder with the candle and puffed himself out like a turkey cock.

And amid all this maddening confusion Karen had disappeared. The postilion Anders sat on the driver's seat; the stable boy stood ready to open the door; the travelers in the mail coach were impatient and so were the horses, although they had nothing pleasant to look forward to, and the wind still rattled and whistled through the stable. At last the conductor, whom they all awaited, came. He carried his mantle over his arm as he stepped into the coach and excused his delay with a few curt words. He laughed to himself as he drew his cloak about him and took his seat. The door was closed; the mail coach rolled on. Anders let the horses trot gently, now there was no more need of haste. From time to time he glanced slyly at the conductor, who still laughed to himself, while the wind ruffled his hair. The postilion laughed, too. He suspected something. The wind followed the coach to a turn in the road, then threw itself again over the plain and sighed mysteriously through the heather bushes.

The fox lay at his post. All was ready now, the hare must soon come. Yonder at the inn harmony was restored, the anxious farmer was relieved of his candle, and received his change, and the travelers consumed their hare. The hostess complained a little, but she did not blame Karen. No one in all the world had ever scolded Karen. Quietly, unconsciously she hastened from one to the other, and the serene satisfaction that always followed her footsteps spread through the cozy half-dark inn parlor.

The two fish pedlers that had ordered a second cup of cognac and coffee, to follow the first, were specially pleased with her. A soft pink flush rested on her pale cheek, the glimmer of a smile on her lip, and once when she raised her eyes their light was dazzling. When she felt the men's eyes followed her she went into the next room where the travelers sat, pretending that she wanted some teaspoons from the cupboard. "Did you notice the conductor?" asked one of them.

"No; not till he went out. He left very quickly," answered the other with his mouth full of roast hare.

"A devilish handsome fellow. I attended his wedding."

"So, is he married?"

"Yes, indeed; his wife is the daughter of the landlord at Ulstrup, and I got there the night of the wedding. That was a jolly time, I assure you. They have two children, I believe."

Karen dropped the teaspoons and went out. She heard nothing that was called after her from the inn. She went across the court to her room and began mechanically to make her bed. Her eyes stared into the darkness. She pressed her hands to her head, to her breast; she groaned. She could comprehend nothing—nothing! She heard the landlady's complaining voice: "Karen, dear Karen!" it called. She ran out across the court, behind the inn, across the moor.

The winding strip of grass glimmered in the half-light as if it were a path, but it was no path. No one dared to follow it, for it led abruptly to the brink of the great pond. The hare quickened his steps. He heard a rustling. He gave long jumps as if he were mad to escape; not knowing what he feared, he fled over the plain. The fox stretched out his sharp nose and stared in surprise at the hare. He had heard nothing. According to the instincts of his kind he had crouched there in the hollow—he was conscious of no error. He could not understand the action of the hare. He stood long with outstretched head and slinking body. His bushy tail was hid by the heather bushes, and he began to wonder if foxes were getting duller or hares wiser. But when the west wind had run its long course it turned into a north wind, and then into an east wind, and then into the south wind, and at last came back over the sea as the west wind again, threw itself upon the dunes, and long, mysterious sighs moaned through the heather bushes.

But there were wanting in Kraruper Inn two wondering gray eyes, a little blue woolen gown that had grown too small, and the hostess complained more than ever. She could not understand it at all. No one could understand it, save the postilion Anders, and one other!

LOVE AND BREAD

BY JEAN AUGUST STRINDBERG

Strindberg, renovator of the literary language of Sweden, one of the most conspicuous, prolific, and versatile of the newer realists of that country, was born in 1849, at Stockholm. In spite of early struggles he obtained an education at Upsala, and eventually the post of Orientalist at the Royal Library.

It was his "Red Room," written in 1879, that is supposed to have introduced naturalism into Swedish literature; at any rate, it helped the author to his first literary honors. It is a picture of Stockholm bohemianism, a satire on all artistic hypocrisy, as his later book, "The New Kingdom," was a satire on social hypocrisy that raised a scandal which drove him abroad for a while.

Strindberg has formulated no philosophy, but he is thought to be an atheist, a misogynist, and has more than once proved himself an enemy to all tyranny of the majority. His books breathe violence, sarcasm, melancholy. And as such Strindberg appears in "Love and Bread."

LOVE AND BREAD

BY AUGUST STRINDBERG

WHEN young Gustaf Falk, the assistant councilor, made his ceremonial proposal for Louise's hand to her father, the old gentleman's first question was: "How much are you earning?"

"Not more than a hundred kroner[1] a month. But Louise—"

"Never mind the rest," interrupted Falk's prospective father-in-law; "you don't earn enough."

"Oh, but Louise and I love each other so dearly! We are so sure of one another."

"Very likely. However, let me ask you: is twelve hundred a year the sum total of your resources?"

"We first became acquainted at Lidingö."

"Do you make anything beside your government salary?" persisted Louise's parent.

"Well, yes, I think we shall have sufficient. And then, you see, our mutual affection—"

"Yes, exactly; but let's have a few figures."

"Oh," said the enthusiastic suitor, "I can get enough by doing extra work!"

"What sort of work? And how much?"

"I can give lessons in French, and also translate. And then I can get some proofreading."

---

[1] A krone is worth about twenty-eight cents.

"How much translation?" queried the elder, pencil in hand.

"I can't say exactly, but at present I am translating a French book at the rate of ten kroner per folio."

"How many folios are there altogether?"

"About a couple of dozen, I should say."

"Very well. Put this at two hundred and fifty kroner. Now, how much else?"

"Oh, I don't know. It's a little uncertain."

"What, you are not certain, and you intend to marry? You seem to have queer notions of marriage, young man! Do you realize that there will be children, and that you will have to feed and clothe them, and bring them up?"

"But," objected Falk, "the children may not come so very soon. And we love each other so dearly, that—"

"That the arrival of children may be prophesied quite safely." Then, relenting, Louise's father went on:

"I suppose you are both set on marrying, and I don't doubt but what you are really fond of each other. So it seems as though I should have to give my consent after all. Only make good use of the time that you are engaged to Louise by trying to increase your income."

Young Falk flushed with joy at this sanction, and demonstratively kissed the old man's hand. Heavens, how happy he was—and his Louise, too! How proud they felt the first time they went out walking together arm in arm, and how everybody noticed the radiant happiness of the engaged couple!

In the evenings he came to see her, bringing with

him the proof-sheets he had undertaken to correct.
This made a good impression on papa, and earned the
industrious young man a kiss from his betrothed. But
one evening they went to the theatre for a change, and
drove home in a cab, the cost of that evening's enter-
tainment amounting to ten kroner. Then, on a few
other evenings, instead of giving the lessons, he called
at the young lady's house to take her for a little walk.

As the day set for the wedding drew near, they had
to think about making the necessary purchases to furnish their flat. They bought two handsome beds of
real walnut, with substantial spring mattresses and
soft eiderdown quilts. Louise must have a blue quilt,
as her hair was blond. They, of course, also paid a
visit to the house-furnishers', where they selected a
lamp with a red shade, a pretty porcelain statuette of
Venus, a complete table service with knives, forks, and
fine glassware. In picking out the kitchen utensils
they were benefited by mama's advice and aid. It was
a busy time for the assistant councilor—rushing about
to find a house, looking after the workmen, seeing that
all the furniture was got together, writing out checks,
and what not.

Meanwhile it was perfectly natural that Gustaf
could earn nothing extra. But when they were once
married he would easily make it up. They intended
to be most economical—only a couple of rooms to start
with. Anyhow, you could furnish a small apartment
better than a large one. So they took a first-floor
apartment at six hundred kroner, consisting of two
rooms, kitchen, and larder. At first Louise said she

would prefer three rooms on the top landing. But
what did it matter, after all, so long as they sincerely
loved each other?

At last the rooms were furnished. The sleeping
chamber was like a small sanctuary, the beds standing
side by side like chariots taking their course along
life's journey. The blue quilts, the snowy sheets, and
the pillow-spreads embroidered with the young people's initials amorously intertwined, all had a bright
and cheerful appearance. There was a tall, elegant
screen for the use of Louise, whose piano—costing
twelve hundred kroner—stood in the other chamber,
which served as sitting-room, dining-room, and study,
in one. Here, too, stood a large walnut writing-desk
and dining-table, with chairs to match; a large gilt-
framed mirror, a sofa, and a bookcase added to the
general air of comfort and coziness.

The marriage ceremony took place on a Saturday
night, and late on Sunday morning the happy young
couple was still asleep. Gustaf rose first. Although
the bright light of day was peering in through the
shutters, he did not open them, but lit the red-shaded
lamp, which threw a mysterious rosy glow over the
porcelain Venus. The pretty young wife lay there
languid and content; she had slept well, and had not
been awakened—as it was Sunday—by the rumbling
of early market wagons. Now the church bells were
ringing joyfully, as if to celebrate the creation of man
and woman.

Louise turned over, while Gustaf retired behind the
screen to put on a few things. He went out into the

kitchen to order lunch. How dazzlingly the new copper and tin utensils gleamed and glistened! And all was his own—his and hers. He told the cook to go to the neighboring restaurant, and request that the lunch be sent in. The proprietor knew about it; he had received full instructions the day before. All he needed now was a reminder that the moment had come.

The bridegroom thereupon returns to the bedchamber and taps softly: "May I come in?"

A little scream is heard. Then: "No, dearest; just wait a minute!"

Gustaf lays the table himself. By the time the lunch arrives from the restaurant, the new plates and cutlery and glasses are set out on the fresh, white linen cloth. The bridal bouquet lies beside Louise's place. As she enters the room in her embroidered morning wrapper, she is greeted by the sunbeams. She still feels a little tired, so he makes her take an armchair, and wheels it to the table. A drop or two of liqueur enlivens her; a mouthful of caviar stimulates her appetite. Fancy what mama would say if she saw her daughter drinking spirits! But that's the advantage of being married, you know; then you can do whatever you please.

The young husband waits most attentively upon his fair bride. What a pleasure, too! Of course he has had good luncheons before, in his bachelor days; but what comfort or satisfaction had he ever derived from them? None. Thus he reflects while consuming a plate of oysters and a glass of beer. What numbskulls they are, those bachelors, not to marry! And how selfish! Why, there ought to be a tax on them, as on

dogs. Louise is not quite so severe, urging gently and
sweetly that perhaps the poor fellows who elect the
single state are subjects of pity. No doubt if they
could afford to marry, they would—she thinks. Gustaf feels a slight pang at his heart. Surely happiness
is not to be measured by money. No, no; but, but—
Well, never mind, there will soon be lots of work, and
then everything will run smoothly. For the present
there is this delicious roast partridge with cranberry
sauce to be considered, and the Burgundy. These
luxuries, together with some fine artichokes, cause the
young wife a moment's alarm, and she timidly asks
Gustaf if they can afford living on such a scale. But
Gustaf pours more wine into the glass of his little
Louise, reassuring her and softening those groundless
fears. "One day is not every day," he says; "and
people ought to enjoy life when they can. Ah, how
beautiful life is!"

At six o'clock an elegant carriage, with two horses,
pulls up before the door, and the bridal pair take a
drive. Louise is charmed as they roll along through
the park, reclining there so comfortably, while they
meet acquaintances on foot, who bow to them in obvi-
ous astonishment and envy. The assistant councilor
has made a good match, they must think; he has chosen
a girl with money. And they, poor souls, have to walk.
How much pleasanter to ride, without effort, leaning
against these soft cushions! It is symbolical of agreeable married life.

The first month was one of unceasing enjoyment—
balls, parties, dinners, suppers, theatres. Still, the time

they spent at home was really the best of all! It was
a delightful sensation to carry Louise off home, from
her parents, at night, when they would do as they
pleased under their own roof. Arriving at the flat,
they would make a little supper, and then they would
sit comfortably, chatting until a late hour. Gustaf was
all for economy—the theory of it, that is to say. One
day the young bride and housekeeper tried smoked
salmon with boiled potatoes. How she relished it, too!
But Gustaf demurred, and when smoked salmon day
came round again he invested in a brace of partridges.
These he bought at the market for a krone, exulting
over the splendid bargain, of which Louise did not
approve. She had once bought a pair for less money.
Besides, to eat game was extravagant. However, it
would not do to disagree with her husband about such
a trifling matter.

After a couple of months more Louise Falk became
strangely indisposed. Had she caught cold? Or had
she perchance been poisoned by the metal kitchen utensils? The doctor who was called in merely laughed,
and said it was all right—a queer diagnosis, to be sure,
when the young lady was seriously ailing. Perhaps
there was arsenic in the wall-paper. Falk took some
to a chemist, bidding him make a careful analysis.
The chemist's report stated the wall-paper to be quite
free from any harmful substance.

His wife's sickness not abating, Gustaf began to
investigate on his own account, his studies in a med-
ical book resulting in a certainty as to her ailment.
She took warm foot-baths, and in a month's time her

state was declared entirely promising. This was sudden—sooner than they had expected; yet how lovely to be papa and mama! Of course the child would be a boy—no doubt of that; and one must think of a name to give him. Meanwhile, though, Louise took her husband aside, and reminded him that since their marriage he had earned nothing to supplement his salary, which had proved far from sufficient. Well, it was true they had lived rather high, but now a change should be made, and everything would be satisfactory!

Next day the assistant councilor went to see his good friend the barrister, with a request that he indorse a promissory note. This would allow him to borrow the money that would be needed to meet certain unavoidable forthcoming expenses—as Falk made clear to his friend. "Yes," agreed the man of law, "marrying and raising a family is an expensive business. I have never been able to afford it."

Falk felt too much ashamed to press his request, and when he returned home, empty-handed, was greeted with the news that two strangers had been to the house, and had asked for him. They must be lieutenants in the army, thought Gustaf, friends belonging to the garrison of Fort Vaxholm. No, he was told, they could not have been lieutenants; they were much older-looking men. Ah, then they were two fellows he used to know in Upsala; they had probably heard of his marriage, and had come to look him up. Only the servant said they were not from Upsala, but were Stockholmers, and carried sticks. Mysterious—very; but no doubt they would come back.

Then the young husband went marketing again.
He bought strawberries—at a bargain, of course.

"Just fancy," he triumphantly exclaimed to his
housewife, "a pint of these large strawberries for a
krone and a half, at this time of year!"

"Oh, but Gustaf dear, we can't afford that sort of
thing!"

"Never mind, darling; I have arranged for some
extra work."

"But what about our debts?"

"Debts? Why, I'm going to make a big loan, and
pay them all off at once that way."

"Ah," objected Louise, "but won't this simply mean
a new debt?"

"No matter if it does. It will be a respite, you
know. But why discuss such unpleasant things?
What capital strawberries, eh, dear? And don't you
think a glass of sherry would go well now after the
strawberries?"

Upon which the servant was sent out for a bottle
of sherry—the best, naturally.

When Falk's wife awoke from her afternoon nap
on the sofa that day, she apologetically reverted to
the subject of debt. She hoped he would not be angry
at what she had to say. Angry? No, of course not.
What was it? Did she want some money for the
house? Louise explained:

"The grocer has not been paid, the butcher has
threatened us, and the livery-stable man also insists
on having his bill settled."

"Is that all?" replied the assistant councilor. "They

shall be paid at once—to-morrow—every farthing. But let's think of something else. How would you like to go out for a little drive to the park? You'd rather not take a carriage? All right, then, there's the tramway; that will take us to the park."

So they went to the park, and they had dinner in a private room at the Alhambra Restaurant. It was great fun, too, because the people in the general dining-room thought they were a frisky young pair of lovers. This idea amused Gustaf, though Louise seemed a trifle depressed, especially when she saw the bill. They could have had a good deal at home for that amount.

The months go by, and now arises the need for actual preparation—a cradle, infant's clothing, and so forth.

Falk has no easy time raising the money. The livery-stable man and the grocer refuse further credit, for they, too, have families to feed. What shocking materialism!

At length the eventful day arrives. Gustaf must secure a nurse, and even while holding his new-born daughter in his arms is called out to pacify his creditors. The fresh responsibilities weigh heavily upon him; he almost breaks down under the strain. He succeeds, it is true, in getting some translation to do, but how can he perform the work when at every touch and turn he is obliged to run errands? In this frame of mind he appeals to his father-in-law for help. The old gentleman receives him coldly:

"I will help you this once, but not again. I have little enough myself, and you are not my only child."

Delicacies must be provided for the mother, chicken and expensive wine. And the nurse has to be paid.

Fortunately, Falk's wife is soon on her feet again. She is like a girl once more, with a slender figure. Her pallor is quite becoming. Louise's father talks seriously to his son-in-law, however:

"Now, no more children, if you please, unless you want to be ruined."

For a brief space the junior Falk family continued to live on love and increasing debts. But one day bankruptcy knocked at the door. The seizure of the household effects was threatened. Then the old man came and took away Louise and her child, and as they rode off in a cab he made the bitter reflection that he had lent his girl to a young man, who had given her back after a year, dishonored. Louise would willingly have stayed with Gustaf, but there was nothing more to subsist upon. He remained behind, looking on while the bailiffs—those men with the sticks—denuded the flat of everything, furniture, bedding, crockery, cutlery, kitchen utensils, until it was stripped bare.

Now began real life for Gustaf. He managed to get a position as proofreader on a newspaper which was published in the morning, so that he had to work at his desk for several hours each night. As he had not actually been declared a bankrupt, he was allowed to keep his place in the government service, although he could hope for no more promotion. His father-in-law made the concession of letting him see his wife and child on Sundays, but he was never permitted to be alone with them. When he left, in the evening, to go to the newspaper office, they would accompany him to the gate, and he would depart in utter humiliation of soul. It might take him perhaps twenty years to pay off all his obligations. And then—yes, what then? Could he then support his wife and child? No, probably not. If, in the mean time, his father-in-law should die, they would be left without a home. So he must be thankful even to the hard-hearted old man who had so cruelly separated them.

Ah, yes, human life itself is indeed hard and cruel! The beasts of the field find maintenance easily enough, while of all created beings man alone must toil and spin. It is a shame, yes, it is a crying shame, that in this life everybody is not provided with gratuitous partridges and strawberries.

IRENE HOLM

BY HERMANN JOACHIM BANG

Bang was born in Seeland in 1858. During his sojourn among foreigners he has been at various times journalist, author, playwright, until he now stands first among Danish writers of the modern realistic school, for Drachmann can not be accounted to any school for any length of time.

Outside of his critical writings his works form a series of naturalistic romances and novels, showing a deep knowledge of the sad side of life, all the way from his first novel, called "Hopeless Struggle," published in 1880, to "Alive or Dead," published in 1900, including the very remarkable play, "Ellen Urne," and his short stories. "Irene Holm" is as inconclusive as life itself, and that is what it is intended to be; that is the author's conception of art when dealing with life.

IRENE HOLM

BY HERMANN BANG

ONE Sunday morning, after service, the bailiff's son announced to the gathering at the
meeting-stone outside the church that Miss
Irene Holm, dancer from the Royal Theatre in Copenhagen, would open a course for dancing and deport-
ment, for children, ladies, and gentlemen, if a sufficient number of subscribers could be found. The
lessons would begin the first of November, in the
inn, and the price would be five crowns for each child,
with a discount for several in the same family.

Seven names were signed. Jens Larsens put up his
three on the discount.

Miss Irene Holm considered the number sufficient.
She arrived toward the end of October, and stopped
in at the Inn with her only baggage, an old champagne
basket tied up with a cord. She was little and wearily
meagre in form, had a childish face with the lines of
forty years in it under her fur cap, and she wore old
handkerchiefs wrapped about her wrists, because of the
gout. She pronounced all the consonants most carefully, and said, "Oh, thank you, I can do it myself,"
for everything, looking very helpless the while. She
wanted nothing but a cup of tea, and then crept into
her bed in the tiny room, trembling in fear of ghosts.

Translated by Grace Isabel Colbron. Copyright, 1907, by P. F. Collier & Son.

Next morning she appeared with a head full of curls, her figure encased in a tight-fitting, fur-trimmed coat, much the worse for wear. She was going to call upon the parents of her pupils. She inquired the way timidly. Madam Henriksen came out to the door with her, and pointed over the fields. At every step Miss Holm bowed once in her gratitude. "Such a looking creature!" thought Madam Henriksen, and stood in the doorway looking out after her. Miss Holm walked toward Jens Larsens', choosing the dike path to save her shoes. Miss Holm was wearing leather shoes and fancy knit stockings.

When she had visited all the parents—Jens Larsens gave nine crowns for his three children—Miss Holm looked about for a place to live. She hired a tiny whitewashed room at the smith's, the window looking out over the level fields. The entire furnishing consisted of a bed, a bureau, and a chair. The champagne basket was placed between the bureau and the window.

Miss Holm moved into her new quarters. Her mornings were given up to busy handling of curling tongs and pins, and much drinking of cold tea. When her hair was dressed she tidied up her room, and then she knitted all the afternoon. She sat on her basket in the corner, trying to catch the last rays of light. The smith's wife would drop in, sit down on the chair and talk, Miss Holm listening with a pleasant smile and a graceful nod of her curly head.

The hostess spun out her stories until it was time for supper. But Miss Holm seldom knew what she had been talking about. With the exception of dance, and positions, and the calculation for one's daily bread —a tiresome, never-ending calculation—the things of this world seldom filtered into Miss Holm's brain. When left alone she sat silent on her basket, her hands in her lap, gazing at the narrow strip of light that came in under the door.

She never went out. The level, dreary fields made her homesick, and she was afraid of wild horses.

When evening came, she cooked her simple supper, and then busied herself with her curl papers. When she had divested herself of her skirts she practised her "pas" beside the bedpost, stretching her legs energetically. The smith and his wife clung to the keyhole during this proceeding. They could just see the high kicks from behind, and the curl papers standing up on the dancer's head like quills on a porcupine. She danced so eagerly that she began to hum gently as she hopped up and down in the little room, the whole family outside hugging the keyhole closely.

When Miss Holm had practised her accustomed time, she crept into bed. While she practised her thoughts would wander back to the time "when she was at dancing school." And she would suddenly laugh, a gentle, girlish laugh, as she lay still in the darkness. She fell asleep thinking of that time—that happy, merry time—the rehearsals, when they pricked each other in the calves with pins—and screamed so merrily— And then the evenings in the dressing-rooms, with the whir and tumult of voices, and the silence as the stage-manager's bell shrilled out— Miss Holm would wake up in a fright, dreaming that she had missed her entrance.

II

"Now, then—one—two"—Miss Irene Holm raised her skirt and put out her foot—"feet out—one—two —three—" The seven pupils toed in, and hopped about with their fingers in their mouths. "Here, little Jens—toes out—one, two, three—bow—one, two, three—now once more." Jens bowed, his tongue hanging out of his mouth. "Now, Maren, left—one, two, three; Maren turns to the right—once more—one, two, three—" Miss Holm sprang about like a kid, so that one could see long stretches of fancy stockings.

The dancing lessons were in full swing, and were held three times a week in the hall of the inn, under the two old lamps that hung from the beams. The long, undisturbed dust in the cold room whirled up under their feet. The seven pupils flew about wildly like a flock of magpies, Miss Holm straightening their backs and bending their arms. "One, two, three— *battement*—one, two, three—*battement*." The seven bobbed at "battement" and stepped out energetically.

The dust gathered in Miss Holm's throat as she called out her orders. Now the pupils were to dance a round dance in couples. They held their partners at arm's length, stiff-armed and embarrassed, and turned in sleepy circles. Miss Holm swung them around, with encouraging words. "Good—now around—four, five—turn again—good—" She took hold of Jens Larsen's second, and little Jette, and turned them as one would turn a top.

Jette's mother had come to look on. The peasant women would drop in for the lessons, their cap-bands tied in stiff bows, and sit motionless as wooden figures against the wall, without speaking a word even to each other. Miss Holm addressed them as "Madame," and smiled at them as she skipped about.

Now it was the turn of the lanciers. "Ladies to the right—good—now three steps to the left, Jette—good—" The lanciers was more like a general skirmish than a dance.

Miss Holm groaned from her exertions. She leaned against the wall, her temples beating with hammerstrokes. "Good—this way, Jette—" The dust hurt her eyes, as the seven hopped about in the dusk.

When Miss Holm came home after her dancing lessons, she wrapped her head up in a handkerchief. But in spite of this, she suffered from an everlasting cold, and sat, most of her leisure hours, with her head over a bowl of hot water.

Finally, they had music for their lessons—Mr. Broderson's violin. Two new pupils, a couple of half-grown young people, joined the class. They all hopped about to the tune of tailor Broderson's fiddle, as the dust flew up in clouds, and the old stove seemed to dance on its rough carved feet.

They had spectators, too, and once the young people from the rectory, the pastor's daughter and the curate, came to look on. Miss Holm danced out more energetically under the two dim lamps, threw out her chest, and arched her feet. "Throw out your feet like this, children—throw out your feet—" She threw out her feet proudly and raised the hem of her skirt—now she had an audience!

. . . .

Every week Miss Holm sent a package of knitting to Copenhagen. The teacher took charge of the package. Each time it was clumsily wrapped or addressed wrong, and he had to put it to rights himself. She stood watching him with her girlish nod and the smile of faded sixteen. The newspapers that had come by the mail lay ready for distribution on one of the school-tables. One day Miss Holm asked timidly if she might look at the "Berlinske." She had gazed longingly at the bundle for a week before she could pluck up courage enough to proffer her request. After that she came every day, in the noon pause. The school-teacher soon came to recognize her timid knock. "Come in, little lady, the door is open," he would call.

She tripped across the schoolroom and took her chosen paper from the bundle. She read the theatrical advertisements, the repertoire, and the criticisms, of which she understood but little. But it was about "those over there." She needed a lengthy time to go the length of a column, following the words with one gracefully pointed finger. When she had finished reading she crossed the hall and knocked once more at the other door. "Well?" said the teacher. "Anything new happened in the city?"

"It's only about—those over there—the old friends—" she would answer.

The schoolteacher looked after her, as she wandered home to her knitting. "Poor little creature!" he sighed. "She's really quite excited about her dancing master—" It was the news of a new ballet, by a lately promoted master of the ballet, that had so excited her. Miss Holm knew the list of names by heart, and knew the names of every solo dance. "We went to school together," she would say.

And on the evening when the ballet was performed for the first time she fevered with excitement, as if she were to dance in it herself. She lit the two candles, gray with age and dust, that stood one on each side of a plaster cast of Thorwaldsen's Christ on the bureau, and sat down on her champagne basket, staring into the light. But she couldn't bear to be alone that evening. All the old unrest of theatrical life came over her. She went into the room where the smith and his wife were, and sat down beside the tall clock. She talked more during the next hour than she had talked for a whole year. She talked about the theatre and about first nights; she talked about the big "solos" and the famous "pas." She hummed and she swayed in her chair while she talked.

The novelty of it all so excited the smith that he began to sing an old cavalry song, and finally called out: "Mother, shan't we have a punch to-night?"

The punch was brewed, the two candles brought out from the little room, and they sat there and chatted merrily. But in the midst of all the gaiety, Miss Holm grew suddenly silent, and sat still, great tears welling up in her eyes. Then she rose quietly and

went to her room. In there she sat down on her
basket and wept quietly and bitterly, before she undressed and went to bed. She did not practise her
steps that evening. She could think of but one thing.
He had gone to school with her.

She lay sobbing gently in the darkness. Her head
moved uneasily on the pillow as the remembered voice
of the old dancing master of the school rang in her
ears, cross and excited: "Holm has no *élan*—Holm
has no *élan*—" He cried it out for all the hall to
hear. How plainly she could hear it now—how
plainly she could see the great bare hall—the long
rows of figurantes practising their steps—she herself
leaning for a moment against the wall with the feeling as if her tired limbs had been cut off from her
body altogether—and then the voice of the dancing
master: "Haven't you any ambition, Holm?"

Then she saw her little home, her mother shrunken
down into the great armchair, her sister bending over
the rattling sewing-machine. And she heard her
mother ask, in her asthmatic voice: "Didn't Anna
Stein dance a solo?"—"Yes, mother."—"Did they
give her 'la grande Napolitaine'?"—"Yes, mother."—
"You both entered the school at the same time," she
asked, looking over at her from behind the lamp.

"Yes, mother." And she saw Anna Stein in her
gay-colored skirts, with the fluttering ribbons on her
tambourine, so happy and smiling in the glare of the
footlights as she danced her solo.

And suddenly the little woman in the darkness
buried her head in her pillow and sobbed convulsive,

heart-breaking, unchecked sobs of impotent and despairing grief. It was dawn before she fell asleep.

The new ballet was a success. Miss Holm read the notices, and two little, old woman's tears fell softly down upon the printed page as she read.

Letters came now and then from her sisters, letters about pawn-tickets and dire need. The days such letters came Miss Holm would forget her knitting and sit with her hands pressed to her temples, the open letter lying before her. Finally, one day, she made the round of the homes of her pupils, and begged shyly, with painful blushes, for the advance of half her money. This she sent home to her family.

. . . .

So the days passed. Miss Irene Holm went back and forth to her dancing lessons. More pupils came to her, a half-score young peasants formed an evening class that met three times a week in Peter Madsen's big room on the edge of the woods. Miss Holm walked the half mile in the darkness, timid as a hare, pursued by all the old ghost stories of the ballet school. At one place she had to pass a pond deeply fringed with willows. She would stare up at the trees that stretched their great arms weirdly in the blackness, her heart hanging dead as a stone in her breast.

They danced three hours each evening. Miss Holm called out, commanded, skipped here and there, and danced with the gentlemen pupils until two deep red spots appeared on her withered cheeks. Then it was time to go home. A boy would open the gate for her, and hold up a lantern to start her on the way. She heard his "Good night" behind her and then the locking of the gate, as it rasped over the rough stone pavement. Along the first stretch of the path was a hedge of bushes that bent over at her and nodded their heads.

It was nearly spring when Miss Holm's course of lessons came to an end. The company at Peter Madsen's decided to finish off with a ball at the inn.

III

It was quite an affair, this ball, with a transparency, "Welcome," over the door, and a cold supper at two crowns a plate, with the pastor's daughter and the curate to grace the table.

Miss Holm wore a barège gown much betrimmed, and Roman bands around her head. Her fingers were full of keepsake rings from her ballet-school friends. Between the dances she sprinkled lavender water about the floor, and threatened the "ladies" with the bottle. Miss Holm never felt so young again on any such festive occasion. The ball began with a quadrille. The parents of the pupils and other older people stood around the walls, each looking after his own young ones with secret pride. The young dancers walked through the quadrille with faces set as masks, placing their feet as carefully as if they were walking on peas. Miss Holm was all encouraging smiles and nods as she murmured her French commands. The music was furnished by Mr. Broderson and his son, the latter maltreating the piano kindly lent for the occasion by the pastor.

Then the round dances began, and the tone grew more free and easy. The elder men discovered the punch bowl in the next room, and the gentlemen pupils danced in turn with Miss Holm. She danced with her head on one side, raising herself on her toes, and smiling with her faded grace of sixteen years. After a while the other couples stopped dancing to watch Miss Holm and her partner. The men came out of the other room, stood in the doorway, and murmured admiration as Miss Holm passed, raising her feet a little higher under her skirt, and rocking gracefully in the hips. The pastor's daughter was so amused that she pinched the curate's arm repeatedly. After the mazurka, the schoolteacher cried out, "Bravo!" and they all clapped hands. Miss Holm bowed the elegant ballet courtesy, laying two fingers on her heart.

When supper-time came, she arranged a polonaise and made them all join in. The women giggled and nudged each other in their embarrassment, and the men said: "Well—let's get in line—" One couple began a march song, beating time with their feet.

Miss Holm sat next the schoolteacher, in the place of honor under the bust of his Majesty the King. They all grew solemn again at the table, and Miss Holm was almost the only one who conversed. She spoke in the high-pitched tone of the actors in the modern society dramas of Scribe. After a while the company became more jovial, the men began to laugh and drink toasts, touching glasses across the table. Things were very lively at the end of the table where the young people sat, and it was not easy to obtain quiet for the schoolmaster, who rose to make a speech. He spoke at some length, mentioning Miss Holm and the nine Muses, and ending up with a toast to "The Priestess of Art, Miss Irene Holm!" All joined in the cheers, and everybody came up to touch glasses with Miss Holm.

Miss Holm had understood very little of the long speech, but she felt greatly flattered. She rose and bowed to the company, her glass held high in her curved arm. Her face-powder, put on for the festive occasion, had quite disappeared in the heat and exertion, and two deep red spots shone on her cheeks.

The fun waxed fast and furious. The young people began to sing, the old men drank a glass or two extra on the sly, and stood up from their places to hit each other on the shoulder, amid shouts of laughter. The women threw anxious glances at the sinners, fearing they might indulge too deeply. Amid all the noise Miss Holm's laugh rang out, a girlish laugh, bright and merry as thirty years before in the ballet school.

Then the schoolmaster said that Miss Holm ought to dance. "But I have danced." Yes, but she should dance for them—a solo—that would be fine.

Miss Holm understood at once—and a great desire grew up in her heart—she was to dance—a solo! But she pretended to laugh, and smiling up at Peter Madsen's wife, she said: "The gentleman says I ought to dance," as if it were the most absurd thing in the world.

Several heard it, and they all called out in answer, "Yes, yes, do dance."

Miss Holm blushed to the roots of her hair, and said that she thought the fun was getting just a little too outspoken. "And, besides, there was no music; and one couldn't dance in long skirts." A man some- where in the background called out: "You can lift them up, can't you?" The guests all laughed at this, and began to renew their entreaties.

"Well, yes, if the young lady from the rectory will play for me?—a tarantella." They surrounded the pastor's daughter, and she consented to lend her ser- vices. The schoolmaster rose and beat on his glass: "Ladies and gentlemen," he announced, "Miss Holm will do us the honor to perform a solo dance for us." The guests cheered, and the last diners arose from the table. The curate's arm was black and blue where the young lady from the rectory had pinched him.

Miss Holm and the pastor's daughter went to the piano to try the music. Miss Holm was feverish with excitement, and tripped back and forth, trying the muscles of her feet. She pointed to the humps and bumps in the floor: "I'm not quite used to dancing in a circus." Then again: "Well, the fun can begin now;" her voice was hoarse with emotion. "I'll come in after the first ten bars," she said to the pianist; "I'll give you a sign when to begin." Then she went out into a little neighboring room and waited there. The audience filed in and stood around in a circle, whis- pering and very curious. The schoolmaster brought the lights from the table, and stood them up in the windows. It was quite an illumination. Then there came a light knock at the door of the little room.

The rector's daughter began to play, and the guests looked eagerly at the closed door. At the tenth bar of the music it opened, and they all clapped loudly. Miss Holm danced out, her skirt caught up with a Roman scarf. It was to be "la grande Napolitaine." She danced on toetips, she twisted and turned. The audience gazed, dumfounded, in admiration at the little feet that moved up and down as rapidly as a couple of drumsticks. They cheered and clapped wildly as she stood on one leg for a moment.

She called out "Quicker," and began to sway again. She smiled and nodded and waved her arms. There was more and more motion of the body from the waist up, more gestures with the arms; the dance became more and more mimic. She could no longer see the faces of her audience; she opened her mouth, smiling so that all her teeth, a few very bad teeth, could be seen; she began to act in pantomime; she felt and knew only that she was dancing a solo—at last a solo, the solo for which she had waited so long. It was no longer the "grande Napolitaine." It was Fenella who knelt, Fenella who implored, Fenella who suffered, the beautiful, tragic Fenella.

She hardly knew how she had risen from the floor, or how she had come from the room. She heard only the sudden ceasing of the music, and the laughter— the terrible laughter, the laughter she heard and the laughter she saw on all these faces, to which she had suddenly become alive again.

She had risen from her knees, raised her arms me- chanically, from force of habit, and bowed amid shouting. In there, in the little room, she stood, supporting herself on the edge of the table. It was all so dark around and in her—so empty. She loosened the scarf from her gown with strangely stiff hands, smoothed her skirts, and went back again to the room where the audience were now clapping politely. She bowed her thanks, standing by the piano, but she did not raise her eyes. The others began to dance again, eager to resume the fun. Miss Holm went about among them, saying farewell. Her pupils pressed the paper packages containing their money into her hands. Peter Madsen's wife helped her into her cloak, and at the door she was met by the pastor's daughter and the curate, ready to accompany her home.

They walked along in silence. The young lady from the rectory was very unhappy about the evening's occurrence, and wanted to excuse it somehow, but didn't know what to say. The little dancer walked along at her side, pale and quiet.

Finally the curate, embarrassed at the silence, remarked hesitatingly: "You see, miss—these people—they don't understand tragic art." Miss Holm did not answer. When they came to her door she bowed and gave them her hand in silence. The rector's daughter caught her in her arms and kissed her. "Good night, good night," she said, her voice trembling. Then she waited outside with the curate until they saw a light in the little dancer's room.

. . . .

Miss Holm took off her barège gown and folded it carefully. She unwrapped the money from the paper parcels, counted it, and sewed it into a little pocket in her bodice. She handled the needle awkwardly, sitting bowed over the tiny light.

The next morning her champagne basket was lifted onto a wagon of the country post. It rained, and Miss Holm huddled down under a broken umbrella. She drew her legs up under her, and sat on her basket like a Turk. When it was time to leave, the driver ran alongside. The young lady from the rectory came running up bareheaded. She had a white basket in her hands, and said she had brought "just a little food for the journey."

She bent down under the umbrella, caught Miss Holm's head in her hands, and kissed her twice. The old dancer broke into sobs, and grasping the young girl's hand, she kissed it violently.

The rector's daughter stood and looked for a long time after the old umbrella swaying on top of the little cart.

Miss Irene Holm had announced a "spring course in modern society dances" in a little town nearby. Six pupils were promised. It was thither she was going now—to continue the thing we call Life.

THE OUTLAWS

BY SELMA LAGERLÖF

Selma Lagerlöf, at one time teacher at Landskrona, has just recently been crowned the people's favorite authoress at the national Swedish festival held in 1907. She was born in 1858, on the ancestral estate of Wärmland, where she found the material for her first stories, "Gösta Berling's Saga," a fantastic collection of child-reminiscences modeled after the problem-literature then in vogue, and rendered enormously popular by reason of a happy linking of the old romanticism with the new realistic truthfulness to nature.

In 1895 she traveled abroad, and soon after produced her famous Sicilian tales. Her "Memoirs of Madame Ristori," the great Italian tragic actress, containing important pictures of Madame Ristori's contemporaries, Tommaso Salvini, Dumas Père, and others, have lately been translated into English.

Selma Lagerlöf's style, ideally represented in "The Outlaws," the best of her tales, is calm, sure, broad, and poetic.

THE OUTLAWS

BY SELMA LAGERLÖF

A PEASANT had killed a monk and fled to the woods. He became an outlaw, upon whose head a price was set. In the forest he met another fugitive, a young fisherman from one of the outermost islands, who had been accused of the theft of a herring net. The two became companions, cut themselves a home in a cave, laid their nets together, cooked their food, made their arrows, and held watch one for the other. The peasant could never leave the forest. But the fisherman, whose crime was less serious, would now and then take upon his back the game they had killed, and would creep down to the more isolated houses on the outskirts of the village. In return for milk, butter, arrow-heads, and clothing he would sell his game, the black mountain cock, the moor hen, with her shining feathers, the toothsome doe, and the long-eared hare.

The cave which was their home cut down deep into a mountain-side. The entrance was guarded by wide slabs of stone and ragged thorn-bushes. High up on the hillside there stood a giant pine, and the chimney of the fireplace nestled among its coiled roots. Thus the smoke could draw up through the heavy hanging branches and fade unseen into the air. To reach their cave the men had to wade through the stream that sprang out from the hill slope. No pursuer thought of seeking their trail in this merry brooklet. At first they were hunted as wild animals are. The peasants of the district gathered to pursue them as if for a baiting of wolf or bear. The bowmen surrounded the wood while the spear carriers entered and left no thicket or ravine unsearched. The two outlaws cowered in their gloomy cave, panting in terror and listening breathlessly as the hunt passed on with noise and shouting over the mountain ranges.

For one long day the young fisherman lay motionless, but the murderer could stand it no longer, and went out into the open where he could see his enemy. They discovered him and set after him, but this was far more to his liking than lying quiet in impotent terror. He fled before his pursuers, leaped the streams, slid down the precipices, climbed up perpendicular walls of rock. All his remarkable strength and skill awoke to energy under the spur of danger. His body became as elastic as a steel spring, his foot held firm, his hand grasped sure, his eye and ear were doubly sharp. He knew the meaning of every murmur in the foliage; he could understand the warning in an upturned stone.

When he had clambered up the side of a precipice he would stop to look down on his pursuers, greeting them with loud songs of scorn. When their spears sang above him in the air, he would catch them and hurl them back. As he crashed his way through tangled underbrush something within him seemed to sing

Selma Lagerlöf

a wild song of rejoicing. A gaunt, bare hilltop stretched itself through the forest, and all alone upon its crest there stood a towering pine. The red brown trunk was bare, in the thick grown boughs at the top a hawk's nest rocked in the breeze. So daring had the fugitive grown that on another day he climbed to the nest while his pursuers sought him in the woody slopes below. He sat there and twisted the necks of the young hawks as the hunt raged far beneath him. The old birds flew screaming about him in anger. They swooped past his face, they struck at his eyes with their beaks, beat at him with their powerful wings, and clawed great scratches in his weather-hardened skin. He battled with them laughing. He stood up in the rocking nest as he lunged at the birds with his knife, and he lost all thought of danger and pursuit in the joy of the battle. When recollection came again and he turned to look for his enemies, the hunt had gone off in another direction. Not one of the pursuers had thought of raising his eyes to the clouds to see the prey hanging there, doing schoolboy deeds of recklessness while his life hung in the balance. But the man trembled from head to foot when he saw that he was safe. He caught for a support with his shaking hands; he looked down giddily from the height to which he had climbed. Groaning in fear of a fall, afraid of the birds, afraid of the possibility of being seen, weakened through terror of everything and anything, he slid back down the tree trunk. He laid himself flat upon the earth and crawled over the loose stones until he reached the underbrush. There he hid among the tangled branches of the young pines, sinking down, weak and helpless, upon the soft moss. A single man might have captured him.

.   .   .   .

Tord was the name of the fisherman. He was but sixteen years old, but was strong and brave. He had now lived for a whole year in the wood.

The peasant's name was Berg, and they had called him "The Giant." He was handsome and well-built, the tallest and strongest man in the entire county. He was broad-shouldered and yet slender. His hands were delicate in shape, as if they had never known hard work, his hair was brown, his face soft-colored. When he had lived for some time in the forest his look of strength was awe-inspiring. His eyes grew piercing under bushy brows wrinkled by great muscles over the forehead. His lips were more firmly set than before, his face more haggard, with deepened hollows at the temples, and his strongly marked cheek-bones stood out plainly. All the softer curves of his body disappeared, but the muscles grew strong as steel. His hair turned gray rapidly.

Tord had never seen any one so magnificent and so mighty before. In his imagination, his companion towered high as the forest, strong as the raging surf. He served him humbly, as he would have served a master, he revered him as he would have revered a god. It seemed quite natural that Tord should carry the hunting spear, that he should drag the game home, draw the water, and build the fire. Berg, the Giant, accepted all these services, but scarce threw the boy a friendly word. He looked upon him with contempt, as a common thief.

The outlaws did not live by pillage, but supported themselves by hunting and fishing. Had not Berg killed a holy man, the peasants would soon have tired of the pursuit and left them to themselves in the mountains. But they feared disaster for the villages if he who had laid hands upon a servant of God should go unpunished. When Tord took his game down into the valley they would offer him money and a pardon for himself if he would lead them to the cave of the Giant, that they might catch the latter in his sleep. But the boy refused, and if they followed him he would lead them astray until they gave up the pursuit.

Once Berg asked him whether the peasants had ever tried to persuade him to betrayal. When he learned what reward they had promised he said scornfully that Tord was a fool not to accept such offers. Tord looked at him with something in his eyes that Berg, the Giant, had never seen before. No beautiful woman whom he had loved in the days of his youth had ever looked at him like that; not even in the eyes of his own children, or of his wife, had he seen such affection. "You are my God, the ruler I have chosen of my own free will." This was what the eyes said. "You may scorn me, or beat me, if you will, but I shall still remain faithful."

From this on Berg gave more heed to the boy and saw that he was brave in action but shy in speech. Death seemed to have no terrors for him. He would deliberately choose for his path the fresh formed ice on the mountain pools, the treacherous surface of the morass in springtime. He seemed to delight in danger. It gave him some compensation for the wild ocean storms he could no longer go out to meet. He would tremble in the night darkness of the wood, however, and even by day the gloom of a thicket or a deeper shadow could frighten him. When Berg asked him about this he was silent in embarrassment.

Tord did not sleep in the bed by the hearth at the back of the cave, but every night, when Berg was asleep the boy would creep to the entrance and lie there on one of the broad stones. Berg discovered this, and although he guessed the reason he asked the boy about it. Tord would not answer. To avoid further questions he slept in the bed for two nights, then returned to his post at the door.

One night, when a snow-storm raged in the tree-tops, piling up drifts even in the heart of the thickets, the flakes swirled into the cave of the outlaws. Tord, lying by the entrance, awoke in the morning to find himself wrapped in a blanket of melting snow. A day or two later he fell ill. Sharp pains pierced his lungs when he tried to draw breath. He endured the pain as long as his strength would stand it, but one evening, when he stooped to blow up the fire, he fell down and could not rise again. Berg came to his side and told him to lie in the warm bed. Tord groaned in agony, but could not move. Berg put his arm under the boy's body and carried him to the bed. He had a feeling while doing it as if he were touching a clammy snake; he had a taste in his mouth as if he had eaten

unclean horseflesh, so repulsive was it to him to touch
the person of this common thief. Berg covered the
sick boy with his own warm bear-skin rug and gave
him water. This was all he could do, but the illness
was not dangerous, and Tord recovered quickly. But
now that Berg had had to do his companion's work
for a few days, and had had to care for him, they
seemed to have come nearer to one another. Tord
dared to speak to Berg sometimes, as they sat together by the fire cutting their arrows.

"You come of good people, Berg," Tord said one
evening. "Your relatives are the richest peasants in
the valley. The men of your name have served kings
and fought in their castles."

"They have more often fought with the rebels and
done damage to the king's property," answered Berg.

"Your forefathers held great banquets at Christmas
time. And you held banquets too, when you were at
home in your house. Hundreds of men and women
could find place on the benches in your great hall, the
hall that was built in the days before St. Olaf came
here to Viken for christening. Great silver urns were
there, and mighty horns, filled with mead, went the
rounds of your table."

Berg looked at the boy again. He sat on the edge
of the bed with his head in his hands, pushing back
the heavy tangled hair that hung over his eyes. His
face had become pale and refined through his illness.
His eyes still sparkled in fever. He smiled to himself
at the pictures called up by his fancy—pictures of the
great hall and of the silver urns, of the richly clad

guests, and of Berg, the Giant, lording it in the place of honor. The peasant knew that even in the days of his glory no one had ever looked at him with eyes so shining in admiration, so glowing in reverence, as this boy did now, as he sat by the fire in his worn leather jacket. He was touched, and yet displeased. This common thief had no right to admire him.

"Were there no banquets in your home?" he asked.

Tord laughed: "Out there on the rocks where father and mother live? Father plunders the wrecks and mother is a witch. When the weather is stormy she rides out to meet the ships on a seal's back, and those who are washed overboard from the wrecks belong to her."

"What does she do with them?" asked Berg.

"Oh, a witch always needs corpses. She makes salves of them, or perhaps she eats them. On moonlit nights she sits out in the wildest surf and looks for the eyes and fingers of drowned children."

"That is horrible!" said Berg.

The boy answered with calm confidence: "It would be for others, but not for a witch. She can't help it."

This was an altogether new manner of looking at life for Berg. "Then thieves have to steal, as witches have to make magic?" he questioned sharply.

"Why, yes," answered the boy. "Every one has to do the thing he was born for." But a smile of shy cunning curled his lips, as he added: "There are thieves who have never stolen."

"What do you mean by that?" spoke Berg.

The boy still smiled his mysterious smile and seemed

happy to have given his companion a riddle. "There are birds that do not fly; and there are thieves who have not stolen," he said.

Berg feigned stupidity, in order to trick the other's meaning: "How can any one be called a thief who has never stolen?" he said.

The boy's lips closed tight as if to hold back the words. "But if one has a father who steals—" he threw out after a short pause.

"A man may inherit house and money, but the name thief is given only to him who earns it."

Tord laughed gently. "But when one has a mother —and that mother comes and cries, and begs one to take upon one's self the father's crime—and then one can laugh at the hangman and run away into the woods. A man may be outlawed for the sake of a fish net he has never seen."

Berg beat his fist upon the stone table, in great anger. Here this strong, beautiful boy had thrown away his whole life for another. Neither love, nor riches, nor the respect of his fellow men could ever be his again. The sordid care for food and clothing was all that remained to him in life. And this fool had let him, Berg, despise an innocent man. He scolded sternly, but Tord was not frightened any more than a sick child is frightened at the scolding of his anxious mother.

. . . .

High up on one of the broad wooded hills there lay a black swampy lake. It was square in shape, and its banks were as straight, and their corners as sharp as if it had been the work of human hands. On three sides steep walls of rock rose up, with hardy mountain pines clinging to the stones, their roots as thick as a man's arm. At the surface of the lake, where the few strips of grass had been washed away, these naked roots twisted and coiled, rising out of the water like myriad snakes that had tried to escape from the waves, but had been turned to stone in their struggle. Or was it more like a mass of blackened skeletons of long-drowned giants which the lake was trying to throw off? The arms and legs were twisted in wild contortions, the long fingers grasped deep into the rocks, the mighty ribs formed arches that upheld ancient trees. But now and again these iron-hard arms, these steel fingers with which the climbing pines supported themselves, would loosen their hold, and then the strong north wind would hurl the tree from the ridge far out into the swamp. There it would lie, its crown burrowing deep in the muddy water. The fishes found good hiding places amid its twigs, while the roots rose up over the water like the arms of some hideous monster, giving the little lake a repulsive appearance.

The mountains sloped down on the fourth side of the little lake. A tiny rivulet foamed out here; but before the stream could find its path it twisted and turned among boulders and mounds of earth, forming a whole colony of islands, some of which scarce offered foothold, while others carried as many as twenty trees on their back.

Here, where the rocks were not high enough to shut out the sun, the lighter foliaged trees could grow.

Here were the timid, gray-green alders, and the willows with their smooth leaves. Birches were here, as they always are wherever there is a chance to shut out the evergreens, and there were mountain ash and elder bushes, giving charm and fragrance to the place.

At the entrance to the lake there was a forest of rushes as high as a man's head, through which the sunlight fell as green upon the water as it falls on the moss in the true forest. There were little clearings among the reeds, little round ponds where the water lilies slumbered. The tall rushes looked down with gentle gravity upon these sensitive beauties, who closed their white leaves and their yellow hearts so quickly in their leather outer dress as soon as the sun withdrew his rays.

One sunny day the outlaws came to one of these little ponds to fish. They waded through the reeds to two high stones, and sat there throwing out their bait for the big green, gleaming pike that slumbered just below the surface of the water. These men, whose life was now passed entirely among the mountains and the woods, had come to be as completely under the control of the powers of nature as were the plants or the animals. When the sun shone they were open-hearted and merry, at evening they became silent, and the night, which seemed to them so all-powerful, robbed them of their strength. And now the green light that fell through the reeds and drew out from the water stripes of gold, brown, and black-green, smoothed them into a sort of magic mood. They were completely shut out from the outer world. The

reeds swayed gently in the soft wind, the rushes murmured, and the long, ribbon-like leaves struck them
lightly in the face. They sat on the gray stones in
their gray leather garments, and the shaded tones of
the leather melted into the shades of the stones. Each
saw his comrade sitting opposite him as quietly as a
stone statue. And among the reeds they saw giant
fish swimming, gleaming and glittering in all colors
of the rainbow. When the men threw out their lines
and watched the rings on the water widen amid the
reeds, it seemed to them that the motion grew and
grew until they saw it was not they themselves alone
that had occasioned it. A Nixie, half human, half
fish, lay sleeping deep down in the water. She lay
on her back, and the waves clung so closely to her
body that the men had not seen her before. It was her
breath that stirred the surface. But it did not seem
to the watchers that there was anything strange in the
fact that she lay there. And when she had disappeared in the next moment they did not know whether
her appearance had been an illusion or not.

The green light pierced through their eyes into their
brains like a mild intoxication. They saw visions
among the reeds, visions which they would not tell
even to each other. There was not much fishing done.
The day was given up to dreams and visions.

A sound of oars came from among the reeds, and
they started up out of their dreaming. In a few moments a heavy boat, hewn out of a tree trunk, came
into sight, set in motion by oars not much broader
than walking sticks. The oars were in the hands of a

young girl who had been gathering water-lilies. She
had long, dark brown braids of hair, and great dark
eyes, but she was strangely pale, a pallor that was not
gray, but softly pink tinted. Her cheeks were no deeper
in color than the rest of her face; her lips were scarce
redder. She wore a bodice of white linen and a
leather belt with a golden clasp. Her skirt was of
blue with a broad red hem. She rowed past close by
the outlaws without seeing them. They sat absolutely quiet, less from fear of discovery than from the
desire to look at her undisturbed. When she had
gone, the stone statues became men again and smiled:

"She was as white as the water-lilies," said one.
"And her eyes were as dark as the water back there
under the roots of the pines."

They were both so merry that they felt like laughing, like really laughing as they had never laughed in
this wamp before, a laugh that would echo back from
the wall of rock and loosen the roots of the pines.

"Did you think her beautiful?" asked the Giant.

"I do not know, she passed so quickly. Perhaps she
was beautiful."

"You probably did not dare to look at her. Did
you think she was the Nixie?"

And again they felt a strange desire to laugh.

. . . .

While a child, Tord had once seen a drowned man.
He had found the corpse on the beach in broad daylight, and it had not frightened him, but at night his
dreams were terrifying. He had seemed to be looking
out over an ocean, every wave of which threw a dead

body at his feet. He saw all the rocks and islands covered with corpses of the drowned, the drowned that were dead and belonged to the sea, but that could move, and speak, and threaten him with their white stiffened fingers.

And so it was again. The girl whom he had seen in the reeds appeared to him in his dreams. He met her again down at the bottom of the swamp lake, where the light was greener even than in the reeds, and there he had time enough to see that she was beautiful. He dreamed that he sat on one of the great pine roots in the midst of the lake while the tree rocked up and down, now under, now over the surface of the water. Then he saw her on one of the smallest islands. She stood under the red mountain ash and laughed at him. In his very last dream it had gone so far that she had kissed him. But then it was morning, and he heard Berg rising, but he kept his eyes stubbornly closed that he might continue to dream. When he did awake he was dazed and giddy from what he had seen during the night. He thought much more about the girl than he had done the day before. Toward evening it occurred to him to ask Berg if he knew her name.

Berg looked at him sharply. "It is better for you to know it at once," he said. "It was Unn. We are related to each other."

And then Tord knew that it was this pale maiden who was the cause of Berg's wild hunted life in forest and mountain. He tried to search his memory for what he had heard about her.

Unn was the daughter of a free peasant. Her

mother was dead, and she ruled in her father's household. This was to her taste, for she was independent by nature, and had no inclination to give herself to any husband. Unn and Berg were cousins, and the rumor had long gone about that Berg liked better to sit with Unn and her maids than to work at home in his own house. One Christmas, when the great banquet was to be given in Berg's hall, his wife had invited a monk from Draksmark, who, she hoped, would show Berg how wrong it was that he should neglect her for another. Berg and others besides him hated this monk because of his appearance. He was very stout and absolutely white. The ring of hair around his bald head, the brows above his moist eyes, the color of his skin, of his hands, and of his garments, were all white. Many found him very repulsive to look at.

But the monk was fearless, and as he believed that his words would have greater weight if many heard them, he rose at the table before all the guests, and said: "Men call the cuckoo the vilest of birds because he brings up his young in the nest of others. But here sits a man who takes no care for his house and his children, and who seeks his pleasure with a strange woman. Him I will call the vilest of men." Unn rose in her place. "Berg, this is said to you and to me," she cried. "Never have I been so shamed, but my father is not here to protect me." She turned to go, but Berg hurried after her. "Stay where you are," she said. "I do not wish to see you again." He stopped her in the corridor, and asked her what he should do that she might stay with him. Her eyes glowed as she answered that he himself should know best what he must do. Then Berg went into the hall again and slew the monk.

Berg and Tord thought on awhile with the same thoughts, then Berg said: "You should have seen her when the white monk fell. My wife drew the children about her and cursed Unn. She turned the faces of the children toward her, that they might always remember the woman for whose sake their father had become a murderer. But Unn stood there so quiet and so beautiful that the men who saw her trembled. She thanked me for the deed, and prayed me to flee to the woods at once. She told me never to become a robber, and to use my knife only in some cause equally just."

"Your deed had ennobled her," said Tord.

And again Berg found himself astonished at the same thing that had before now surprised him in the boy. Tord was a heathen, or worse than a heathen; he never condemned that which was wrong. He seemed to know no sense of responsibility. What had to come, came. He knew of God, of Christ, and the Saints, but he knew them only by name, as one knows the names of the gods of other nations. The ghosts of the Scheeren Islands were his gods. His mother, learned in magic, had taught him to believe in the spirits of the dead. And then it was that Berg undertook a task which was as foolish as if he had woven a rope for his own neck. He opened the eyes of this ignorant boy to the power of God, the Lord of all justice, the avenger of wrong who condemned sinners to the pangs of hell everlasting. And he

taught him to love Christ and His Mother, and all
the saintly men and women who sit before the throne
of God praying that His anger may be turned away
from sinners. He taught him all that mankind has
learned to do to soften the wrath of God. He told
him of the long trains of pilgrims journeying to the
holy places; he told him of those who scourged themselves in their remorse; and he told him of the pious
monks who flee the joys of this world.

The longer he spoke the paler grew the boy and
the keener his attention as his eyes widened at the
visions. Berg would have stopped, but the torrent of
his own thoughts carried him away. Night sank down
upon them, the black forest night, where the scream
of the owl shrills ghostly through the stillness. God
came so near to them that the brightness of His throne
dimmed the stars, and the angels of vengeance descended upon the mountain heights. And below them
the flames of the underworld fluttered up to the outer
curve of the earth and licked greedily at this last
refuge of a race crushed by sin and wo.

.   .   .   .

Autumn came, and with it came storm. Tord went
out alone into the woods to tend the traps and snares,
while Berg remained at home to mend his clothes.
The boy's path led him up a wooded height along
which the falling leaves danced in circles in the gust.
Again and again the feeling came to him that some
one was walking behind him. He turned several times,
then went on again when he had seen that it was only
the wind and the leaves. He threatened the rustling

circles with his fist, and kept on his way. But he had not silenced the sounds of his vision. At first it was the little dancing feet of elfin children; then it was the hissing of a great snake moving up behind him. Beside the snake there came a wolf, a tall, gray creature, waiting for the moment when the adder should strike at his feet to spring upon his back. Tord hastened his steps, but the visions hastened with him. When they seemed but two steps behind him, ready for the spring, he turned. There was nothing there, as he had known all the time. He sat down upon a stone to rest. The dried leaves played about his feet. The leaves of all the forest trees were there: the little yellow birch leaves, the red-tinged mountain ash leaves, the dried, black-brown foliage of the elm, the bright red aspen leaves, and the yellow-green fringes of the willows. Faded and crumpled, broken and scarred, they were but little like the soft, tender shoots of green that had unrolled from the buds a few months ago.

"Ye are sinners," said the boy. "All of us are sinners. Nothing is pure in the eyes of God. Ye have already been shriveled up in the flame of His wrath."

Then he went on again, while the forest beneath him waved like a sea in storm, although it was still and calm on the path around him. But he heard something he had never heard before. The wood was full of voices. Now it was like a whispering, now a gentle plaint, now a loud threat, or a roaring curse. It laughed, and it moaned. It was as the voice of hundreds. This unknown something that threatened and excited, that whistled and hissed, a something that seemed to be, and yet was not, almost drove him mad. He shivered in deadly terror, as he had shivered before, the day that he lay on the floor of his cave, and heard his pursuers rage over him through the forest. He seemed to hear again the crashing of the branches, the heavy footsteps of the men, the clanking of their arms, and their wild, bloodthirsty shouts.

It was not alone the storm that roared about him. There was something else in it, something yet more terrible; there were voices he could not understand, sounds as of a strange speech. He had heard many a mightier storm than this roar through the rigging. But he had never heard the wind playing on a harp of so many strings. Every tree seemed to have its own voice, every ravine had another song, the loud echo from the rocky wall shouted back in its own voice. He knew all these tones, but there were other stranger noises with them. And it was these that awoke a storm of voices within his own brain.

He had always been afraid when alone in the darkness of the wood. He loved the open sea and the naked cliffs. Ghosts and spirits lurked here in the shadows of the trees.

Then suddenly he knew who was speaking to him in the storm. It was God, the Great Avenger, the Lord of all Justice. God pursued him because of his comrade. God demanded that he should give up the murderer of the monk to vengeance.

Tord began to speak aloud amid the storm. He told God what he wanted to do, but that he could not do it. He had wanted to speak to the Giant and to beg him make his peace with God. But he could not find the words; embarrassment tied his tongue. "When I learned that the world is ruled by a God of Justice," he cried, "I knew that he was a lost man. I have wept through the night for my friend. I know that God will find him no matter where he may hide. But I could not speak to him; I could not find the words because of my love for him. Do not ask that I shall speak to him. Do not ask that the ocean shall rise to the height of the mountains."

He was silent again, and the deep voice of the storm, which he knew for God's voice, was silent also. There was a sudden pause in the wind, a burst of sunshine, a sound as of oars, and the gentle rustling of stiff reeds. These soft tones brought up the memory of Unn.

Then the storm began again, and he heard steps behind him, and a breathless panting. He did not dare to turn this time, for he knew that it was the white monk. He came from the banquet in Berg's great hall, covered with blood, and with an open ax cut in his forehead. And he whispered: "Betray him. Give him up, that you may save his soul."

Tord began to run. All this terror grew and grew in him, and he tried to flee from it. But as he ran he heard behind him the deep, mighty voice, which he knew was the voice of God. It was God himself pursuing him, demanding that he should give up the murderer. Berg's crime seemed more horrible to him than ever it had seemed before. A weaponless man had been murdered, a servant of God cut down by the steel. And the murderer still dared to live. He dared to

enjoy the light of the sun and the fruits of the earth.
Tord halted, clinched his fists, and shrieked a threat.
Then, like a madman, he ran from the forest, the realm
of terror, down into the valley.

. . . .

When Tord entered the cave the outlaw sat upon
the bench of stone, sewing. The fire gave but a pale
light, and the work did not seem to progress satis-
factorily. The boy's heart swelled in pity. This superb Giant seemed all at once so poor and so unhappy.

"What is the matter?" asked Berg. "Are you ill?
Have you been afraid?"

Then for the first time Tord spoke of his fear. "It
was so strange in the forest. I heard the voices of
spirits and I saw ghosts. I saw white monks."

"Boy!"

"They sang to me all the way up the slope to the
hilltop. I ran from them, but they ran after me, singing. Can I not lay the spirits? What have I to do
with them? There are others to whom their appearance is more necessary."

"Are you crazy to-night, Tord?"

Tord spoke without knowing what words he was
using. His shyness had left him all at once, speech
seemed to flow from his lips. "They were white
monks, as pale as corpses. And their clothes are
spotted with blood. They draw their hoods down
over their foreheads, but I can see the wound shining there. The great, yawning, red wound from
the ax."

"Tord," said the giant, pale and deeply grave, "the

Saints alone know why you see wounds of ax thrusts. I slew the monk with a knife."

Tord stood before Berg trembling and wringing his hands. "They demand you of me. They would compel me to betray you."

"Who? The monks?"

"Yes, yes, the monks. They show me visions. They show me Unn. They show me the open, sunny ocean. They show me the camps of the fishermen, where there is dancing and merriment. I close my eyes, and yet I can see it all. 'Leave me,' I say to them. 'My friend has committed a murder, but he is not bad. Leave me alone, and I will talk to him, that he may repent and atone. He will see the wrong he has done, and he will make a pilgrimage to the Holy Grave.'"

"And what do the monks answer?" asked Berg. "They do not want to pardon me. They want to torture me and to burn me at the stake."

"'Shall I betray my best friend?' I ask them. He is all that I have in the world. He saved me from the bear when its claws were already at my throat. We have suffered hunger and cold together. He covered me with his own garments while I was ill. I have brought him wood and water, I have watched over his sleep, and led his enemies off the trail. Why should they think me a man who betrays his friend? My friend will go to the priest himself, and will confess to him, and then together we will seek absolution?"

Berg listened gravely, his keen eyes searching in Tord's face. "Go to the priest yourself, and tell him the truth. You must go back again among mankind."

"What does it help if I go alone? The spirits of the dead follow me because of your sin. Do you not see how I tremble before you? You have lifted your hand against God himself. What crime is like unto yours? Why did you tell me about the just God? It is you yourself who compel me to betray you. Spare me this sin. Go to the priest yourself." He sank down on his knees before Berg.

The murderer laid his hand on his head and looked at him. He measured his sin by the terror of his comrade, and it grew and grew to monstrous size. He saw himself in conflict with the Will that rules the world. Remorse entered his heart.

"Wo unto me that I did what I did," he said. "And is not this miserable life, this life we lead here in terror, and in deprivation, is it not atonement enough? Have I not lost home and fortune? Have I not lost friends, and all the joys that make the life of a man? What more?"

As he heard him speak thus, Tord sprang up in wild terror. "You can repent!" he cried. "My words move your heart? Oh, come with me, come at once. Come, let us go while yet there is time."

Berg the Giant sprang up also. "You—did it—?"

"Yes, yes, yes. I have betrayed you. But come quickly. Come now, now that you can repent. We must escape. We will escape."

The murderer stooped to the ground where the battle-ax of his fathers lay at his feet. "Son of a thief," he hissed. "I trusted you—I loved you."

But when Tord saw him stoop for the ax, he knew

that it was his own life that was in peril now. He tore his own ax from his girdle, and thrust at Berg before the latter could rise. The Giant fell headlong to the floor, the blood spurting out over the cave. Between the tangled masses of hair Tord saw the great, yawning, red wound of an ax thrust.

Then the peasants stormed into the cave. They praised his deed and told him that he should receive full pardon.

Tord looked down at his hands, as if he saw there the fetters that had drawn him on to kill the man he loved. Like the chains of the Fenrir wolf, they were woven out of empty air. They were woven out of the green light amid the reeds, out of the play of shadows in the woods, out of the song of the storm, out of the rustling of the leaves, out of the magic vision of dreams. And he said aloud: "God is great."

He crouched beside the body, spoke amid his tears to the dead, and begged him to awake. The villagers made a litter of their spears, on which to carry the body of the free peasant to his home. The dead man aroused awe in their souls, they softened their voices in his presence. When they raised him on to the bier, Tord stood up, shook the hair from his eyes, and spoke in a voice that trembled:

"Tell Unn, for whose sake Berg the Giant became a murderer, that Tord the fisherman, whose father plunders wrecks, and whose mother is a witch—tell her that Tord slew Berg because Berg had taught him that justice is the corner-stone of the world."